Singularity

Joe Hart

To Jim,

Hope you enjoy the book!

Singularity

For my mother and father, who dreamed for me before I could do it myself.

Contents

Special Thanks

There are a few people who were indispensable in the birthing of this book I'd like to point out. First off, my sister, Ang. Thank you for providing great info on the specific inner workings of the BCA; your advice and input were invaluable. Special Agent Paul Gherardi with the BCA for walking me through the typical death investigation procedure. Thanks so much, Paul, for without your help, I would have missed the visceral feeling of being on a case and everything that goes with it. My family for their utmost support and patience over the months that I spent behind the desk; you all mean the world to me. And to you, Reader. Without you, I would merely be writing for my own enjoyment; and while that is great, it's not nearly as fun to be scared by yourself.

Prologue

Summer 1958

The man in the white T-shirt and black slacks breathed a prayer between a set of cracked lips and realized that the moment was finally here. The moment he'd dreamed of for nearly three years. Every hypothesis, plan, and drawing culminated in this last second, as he felt sweat run down the middle of his spine and his finger lit on the faded red button before him.

His eyes searched out each member of his team. "Ready?" he yelled. Their faces looked toward him, his moment. They nodded in turn. Mallory, his second in command, began to call out questions above the humming massive piece of steel that sat before them, enshrouded with bundles of wires and electrical panels. His voice echoed against the walls of the cave.

"Power control?"

"Check!" a voice answered from behind a lead shield nearly a foot thick.

"Cameras?"

"Check!"

"Override?"

"Check!"

"Radiation monitor?"

"Check!"

The man in the white T-shirt stepped closer to the machine and gazed through its plate-glass window, which made the view hazy and indistinguishable. He would have to amend the sighting plane with a different medium—something that could be seen through while withstanding short bursts of radiation. He felt the button beneath his fingers, rough and so real. He was here, at the edge of the rest of his life. He breathed again and stared through the glass at the boulder lying a hundred yards away. The cave walls and high ceiling dwarfed the rock, but he knew it was immense, weighing well over five tons.

Not for long, he thought. "Firing on three!" he yelled. He watched his team slide behind their barriers, and he wondered if they were ready to die. Were they willing to give their lives like he was in the name of discovery, of science? Either way, after he pushed this button, he would never know for sure. "One, two, three!"

The button snapped down beneath his fingers and there was a sound like an x-ray being triggered as the machine fell silent. The cave lit up in a white flare and then darkened once again except for the sparse string of incandescent lights hanging from the ceiling. For a moment he thought the machine had simply shut off, but then he realized that everything was silent. The sounds that normally rebounded off the underground walls were gone, along with all other noises. The world had died when he pressed the button, its breath cinched off by what he'd done. He blinked and looked through the glass for the boulder.

It was gone.

He leaned forward and pressed his face against the surface of the sighting chamber. The glass felt warm to the touch. Yes, the boulder was definitely gone, but something was wrong. There was a hole where the rock sat moments before. He squeezed his eyes shut and wondered if it was an afterimage of the beam. *No.* When he looked again, the hole was still there. The beam must have torn through the far wall some three hundred yards beyond the target point.

He cursed, and for the first time looked to the control station on his left. As he stared at the bodies on the ground, their ears dribbling blood into wider pools on the dirt floor, he marveled at how perfect the silence was. It wasn't the quiet of a library on a Sunday evening, and definitely not the same as being immersed underwater. It was perfect. Clean and pure. It was like he had never known sound.

He glanced to his right, not surprised to see Mallory face-down in the dirt. One of the man's arms stretched toward him, and it looked as if there was a crack running down the middle of his skull.

He rubbed his eyes and ran his fingers through his hair, which had grown much too long in the last year. He stretched a shaking hand out and punched the emergency off button several times, then saw that the machine had indeed shut down. No, not shut down. He looked through the sighting window again and saw the barrel was gone, as was the firing chamber behind it. How had he missed that?

Rubbing sweat from his eyes with claw-like fingers, he walked around the machine and stared at the areas where the rest of it should have been. Gone. He shook his head and looked down the length of the cave to the hole punched through the wall.

His stomach fluttered.

He had been mistaken. The hole wasn't in the wall at the far end of the chamber. It was where the boulder used to be. It stood in the middle of the cave, like a black mirror, oval in shape and nearly ten yards across. He walked a few steps toward it and then stopped, taking in its perfection, its *depth*.

He and Mallory used to theorize on this very thing over coffee and whiskey alike. The probability for it ever occurring was so low they hadn't even brought it up to the council, hadn't mentioned it in any of the briefs. It was nearly impossible. *Nearly.* Yet here it was, staring him full in the face. Something so much more exciting, brimming with possibilities, than the machine's original purpose.

He began to run, his hearing and dead team forgotten. He ran toward the hole and it seemed to grow, as its outer edges wavered like black-tongued flames in the deeper darkness. He skidded to a stop a few feet from it and his jaw slackened. He could see something in the center of the black. Dual shining points a few feet apart, like moonbeams glancing off a pond. Everything in his body told him to halt, not to go any closer. He would regret it if he didn't stop, but he ignored the warnings; his innate curiosity was the epicenter to his creativity. It would not let him stop.

He reached toward the oval and noticed its edges fluctuating faster. *It's dissipating,* he thought. He and Mallory discussed this too. Only a brief tear had occurred. Already, the fabric of the world was trying to repair itself. He looked into the darkness at the two spots of light that were closer now, and he felt a sense of privilege wash over him. Was he seeing stars that were not of his own sky? Were they supernovas dying out in a dull shade after burning for hundreds of millions of years? He was within reaching distance of the hole now, its diameter shrinking with each second. He leaned closer. He needed to see something of value. The machine was ruined. It would take years of appropriations and materials to restore it to working order. That is, if he could convince the council to try again after the decimation of his entire team during the initial test. He needed to be able to tell them he'd seen through a window into a place upon which no other human had laid eyes. He needed to make them understand what this was: the most significant discovery in all of human history. He squinted at the two points of light, trying to discern their details.

The two lights blinked.

Much too late, he realized that the eyes were only feet from the other side, and he glimpsed the rest of a body as it fell through the diminishing hole, onto the rough floor of the cave. A scream ripped out of his lungs, which he could only feel without his hearing, as he turned and raced away from it. His feet tripped on a ridge of the cave floor and he fell so hard he saw flashes of light sparkle across his vision. The image of what had come through the hole replayed in his mind as he struggled to his knees, his hands clawing at the floor to get away. He had to get away from it.

A dagger of pain shot through his right thigh, and as he looked down to see the thing that jutted from his leg, he realized his auditory sense was back, because now he could hear as well as feel the scream that flew from his mouth and danced back to him from the earthen ceiling.

Chapter 1

Present

He chased her again.

The walls were blurry and surreal as they scrolled past, she in the lead, he just behind. She wore the dress that she'd had on when they'd met. White and long, it flowed out behind her like a pallid comet's tail, rippling with each hurried step.

He could hear his breath rasping in and out of his chest as if he were in the last five miles of a marathon, not fifteen feet from the front door of their one-bedroom apartment. He heard her name being called and he wondered who had yelled it with such panic and desperation. Then he felt his throat constrict again and knew it was him screaming her name. She glanced back over her shoulder, one violet eye searching him out, pinning him to the wall as he ran, teasing and accusing at the same time. He hated her then. He wanted nothing more than to hurt her, to make her cry out for him to stop, so he could gather her thin frame in his arms and hold her. Just hold her.

He felt himself slow. He knew this part. She gained a bit of ground, and now he could see the balcony and its thin, black railing. The afternoon city lay beyond, ten stories below, cars winding their way between buildings on the streets like ants finding alternate ways to their hills. He could see his hand reach out and it looked so small and faint compared to the glaring white of her dress. How it ruffled and swayed as she ran.

She reached the balcony and paused only a moment, perhaps to survey the view one last time. Her hands gripped the wrought iron and for a second her knuckles matched her dress. She looked back at him through the veil of dark hair and smiled sadly this time. There was so much in that smile. A lifetime of happiness waiting there that would never be realized. Children unborn and anniversaries that would linger only in his mind.

He ran faster as she leaned out, more than the average curiosity would push a normal person over such a height. Her feet left the cement of the balcony and she tipped forward. She slid out of sight toward the ground in wisps of white fabric that flapped with a breeze he couldn't feel as he said the only word he could that would make it all go away. No. No. No.

==

"No!"

The word rang out in the bedroom as Sullivan Shale sat up, chest heaving in lungfuls of air. He looked around at the darkened room. The wood floors. The dresser that held his clothes against the far wall. The black outline of the bathroom door that opened up in the corner. His breath shuddered and he ran his hand through a tangled nest of dark hair. His eyes found the curtained window, and out of habit he immediately guessed the time: *4:23,* he was sure of it. He glanced at the clock on the bedside table: 4:44. He sighed and dropped his face into a sweat-slicked hand. He hated it when the time was all the same numerals. For some reason it felt wrong. As if time shouldn't line up that way. It should always be changing, moving forward, moving away. Not the same. Not ever the same.

He swung his feet out from beneath the light sheets and put them on the floor. The boards felt warm. It hadn't cooled off overnight and he wasn't surprised. The heat wave was slated to last through today and into the following evening. Then the rain would begin again, or so the weatherman said.

Thoughts of using the bathroom and then trying to return to a few more hours of sleep crossed his mind, but the memory of the dream resurfaced and he tried to swallow the dryness that crept into his throat. He'd never been able to sleep after having the dream. Not in two years. There was no reason this morning would be an exception. The chirping of his cell phone as it vibrated across his nightstand put any other thoughts of sleep to rest. He knew the number on the screen and answered without hesitation.

"I thought I had a few days off," he said, his words thick with sleep.

"You did. That was yesterday and this is today," the gruff voice said.

"I'm assuming that I'm back on?"

A long sigh issued from the earpiece. "Yes, I need you here in the next half-hour. There was a death over at Singleton Penitentiary last night, the local sheriff called it in. Asked for help."

Sullivan leaned forward, his eyes narrowing at a spot on the floor. "Singleton? Inmate kill an inmate?"

"No."

"Inmate kill a guard?"

"I'm not sure, but it's …" Hacking paused on the other end of the phone. "Strange," he finished.

Sullivan sat back on the bed and scrubbed a few granules of stubborn sleep from his right eye. "'Strange.' Okay. What do you mean by that, boss?"

"I mean, you need to get your ass into the office and get briefed before you get to the crime scene."

Sullivan's eyebrows shot up at his superior's tone. Cameron Hacking had never before sounded like this on the phone.

"I thought my mandatory leave lasted until next week."

"You've been fully reinstated as of now," Hacking said.

Sullivan scanned the dresser for his necessities: ID, keys, and gun. They were all there. "Okay. Anything else I need to know?"

The silence in the phone sounded almost like that of a dead line. He wondered for a moment if his SAIC had hung up without further comment, but then he heard the familiar intake of breath before Hacking spoke.

"The victim was killed in solitary confinement."

==

The leaden sky hung just above the reaching tips of the pine trees surrounding the North Central Bureau of Criminal Apprehension building. Sullivan studied it as he stepped from his black Trailblazer. His left eyebrow hung irritatingly low and he scrunched his forehead up in frustration at seeing it enter his field of vision. He needed to do the exercises the doctor suggested to perform on a daily basis. He'd start on them again tonight, when he was alone. He rubbed the pale scar line above his eyebrow, which snaked off his face and ended in the middle of his temple. He couldn't be seen in public working his brow up and down like a confused drunk. The air felt just as heavy and oppressive as the clouds above, and already sweat started beading on his skin. The air conditioning of the car seemed like a dream from another life.

He strode to the side entrance of the building and swiped his magnetic keycard through the slot beside the heavy door. The interior of the building was cold and he welcomed the crisp, cool air on his face. He had lived in Minnesota his entire life and had never seen weather like this. It was too hot. And when it got too hot, people did weird things. Steal, cheat, murder. It was always this way in the summer, but a feeling of apprehension settled over him as he made his way down the corridors, past darkened offices, toward the back of the building. It felt like he wasn't prepared. Like he'd forgotten some essential piece of equipment at home.

He could see Hacking's office now, behind the other cubicles in the main area of the building. Hazy light shone through the window and outlined the man who sat behind the desk. Cameron Hacking was almost fifty, but he looked a decade younger. Only a faint hint of gray near the temples tainted the man's full head of black hair. He had a high forehead and a thick-lipped mouth, without a line in his face to mar the persona of the collected senior agent that he was. Hacking's cobalt eyes were trained on the computer screen before him, and when Sullivan knocked on the ajar door, they locked on to him and pulled him inside the room. Without a word, Hacking motioned to an empty chair on the far side of the desk. Sullivan sat and unbuttoned the top of his black dress shirt, letting the cool air of the office circulate around him. He stared across the room at his superior, and waited. Hacking tapped momentarily on his keyboard, and then sat back from the desk to study the younger man.

"This one's gonna be a bastard," Hacking said.

Sullivan raised his eyebrows and adjusted himself in the chair. "Why do you say that?" Sullivan asked.

"Number one, we have a dead inmate, which means the warden and senior officers over there are going to be watching your every move. They're going to want to help or provide support in every possible way."

Sullivan licked his lips. "If what you told me is accurate, they have to realize we'll be looking at their staff as possible suspects."

Hacking nodded and pointed a finger at Sullivan's chest. "Exactly. So it's imperative that they be kept at arm's length. Until we know more, we can't rule anyone out."

"What exactly are we looking at here, boss?" Sullivan said.

"Let's wait until Stevens gets here. He's coming with you as support." Hacking eyed the darkened lobby and looked at his watch. "Where the fuck is he?"

"I'm guessing he'll be here soon. He was on vacation, wasn't he?"

"Yeah, first day back is today."

Sullivan stood and stepped to the door. "You want a coffee while we wait?"

Hacking nodded, turning back to his computer screen. Sullivan made his way out to the dark kitchenette that stood at the far end of the room, and flipped the coffeemaker on after adding enough water and grounds for three cups. He stood waiting for the dripping of the dark liquid to cease and wondered again why he'd felt such uneasiness earlier. He'd never investigated a prison case before, but protocol was the same. Wait for the invite from the locals, have the forensics team scour the area, interview each and every person involved, formulate a suspect list, and bring them in for questioning. He shook his head as anxiety squirmed in his stomach once again and tried to push the strange feeling away.

As he made his way back toward Hacking's glowing office, he heard a door in the hallway slam. A few seconds later Barry Stevens appeared from the darkened corridor. Barry was thirty-seven, five years Sullivan's senior, and had thinning blonde hair and a spare tire of twenty pounds hanging around his midsection. His face was long, with a hooked nose and eyes that were nearly always watery. Sullivan had worked with him on dozens of death investigations, attended his children's birthday parties, and been so drunk with him on two occasions that all he could remember were snippets of conversation and bellyaching laughter. The man was rock steady and Sullivan was glad Barry would be coming with him on this one.

Stevens's eyes found Sullivan in the dark and his smile lit up a newly sunburned face. "Sully, how goes it?"

"Better than you, it looks like. There's this new thing called sunscreen, you should look into it," Sullivan said as he handed a cup of coffee to the older man.

Stevens laughed. "That Mexican sun is hotter than shit. You should see my kid's back. We thought we were going to have to take him to an emergency room down there."

"Better than the rain we've been having up here, though," Sullivan said.

The two agents walked into Hacking's office. After Hacking greeted Stevens, both men sat and looked expectantly at the senior agent. Hacking opened a manila folder and pulled two sheets of paper out and handed one to each man. Sullivan studied the top portion, which held directions to Singleton Penitentiary, and then the bottom, which contained some brief information gathered since the call came in earlier that morning.

"Like I told you both, this one's fucked-up," Hacking said. "The deceased's name is Victor Alvarez. He was a runner and dealer for a Mexican supplier specializing mainly in cocaine and heroin. Got busted last fall in central Minnesota selling to a minor. His trial date was set for later this summer, and he was transferred to Singleton only ten days ago. Yesterday, he got in an altercation with another inmate and hurt the other guy pretty bad. He also attacked several prison officers when they tried to intervene. Subsequently, he was thrown in one of their cells that serve as solitary on the lower level. At about one o'clock this morning, a guard went to check on Alvarez after hearing noises coming from his cell."

Hacking rubbed his eyes with a thumb and forefinger before continuing. "This is where it gets strange, boys. The guard called the local sheriff's office in the neighboring town of Brighton and said that Alvarez had been torn apart."

Silence invaded the room, cut only by the low hum of the single fluorescent overhead. Sullivan glanced over at Stevens before shifting his gaze back to Hacking.

"He was torn apart? Like, dismembered?" Sullivan asked.

Hacking nodded. "From what I can gather, it was a bloodbath. The guard was pretty shaken up. Apparently this was his first week on the job. A Sheriff Jaan called it in shortly thereafter. He said the crime scene was too much to deal with for their local staff and requested our help."

"Forensics already been dispatched?" Stevens asked.

Hacking nodded again. "They should be getting there in about a half-hour."

Sullivan studied the overview of the case before looking at Stevens. The older agent also was re-reading the text, and when he looked up and shrugged, Sullivan asked the question that had been on his mind from the moment Hacking called him about the murder an hour earlier.

"So we're thinking it was one of the staff?"

"Everything points to that, but I want you two on your toes on this one. There's no room for fuckups here. The warden over there is highly respected and runs a tight ship. If we go into this directly accusing his guys of something like this, there could be ramifications that might throw a wrench into the investigation. We want all the help we can get, so let's be diplomatic." Hacking looked back and forth to each man. "Anything else?"

Sullivan lifted a hand, and then set it back on his leg. "The internals on the Lemanski case will be—"

"Taken care of," Hacking finished as he flipped the folder closed on his desk. "You're cleared for active duty, Shale."

Sullivan nodded, and both he and Stevens stood and made their way to the office door. Before they could exit, Hacking spoke again without looking away from his computer screen.

"And Shale? Can you do me a favor on this one, and shoot after the questions have been asked?"

Sullivan gritted his teeth, then nodded as he shut the door behind him slightly harder than necessary.

==

The soft swish of the wipers was the only sound in the vehicle as they swept the light rain away from the windshield. Sullivan tapped an idle finger against the top of the coffee he'd bought at the gas station and watched through the drizzle for the form of Stevens returning to the car. The drenched landscape around the car resembled a page from a black-and-white graphic novel; each object lost its color and faded into a semblance of itself. The rain began to fall shortly after they'd left the bureau, and had only increased in intensity since then. It was Barry's idea to get more coffee, since there weren't many stops before they reached Singleton.

Sullivan rubbed his forehead and glanced at the digital clock in his dashboard: 6:15. The forensics team would be arriving at the crime scene in a few minutes and the investigation would begin in earnest. He could already sense the familiar feeling building in the pit of his stomach: the anticipation of catching someone who had done something very wrong. It was the same every time he went on a death investigation, and he felt relief when he noticed the earlier unease was gone. He held his fingers to his nose and breathed deeply. Cordite. He could still smell it. Even after washing his hands over a dozen times, it was still there. Death incarnate. The only smell that was synonymous with firing a weapon.

Movement in front of the windshield caught his eye, and he saw the hunched outline of Stevens as he rushed to the Trailblazer in an effort to stay relatively dry. The door flew open and slammed shut as Barry threw himself into the passenger seat. Water glinted in his light hair and rolled down the sleeves of his oxford shirt.

"Cats and fucking dogs," he muttered and placed his coffee into the vacant spot in the center console.

As Sullivan began to guide the SUV back onto the highway, Stevens pulled a crinkled wrapper from a small plastic bag near his feet. Carefully, he drew out a dripping sausage-and-egg croissant and bit into it wholeheartedly. Sullivan watched him in mild horror as grease and bits of processed flour dribbled down the other man's dimpled chin.

Stevens finally glanced over at him, and narrowed his eyes. "What?"

"That shit will kill you," Sullivan said before looking back to the rain-slicked road.

"What else am I going to eat?"

"Something healthy."

"Okay, smart-ass. What, pray tell, is healthy at a gas station?"

Sullivan smiled and shrugged. "Boiled eggs, jerky, string cheese, apples, oranges, protein shakes—"

"Oh, fuck you," Stevens said, and bit another mouthful off the drooping sandwich. "Better than not eating anything," he retorted.

Sullivan smiled and picked up his coffee, sipping at the steaming opening in the plastic top.

The two agents rode in silence for several miles, save for the incessant patter of rain on the roof and the hissing of the tires. Stevens finished his croissant and balled up the wrapper before tossing it into the plastic bag. After sipping his coffee, he turned toward the younger agent and furrowed his brow.

"So what do you think?"

Sullivan glanced at him before looking back at the road. "I think we might have a gang retaliation. I'm guessing Alvarez was set to testify against someone higher up for a plea. That someone got to him before he could."

Stevens scratched a piece of dry sunburned skin from his cheek. "Dirty prison officer?"

"That's just my guess. You?"

"I'll hold my tongue till we see the crime scene."

Sullivan nodded. Stevens was right. There would be no way to tell exactly what happened until they were knee-deep in the death itself. Even then it might be difficult to extract any inkling of a suspect.

"Rain just won't quit." Barry's voice broke Sullivan out of his reverie. He looked over at the older man, who stared out of the passenger window. "I've never seen this much rain in my life."

Sullivan nodded. "They're saying Duluth is headed for over a hundred million dollars of repair. Hopefully we can make it into Singleton." Stevens shifted in his seat and continued to stare out of the window. Sullivan examined his friend, and finally brought his eyes back to the road. "I'm guessing you heard about it?"

Barry turned toward him, studied him for a moment, before shaking his head. "I just heard the bare bones of what happened, that Richardson is still in the hospital."

Sullivan rubbed his right eye and took another sip of coffee. "Yeah, he's got a fractured skull and bleeding on the brain. He's not awake yet, but they're saying he's going to be fine. He looks terrible. I went to see him yesterday." Sullivan paused. "We went out to see about a witness, maybe a suspect on that shooting a few weeks ago in the southern part of the county. Woman and guy were blown almost in half by a shotgun in a trailer just outside of Littleton. Looked like a drug hit. Money was gone and everything was torn apart. I called that informant, Maxwell, I use sometimes. He told me that this guy named Todd Lemanski ran with both of the deceased on a regular basis, and that he had a house a few miles from the crime scene."

Sullivan flicked the lever for the high beams, as the sky darkened further and night seemed to fall instead of the expected dawn. The rain pelted down harder, creating a cacophonous symphony around them.

"Richardson and I went out there to ask him a few questions and walked into a nice little meth lab. Lemanski must've been brewing the shit for years. There was enough stuff in there to light up half of the state. We saw all this through a window as we were knocking, and Richardson spots Lemanski making a run for it toward the back door. He goes in through the front and draws. I ran around the opposite side of the house and came into the backyard just in time to see Lemanski smash Richardson in the side of the head with a brick. He'd been waiting just outside the back door for him. Lee hit the ground like he'd been shot. All I see is Lemanski raising the brick over his shoulder, ready to bash Lee in the head again."

Sullivan took another drink of his coffee and swallowed thickly. "I think I yelled, but I'm not sure. All I remember is hearing my slide lock back on empty and seeing Lemanski lying on top of Lee like a bloody sack."

The car was quiet as Barry absorbed the information. Sullivan glanced at his friend a few times, trying to gauge his reaction. "I know that's the only reason Hacking sent you along on this one. He wanted someone to be right behind me the whole time, make sure I was steady."

Barry stared out of the windshield, and then looked over at Sullivan. "You did the right thing, Sully. You only had enough time to react and that's what you did. Richardson's alive *because* you did. Maybe Lemanski would've stopped if you'd waited another second, but maybe he wouldn't have. You made sure Lee will go home to his wife after he's healed up, and that's good enough for me."

Sullivan nodded and focused again on the gray road, replaying Barry's words of comfort over and over, but for some reason they did nothing to dispel the clinging doubt surrounding him.

==

The narrow paved road marked only by a small sign reading *Singleton Penitentiary/New Haven Mental Facility* came up fast. No other notations or markers warned of the turnoff, and Sullivan had to brake hard to avoid driving past it.

"That came out of nowhere," Barry commented as he gripped the handle above his window to keep from getting plastered against the door.

"Sorry, didn't realize it was so close," Sullivan said. He stared down the one-lane path that led out of sight over a slight rise. Pines and poplars alike grew alongside the edges of the drive, hanging over it, dripping water from their limbs, and shutting out the meager light that fell from the dismal sky.

"Did I see *mental facility* listed on that sign too?" Stevens asked as he looked out of the windshield at the rain-slicked road.

"Yeah. From what I understand, New Haven is a subdivision of Singleton. A lot of the state's criminally insane end up there. I love how they've switched *asylum* to *mental facility* too. Love the PC," Sullivan said, shaking his head.

Stevens adjusted his shoulder holster and finished the last of his coffee. Very few words were said during the final hour of the ride to the prison turnoff. Both men had been lost in their own thoughts, not needing to speak them aloud but instead riding in a comfortable silence.

The drive dove down after the slight rise and curved around a sharp corner, until it abruptly ended in water that reached up past the confines of the ditches and completely concealed the blacktop from sight. A small aluminum boat with an outboard motor was beached unceremoniously on the road, a figure in a green rain poncho standing off to its right. A truck with a boat trailer attached to it sat almost in the middle of the drive, and a full-size pewter van was parked on the left-hand side of the road.

Forensics made it okay, Sullivan thought, as he stepped on the brake and glided the Trailblazer to a stop thirty yards before the edge of the water. Both agents looked out of the windshield at the sight before them.

"Holy shit," Sullivan finally said.

"No kidding," Stevens said.

The figure in the poncho approached the SUV and stood, dripping, outside of the driver's-side window. Sullivan could see a wrinkled face patched with stubble beneath the hood of the rain slicker as he rolled down the window and the man stepped closer to the car.

"You guys BCA?"

"Yes, sir. I'm assuming you're Sheriff Jaan?" Sullivan asked.

The sheriff nodded and narrowed his eyes at the two agents in the vehicle. "Road's been blocked up here for almost a week with the rain. You'll have to get your things and I'll take you in the rest of the way with the boat."

Sullivan turned to Barry and gave him a glance. Stevens nodded and grabbed a few papers from the dashboard.

"You two have slickers?" Jaan asked, eyeing both of the men with something that bordered distaste.

"No, not with us," Sullivan answered.

The sheriff huffed and made his way to the boat, and after a minute, returned with two folded ponchos protected in plastic cases. He tossed them through the window, onto Sullivan's lap. "You'll need 'em. Wet out here."

==

The boat's motor churned through the black water as the rain continued to pour down. The three men sat on separate seats; Jaan piloted the craft from the back, his hand lying lightly on the tiller and his dark eyes shifting between the two agents and the waterway ahead. Sullivan sat in the middle on the aluminum seat and Stevens rested in the bow, hunched in a Quasimodo sort of way that Sullivan would have found funny on any other day. At the moment all he wanted to do was make it to an actual structure and get inside out of the unending rain.

Sullivan gazed out from beneath the hood of the poncho and surveyed the way ahead. It felt so strange looking at the water rippling with the drops of the rainstorm, knowing they floated above an actual roadway where cars drove only a week before the storms invaded the area.

"Glad you could come. I didn't want any part of this, actually," Jaan said from the back of the boat over the hum of the outboard.

Sullivan did his best to put on an amiable expression. "Happy to help. How bad is the flooding at the prison?"

Jaan rubbed his chin with a wet hand as the boat bounced over a small wave that jounced each man in his seat. "It's almost up to the gate, but the staff sandbagged nearly the whole perimeter, so they're not actually in danger of flooding quite yet. Horseshit spot for a prison, if you ask me. The area's the lowest spot in the county, the runoff all collects here and there's really nowhere for it to go 'cept Willow Creek, but that's overflowing too." Jaan made a disdainful face, as if disappointed in the weather itself. "Shoulda picked high ground, if you ask me."

Sullivan nodded in agreement and the sheriff seemed appeased. He could tell Jaan was a student of the old school. He had no time for anything out of his realm of reckoning, which seemed to stop just outside of his jurisdiction. All of Sullivan's questions received replies in the same clipped phrases, as if the sheriff thought the agent should have already known the answers.

The watery path encased by the thick trees on either side twisted two more times, left then right, before Sullivan saw that the darkened sky opened up into a clearing ahead.

The dull steel of chainlink fence materialized in the rain, and the black head of the road appeared out of the water a few hundred yards before the prow of the boat. A small guard shack stood at the base of the lapping water, and a stack of sagging sandbags ran in a crooked line several yards in front of it. The prison itself sat on top of a rise, like a mastiff overlooking its territory. The building was two stories and made up mostly of faded brick. Windows adorned its sides sporadically, like dark wounds in the flesh of a fallen beast. Sullivan saw an entryway at the head of the building, lower than the rest of the structure, with two dark red doors encasing its front.

Stevens stared back at Sullivan through the falling rain as the boat slowed and finally idled through the last few yards of water. His eyes said several different things, but Sullivan read one the clearest: *Really? Fucking really?* Sullivan tilted his head to the side and shrugged his shoulders. There would be no turning back now. They were here.

The blacktop growled against the aluminum as the boat slid up onto the rough shore. Stevens climbed out and horsed the small craft up farther, to ensure it wouldn't escape with their disembarkment. Sullivan's hand ran across his poncho and pressed against the familiar form of his Heckler & Koch .45 ACP. The weapon had been with him for years and he needed nothing else to feel secure. He wondered absently if the barrel still smelled like his hands, or if the solvent he'd used to clean it was more powerful than the soap he'd washed with.

Barry steadied the boat as Sullivan climbed over the side and felt the blacktop meet the sole of his shoe. Jaan slid out of the boat last, and gazed up at the oppressive building behind the two agents.

"Well, this is where I leave you," the sheriff growled.

Both men turned toward Jaan, and then looked back and forth to one another.

Stevens stepped forward and flinched as a blast of thunder erupted over their heads. "Aren't you accompanying us to the crime scene?"

The sheriff shook his head. "No, I've been up since yesterday morning and I need some rest. I boated your buddies here, so they should be able to tell you more than I ever could." Jaan eyed the prison's walls again and bit a cracked lip with a few yellowed teeth. "Most fucked-up thing I ever saw. And boys, I seen a lot." He groped for a moment beneath his slicker and then produced a business card with his information, which he handed to Barry. "You can call me in a while if you have questions or you need to get back to the other side."

Without another word, the sheriff proceeded to push the boat back off the road and hopped inside. A few seconds later the motor roared to life, and the sheriff was gone behind the last turn in the channel, leaving a small wake.

Lightning flashed above the agents and they both turned to look at the sandbags, the fence, and the prison beyond.

"Well," Sullivan said.

Stevens breathed in deeply and blew water from the overhanging poncho hood as he exhaled. "Yeah, let's go."

Both men started walking up the wet, rising road to the gate.

Chapter 2

The guard house was empty.

Sullivan cupped his hands to the glass and looked into the small space, then reached out and pressed the red button mounted beside a battered-looking speaker. The button elicited no response, and he wondered how long they would have to wait outside in the rain before someone noticed them standing here. He pressed the button again, beginning to lose his patience, and squinted through the rain at the front doors, willing one of them to open.

"This sucks," Stevens said, as he turned in a slow circle, taking in their surroundings.

Sullivan muttered his agreement and punched the button again. "And what's up with the sheriff not coming to the crime scene? I know he's been up all night, but come on. You don't just toss this kind of shit off to someone else."

Barry shook his head, equally agitated. "Let's just get up there and take a look at the dead guy and get out of the weather. I'm getting fucking soaked through this plastic."

Sullivan was about to press the button a fourth time when both men heard a sound and looked up to see a covered Rhino speeding toward the gate; a lone occupant sat in the driver's seat. The agents watched as the figure tapped in a code on a control box next to the gate and the chainlink began to roll to the side. After a few seconds, the ATV sped down to them. Once he arrived, the driver stared at them from beneath the plastic canopy.

The man looked to be in his early thirties and had narrowed eyes, which Sullivan doubted had ever fully opened, and a large nose, which sat obtrusively on his thin face. He wore a dark blue guard uniform that consisted of a button-up long-sleeve shirt, matching cargo pants, and a baseball hat that had the words *SINGLETON PENITENTIARY* outlined in bold white letters.

Sullivan stepped forward and offered the man his hand. "Hi. Special Agent Sullivan Shale, and this is Senior Special Agent Barry Stevens." The man looked down at Sullivan's hand for a moment before returning his narrow stare back to the agent's face.

"Everett Mooring. Your people are already in the cell."

Sullivan dropped his outstretched hand when he realized that there would be no reciprocation, and glanced over his shoulder at Stevens. Barry rubbed his forehead, and then walked around Sullivan, sitting down in the rear seat of the vehicle. Sullivan followed suit and sat next to Mooring.

The prison guard spun the Rhino around and accelerated up the wet drive toward the still-open gate. Sullivan studied the prison's exterior again. The dull brick walls were reminiscent of several schoolhouses he attended as a child. A small but intricate arch of stone sat atop the building just above the entrance, the prison's name carved deeply into the rock. Two paved pathways led to either side of the building. To the left sat a forlorn basketball court, its hoops devoid of nets and its floor covered with standing water. The path to the right disappeared into a thick grove of trees. Mooring pulled the Rhino under the awning that covered the entrance of the building and stopped a few feet from the doors.

Without bothering to look at either agent, he said, "The desk attendant will direct you to your friends."

Sullivan saw Stevens lick his lips and then begin to say something, but Sullivan cut the other man's words off before they began. "Thank you, Officer Mooring."

Without a glance back, Sullivan stood from the vehicle and relished the feeling of being out of the insistent patter of rain. He heard Barry exit the Rhino, and then watched as Mooring drove from under the awning and disappeared around the side of the building.

"What a fucking ass," Barry said. "I'll have to send a special thanks to Hacking for this one."

Sullivan turned and looked at him from beneath his still-dripping hood. "That guy's not just an ass. He's not happy we're here."

Stevens nodded in agreement, and both agents turned to the swinging double doors and made their way inside the prison.

The lobby wasn't very deep, but it ran the width of the building, and with a ceiling that opened into the second story, it gave the impression of a large space. To the left a door led off into an area encased in reinforced Plexiglas, with several rooms containing simple desks and chairs. To the right was an unmarked oak door with a brass handle. A nameplate sat at eye level, but Sullivan was too far away to read the name etched there. A wooden desk shaped like the prow of a ship sat directly in front of the two agents, and their wet footsteps clacked and echoed off the poly-coated concrete floor and slate walls as they approached it.

A heavyset black woman in a uniform that matched Mooring's sat behind the desk typing on an aged keyboard, and only looked up from the screen before her when Sullivan placed his hand upon the desk and leaned forward.

"Yes?" she said, looking surprised to see them standing there.

"Special Agents Shale and Stevens from the BCA. We're looking for the rest of our crime-scene team."

"Identification?" she asked. Sullivan and Barry both pulled out their wallets and opened them to their photo cards that confirmed who they were. The woman studied both IDs, then nodded and turned in her seat. "See that door there?" she said, pointing to a solid steel door set into the back wall of the room. "I'll buzz you through in a moment. An officer is positioned on the other side. He'll direct you to the rest of your team."

"Thank you," Sullivan said before stepping around the desk and heading for the door. A moment later a loud buzzing sound filled the lobby and Sullivan grasped the cold handle and pulled the heavy door open with a resounding clack.

Behind the steel door the prison expanded into an impressive two-story block of cells that ran away from the men in an almost illusionary impression of infinity. Two steel staircases shot up from the floor on opposite sides of the enormous room and ended on the second level. Doorway after doorway encased with chunky bars of iron lined both the first and second stories. The white paint that covered the cells no longer remained intact and chunks were missing here and there, giving the rows a speckled, shabby look. Several sets of disembodied hands could be seen poking out from the mouths of the cells, but other than the sound of the door slamming solidly shut behind them, the holding area was silent.

A young prison officer sat behind a wooden desk to their immediate left, and he shot up out of his seat as the two agents stepped through the doorway.

"Are you BCA agents?" the officer asked in a voice that cracked with what could have been something bordering on panic.

Sullivan nodded and opened his billfold again, revealing his ID. "Special Agent Shale, and this is—"

The young prison guard moved around the desk and began walking down the long first-floor corridor, his footsteps snapping like gunshots off the concrete. Sullivan looked at Stevens, and the other man merely shrugged.

"You have a more intimidating name anyway," Barry said and brushed past Sullivan, with a smirk on his face.

The prison stretched out before them like an indoor runway. Sullivan looked back and forth from one side of the walkway to the other. Inmates of all ethnicities, wearing orange jumpsuits, stared back at him. Most sat on their beds and their heads turned as the guard and two agents passed by—new scenery in an otherwise drab and routine-enforced world. A few prisoners stood at the doors to their cells, but their eyes did not meet Sullivan's as he looked at them. Instead, they stared either at the floor or to the side, the direction in which the group headed.

As they walked, Sullivan realized that the prison's shape was that of a T. At the very end of the corridor, the building shot outward in either direction and ended in a solid brick wall. Two more staircases accessed the upper level of the rear wall, and he could see a few more sets of eyes peering out at him from both the first and second floors. Their footsteps were the loudest noise in the airy space, and soon Sullivan realized why he felt the edges of unease grating against him: there were no yells of anger or defiance from the cells. No catcalls or agitated mutterings filtered out to them.

The prisoners were quiet.

Sullivan looked around again, searching for a jeering face or a middle finger being raised behind the bars, but saw only darkness and silhouettes.

The guard swung left at the far end of the vaulted hall and proceeded toward a set of steps that turned 180 degrees on a wide landing and descended into an eerie yellow glow. Stevens threw a look over his shoulder and Sullivan followed.

The stairway dropped down two levels and emptied out into a narrow passage, the floor they walked on earlier closing over their heads like a cave. The right side of the hall was poured concrete, unpainted and stained from things Sullivan didn't want to guess at. The left held five doors made of solid steel and resembled the entry into the holding area. All of the doors were shut tight and had small portholes at head height roughly the size of a softball and reinforced with wire mesh. A thin slot only a few inches wide and a foot long had been cut in the middle of each door. The entire area felt like being in a submarine—the bolted bulkheads, the painted doors, and the close ceiling.

Sullivan gazed past the shoulders of Stevens and the guard. The last door in the line was wide-open. Sour light cast a pale urine-colored wedge onto the floor of the hall. He could see one of the forensic specialists standing outside the swath of the door. Sullivan recognized the man as Don Anderson, a veteran and the technical head of the crime-scene unit. Unshakeable, Don was easily the most calm and collected man on the team. At the moment he had both hands shoved deeply into the wide pockets of the white smock over his street clothes; elastic booties encased both of his feet. His graying and partially bald head drooped toward his chest.

The guard leading them suddenly stopped several yards from the open doorway and leaned back against the wall opposite the doors. Barry and Sullivan stopped before him and eyed the young officer, who seemed to want nothing more than to melt into the surface behind him.

"Are you okay?" Stevens asked the guard.

The young man nodded tightly and Sullivan saw his jaw clench, the muscles beneath his cheek going taunt. "I'm going to go back up. If you need me, I'll be at my desk."

The guard tried to slip by Sullivan, but he reached out and snagged the younger man's uniformed wrist, stopping him in his tracks.

Sullivan leaned closer. "Are you the one that found the victim?"

The guard's eyelids fluttered, and then he nodded in a jerky motion, his head snapping up and down.

"Are you okay?" Sullivan repeated Stevens's inquiry, studying the pale unlined face of the officer.

The man roughly pulled his sleeve out of Sullivan's grasp, and without looking back, hurried away from the two agents and disappeared back up the stairway.

Sullivan glanced at Stevens. "Shaken up."

"Hacking said he's fresh here. Probably the first body the poor kid ever saw," Barry said.

Anderson turned toward the agents as they approached, and his eyebrows rose in surprise at the sight of Sullivan alongside Barry. "Wow, that's not much of a mandatory leave," the forensic specialist said.

Sullivan shrugged. "I guess Hacking just loves me that much." Don huffed laughter as both men stepped into the mouth of the doorway. Sullivan was about to ask what had been done so far, when he looked into the interior of the cell and blanched.

The room was small, about half the size of the other cells on the level above them. A single incandescent bulb jutted from the ceiling, encased in a steel cover that leaked light through the gaps. A bed extended from the left wall, just wide enough for a man to lie on. A stainless toilet-and-sink combo sat against the far wall.

Blood. Everywhere.

Gore splashed each wall like a paint mixer had exploded within the room. Chunks of what could only be flesh and bone were speckled here and there among the stains. Something dark and misshapen protruded from a small heating-cooling vent in the floor. Two other members of the forensics team stood in the only bare patches of concrete within the room. Their eyes found Sullivan's, and he registered the same thing he felt at the moment—revulsion. The room smelled like a slaughterhouse, coppery with a hint of decay at the edges.

"What—in—the—fuck?" Barry said in a low voice.

Anderson shuffled closer to the doorway and leaned into the threshold. "Yeah, my sentiments exactly. We were just beginning our layout, but I'll tell you what we've got so far, and this is mainly from the file we were given by the sheriff when we arrived. Victim is male, Mexican descent, age thirty-four. As you can see, there's not much left of the body."

"Not much left?" Sullivan asked as he stepped into the doorway, keeping the tips of his shoes a few inches away from the nearest pool of blood. "I don't see anything."

Anderson motioned the closest forensic tech out of the room, and pointed to the spot he'd been standing in. "Step in there and look at the vent."

Sullivan moved carefully over a stream of blood and took the vacated position on the island of bare concrete. He bent at the knees, drawing closer to the vent in the corner of the room. It was three to four inches in diameter and circular in shape. A thick grate cover matching the vent's width sat on the floor; the headless bolts securing it were snapped in the middle and lay strewn in the blood.

The dark shape growing from the vent's mouth looked like a squashed mushroom. The top was flattened and broken in places, and its sides were crushed and disappeared into the floor. It took Sullivan a moment to realize the dark top of the object had strands that were matted together, giving the illusion of a solid piece.

Hair. He was looking at the top of a head.

Sullivan sucked in a breath and leaned back, horrified at the state of the remains. Slowly, mangled features began to take shape on the decapitated head. A flattened nose here, two smashed orbital sockets there, fractured bone stained black with blood poking through flayed cheeks.

Sullivan pivoted on the dry spot and looked at Anderson and Stevens, who still stood in the doorway. "They jammed his fucking head into the air vent?"

Don nodded. "It appears so. Severe blunt-force trauma to the top of the skull. The jaw was fractured as it was forced into the vent, but it looks like the zygomatic bones were too bulky, along with the rest of the skull's rigid structure, to be pushed farther in."

Sullivan turned back to look at what was left of Victor Alvarez as he heard Barry curse under his breath. He ran through what he was looking at again, beginning the process of categorizing and committing the facts to memory. Head cut off, shoved chin-first into the narrow vent. Skull crushed.

Skull crushed, blood arcing out in a halo around her body.

Sullivan closed his eyes and shook his head. He blinked as the room swayed and then steadied. Not now. He had too much to think about. Not now.

"So where is the rest of him?" Sullivan heard Barry ask behind him. Sullivan stood and faced the two men in the entry.

Anderson rubbed his balding pate. "Off the top of my head?"

"That's not funny," Barry said, grimacing at the forensic specialist. Sullivan smiled grimly.

"I would say whoever did this dismembered the victim systematically, then shoved the pieces down the vent. I guess we'll know for sure once we extract the remains from the floor and see for ourselves," Anderson said.

Sullivan turned in a circle and extended his arm, pointing at a large splash of blood on the wall above the bed. "Am I wrong, or does it look like he was bashed into the walls?"

"It appears so. I think that's the contact point for the first blow," Anderson said, motioning to the spot Sullivan pointed out. "Then the wall behind you, and then perhaps off the floor several times."

"So you're saying he was beaten to death against the walls? How strong would you have to be to do something like that?" Barry asked.

"Or, how many guys would you need?" Sullivan said.

"We won't know for sure until we examine the tissue samples and extrapolate velocity, angle, that sort of thing," Anderson replied. "We also might come up with an idea of a murder weapon that's not currently obvious."

"Were you the first ones in, or was it open before you got here?" Sullivan asked.

"From what the sheriff said, he took one look through the window and called the office, he wanted nothing to do with this. Other than him, no one's said they went in before us," Don replied.

Sullivan looked down at the remains poking from the vent. "Why would they shove him down the vent in the first place? Why not just beat him to death and leave him here?"

Both Anderson and Barry shrugged and stared at the blood coated floor.

Footsteps echoed down the hallway outside of the room, and Sullivan stepped out of the cell and let the technician return to his position.

Two men strode down the corridor toward the group. The man in the lead wore a charcoal suit and appeared to be in his late fifties or early sixties. He was well over six feet tall and wisp thin. Feathery gray hair that might have been blonde at one time was combed neatly to one side of the man's head. His face was slightly horse-like, with large but even teeth that already were beginning to poke from beneath a pair of narrow lips in a polite smile. The second man, who strode a few paces behind, was a glowering Everett Mooring.

The older man extended a hand to Stevens as he neared, the smile spreading warmly across his features. "Agents Stevens and Shale, I presume?" the man said.

Barry shook the man's hand. "Yes, sir. I'm Barry Stevens, and this is Sullivan Shale and our forensic pathologist, Don Anderson."

"David Andrews, I'm the warden. I believe you've already met my chief officer?" Andrews said, motioning over his shoulder at the impassive guard behind him.

"He was kind enough to give us a lift earlier this morning," Sullivan said congenially, hoping to crack Mooring's stony façade. The guard only stared at him as if he were part of the wall.

The warden nodded and smiled again. "Yes, I'm sorry that you've been called here on such grim circumstances, and with the current uncooperative weather conditions. I was just telling Everett that a possible evacuation might be needed if the rain doesn't let up soon."

Silence fell over the group of men and Sullivan glanced at Barry before addressing the warden. "We were hoping we could have a word with you. Go over some basic information before we begin the investigation?"

The warden closed his eyes and nodded. "Of course, gentlemen. Any help my staff and I can provide. We are at your service."

"Thank you," Barry said, and turned back to Anderson, who placed a set of safety glasses on his round face and began pulling on a pair of latex gloves. "Don, you'll let us know when you're done and if you find anything significant?"

"We'll be right here for a while," the team leader said.

The warden motioned to the stairs leading back up to the main holding area. "Follow me, gentlemen."

Chapter 3

Thunder grumbled outside the window of the warden's office and rain clicked against the glass like a hundred metronomes.

"Would either of you like a cup of coffee or tea?" Andrews asked as he shut the wooden door behind them and motioned to the two leather seats in front of a wide mahogany desk.

"Coffee would be great," Barry answered as he settled into the left chair.

Sullivan nodded as the older man busied himself near a small coffee station in the corner of the room. As Sullivan dropped into the right chair, he took a moment to study the warden's office.

Andrews had led them back through the holding area and, wordlessly, Mooring split off from the group when they entered the lobby, disappearing behind a single door on the far side of the large room. Andrews brought them to the wooden door with the brass plate Sullivan had noticed on their way in, and ushered them inside. The interior of the room had high ceilings, mirroring the lobby, with ornate woodworking that extended from either wall and joined in the center with a low-hanging chandelier made of brass and stainless steel. The walls were rather bare, a single painting of the prison's grounds hanging on the wall behind Andrew's desk and half a dozen headshots of middle-aged men adorning the space to the right. A tall bookshelf beside the pictures held numerous volumes that would've looked at home in any lawyer's office or judge's chambers. The windows were reinforced with steel mesh and sat just out of reach of even the tallest man's grasp.

"Sugar? Cream?" the warden asked from the corner.

"Cream in mine, please," Barry said.

"Black is fine for me," Sullivan said.

Andrews made his way back to where the agents sat and handed each their respective coffees. After retrieving a steaming cup of tea from the beverage tray in the corner, the older man sat behind the desk, with a sigh and a weary smile at the two agents.

"So, where to begin?" the warden said, looking from Sullivan to Barry and then back again.

Sullivan sat forward after sipping from the hot mug of coffee in his hand. "We'd like to start by just laying out what transpired prior to the call our office received last night. What can you tell us about the victim?"

Andrews sighed and cupped his tea in both hands as if chilled. "Mr. Alvarez came to us just a short time ago—a little over a week, perhaps? Brought up on drug trafficking and selling to a minor. His stay here was only temporary, as he was scheduled to stand trial later this summer. Until yesterday, his record here was fairly uneventful." The warden set his cup down and interlaced his fingers as he looked across the desk at the two agents. "Do you gentlemen know how many altercations between inmates we've had here at Singleton?"

Both men shook their heads.

"We've had five since I began here almost six years ago. Five." The warden sat back in his chair and grasped his tea once again. "Alvarez was the first in a while to disturb our relative peace that we enjoy here. He was a difficult man to understand from the beginning."

"You speak as if you know almost everyone here, Warden," Sullivan said, his eyes narrowing a bit as he spoke.

"I try to be very hands-on in my position, gentlemen. I run a well-oiled machine here, but it doesn't mean that I am without compassion."

"We understand, please go on," Barry said.

"Each and every man here has a story and is serving justice in his own right. Victor had a bad attitude, I could tell it from the day he came here, but up until last night he hadn't caused any real trouble."

"What happened exactly?" Sullivan said, turning on his phone and opening his dictation application. Andrews stared at the phone for a moment before raising his eyes to Sullivan's face. "Do you mind if I record the conversation for later reference?" Sullivan asked.

The warden's face softened and he smiled benignly once again. "Of course not. Mr. Alvarez shared a cell with another inmate, named Henry Fairbend. Yesterday evening the guard on duty heard yelling coming from their cell, and when he got there, Victor was on top of Henry yelling obscenities and choking the life out of him. He was tased after being warned, but as soon as he was able, he began to attack the guards who had come to attend to Henry's injuries. We had no other choice than to detain him in solitary confinement, a rather unheard of occurrence here."

"Can you tell us what events led up to the deceased being discovered?" Sullivan asked as he adjusted his phone so that it lay closer to Andrews on the desk. The older man paid no attention to the agent's passive tactic.

"From what I understand, at around midnight the guard on duty heard sounds coming from the lower level. He went to investigate, and when he looked through the door to check on Alvarez … well, you yourselves saw what the inside of the room looked like."

Sullivan's gaze didn't waver as he scrutinized the warden. He hadn't heard any inflections in the man's narration. No pitch changes or backpedaling that would indicate a lie. He seemed to be telling the truth.

"That's it? The guards on duty saw nothing out of the ordinary? No other inmates heard or saw anything either?" Sullivan asked, dropping his hand away from the side of his face.

The warden shrugged and his white eyebrows rose at the same time. "Nothing of use. Several of our officers were outside sandbagging at the time, since we had reports that the water level was quickly on the rise."

The warden stood from the chair and turned to look out of the high windows, which still drummed with raindrops. He sighed and turned back to the agents. "Gentlemen, it's been a rough couple weeks. Since the flooding started, I've had little else on my mind other than the safety and security of this facility. Right now the runoff is flowing into Willow Creek. A mile or so to the east the Isle River takes it down to Lake Superior itself, but it hasn't been keeping up. Our next option is to evacuate the prison to New Haven, across the compound."

"The mental facility?" Barry asked.

"Yes. The flooding is really the only thing that could actually harm this place. We are very self-sufficient. We have our own well, rations to last a month, and a full arsenal. New Haven is on slightly higher ground and it might give us some more time."

The warden sighed again and slumped back into the chair behind the desk. His long form seemed to bow under the strain of worry, and Sullivan felt a twinge of pity for the old man.

When he looked up, the warden's eyes appeared tired but clear. "I'm telling you gentlemen this because, in all honesty, I don't know how to deal with what happened last night in that cell, it goes beyond my understanding. My plate is already full, and although we would have been able to work with the local law enforcement on this matter, I think it's a blessing the sheriff called you in."

Both Barry and Sullivan nodded. "We'll work as hard as we can to bring this to a close," Barry said, his voice low and soothing in the large office.

A look of relief crossed the warden's face. "What do you need from me?" he asked.

"We'll need to take a look at the surveillance tapes from the last twenty-four hours, as well as interview the guard who found the remains this morning," Sullivan said. "Also, if Fairbend is well enough to speak to us, we'd like to talk to him."

Andrews nodded and began to scribble on a pad of paper before him. "I'll have Everett take you to the control room shortly, and I'll send a note to our medical staff to see if Henry is awake. The guard's name who found Victor this morning is Nathan Hunt, but I'm not sure if he'll be much help until he's calmed down and gotten some rest. Poor boy, it's his first week on the job, and to have this happen." Andrews shook his head and blinked as if he himself were on the brink of exhaustion.

Both agents stood and reached across the desk to shake the warden's hand. "We'll let you know if we come across anything else or if we need further assistance," Barry said as they headed for the door. Andrews murmured his acknowledgement as they stepped back out into the lobby and closed the door behind them.

Barry breathed out heavily and pinched the bridge of his nose. "So what do you think?"

When he saw the female guard peering over the top of her monitor at them, Sullivan glanced around the area and motioned Barry to follow him closer to the entrance. When he was sure they were out of earshot, Sullivan leaned toward his friend so that their heads were only inches apart.

"I think there's something seriously fucked here. Did you not notice how quiet it was in the holding area? You ever been to a jail or lockdown that was that still? You could've heard a mouse fart in there. The other thing is, have you ever not been asked to leave your weapon at the front desk? Or how about most of the guards being armed? That's not standard protocol anymore, is it?"

Barry seemed to mull this over for a moment. "So what's your theory?"

Sullivan leaned against the wall and hissed air between his teeth as he thought. "Don't have one yet. But I'll tell you this, there's no way one person pulled off what happened in that cell. It looked like a bunch of crack heads went to work on that guy with a dozen hammers after someone told them he was full of coke."

"Well, let's hope there's not an army of jonesing crack heads with hammers running rampant around here. That would make things go less smoothly," Barry said.

"Yes, it would. Let's find that surveillance room, I don't want to wait around for that asshole Mooring."

==

Sullivan rapped his knuckles against the steel door and the sound echoed down the hallway like a tomb sealing shut. Barry stood to his left and shivered in the cool air of the prison.

"Can't get warm after being out in the rain," Barry said, rubbing his thick arms over the material of his shirt.

"Don't catch cold now and leave me here with all this fun," Sullivan said as he reached out and knocked on the door again.

The guard at the front desk had directed them to the door to their left and buzzed them through, into what Sullivan suspected was the interview/visitor area. Several rooms with plain tables and chairs were positioned to their left as they'd made their way along the first floor. A few doors led off to the right, no doubt traveling to the main holding area as a passage for inmates who needed to be brought out for visitors or interrogation. At the end of the hall an unmarked door stood by itself, ominously touting two separate deadbolts and no handle. A set of stairs shot up to the left and emptied into a matching hall a floor above. They'd stopped in front of a door marked "Surveillance," and with no other means of announcement, began knocking.

"Didn't she say there was a guard stationed here at all times?" Sullivan asked as he listened for a sound from behind the door.

"Yeah, she did. Maybe we should go back down and have her call up—"

Sullivan kicked the door hard with the ball of his foot. The door rattled in its frame and then fell silent.

"Jesus, Sully," Barry said, but then the door flew open and both men stepped back slightly, surprised.

A disheveled-looking overweight guard stood in the doorway. His dark hair hung down past his ears and a pair of modernly old eyeglasses sat skewed on his paunchy face. A silver hoop earring hung from his left earlobe and shook a little when the man began to speak.

"Can I help you guys?"

Sullivan stepped forward. "Special Agents Shale and Stevens from the BCA. We're here for the homicide that occurred last night. We'd like to take a look at the footage, if you don't mind."

The guard glanced back and forth between the two agents, and then a smile broke out on his wide face. "You guys are from the BCA?" Sullivan nodded, his eyebrows wrinkling despite his effort to keep his annoyance from surfacing completely. "That's so cool!" the guard exclaimed.

Sullivan and Barry exchanged looks as the guard continued. "I've always wanted to meet an actual BCA agent and I never have. Been here for four years now, and pretty much all I've seen is the inside of this box." The guard's face was alight with something like awe and Sullivan had the urge to laugh. Here, in the middle of one of the strangest crime scenes and the most inhospitable weather he'd ever experienced, they'd found a fanboy. Unreal.

Sullivan smiled and nodded, and out of his peripheral vision he saw Barry doing the same. The guard kept grinning and looking at each of their faces, as if they were movie stars and had suddenly stepped off the silver screen into real life. The silence in the hall lengthened into something uncomfortable, and finally Sullivan motioned toward the small room behind the guard.

"Could we come in?"

Realization flooded the other man's features and his cheeks reddened. "Yeah, sorry, of course. My name's Benjamin Strous, but you can call me Benny, everyone does."

Sullivan grasped the man's pudgy hand in his own and shook, not sure if he was bemused or irritated.

Benny spun in place and waved them into the room after his considerable bulk cleared the doorway. "Come on in, guys. Make yourselves at home."

The room was windowless and perhaps twelve by twelve. The aroma of old coffee and stale chips hung in the air. After looking around the crowded space, Sullivan spotted several coffee cups with drying stains in their bottoms and errant Doritos wrappers on the floor beneath a cluttered desk. Computer equipment of all types sat at odd angles against the walls and invaded the floor with their wires. Towers, blinking servers, and data-storage racks hung from different areas, and video screens were mounted every foot or so at varying heights along the gray wall. A chair with a seat so flattened it looked one-dimensional sat in front of what looked like the main terminal. A keyboard and mouse lay on the desk before it.

"Home sweet home," Benny said as he stood behind the chair and swept an arm around the room. "This is the brainpan of Singleton. Everything that happens comes through here either in data entry or in video feed."

Sullivan stepped behind the chair and began to place his hands on its back but noticed some unsavory stains there, and instead put them in the pockets of his slacks. "Mr. Straus, I'm sure you're—" Sullivan stopped as the guard held up a hand and pushed his black-framed glasses tightly onto his face with a fingertip.

"Please, guys. Call me Benny."

Sullivan smiled. "Benny, I'm sure you're aware of what happened last night?"

Benny's face lit up and his eyes seemed to sparkle in the glare of the overhead fluorescents. "Yeah, that was really weird, huh? I heard the guy was torn apart. I mean, can you imagine? What do you guys think happened?"

Sullivan exhaled and licked his lips. "Well, we were hoping you'd be able to rerun the footage from last night for us."

Benny spun the chair around to accept his egg-shaped body, and pulled himself tight to the console. "I already took a look, and I'm sorry to say that there's not much to see, guys." Benny's hands flew over the keyboard, and with a last click of the mouse, a gray-tinged video began to play on four of the main screens sitting on the wall directly opposite the three men.

Sullivan glanced at the flickering white numerals of time in the upper right-hand corner: *0.1.12/6/2/12*. A few minutes before Hunt found Alvarez. The picture itself Sullivan recognized as the solitary corridor. Although the video was nowhere near clear, he could make out the five doors on the left side and the row of lights lining the ceiling. The agents along with the guard watched the screens, and soon a soundless figure stepped into view. Sullivan knew the man at once as the guard that led them to the crime scene earlier. Hunt walked unsurely down the corridor like he was listening to something that puzzled him. His head was cocked at a strange angle, and Sullivan saw one of the guard's hands stray to the handgun holstered on his belt. Hunt made his way closer and closer to the end cell, and Sullivan felt himself leaning forward and noticed Barry did the same. Hunt neared Alvarez's door and looked through the porthole. He staggered back as if he'd been struck and nearly fell against the opposite wall.

"Oh! There it is!" Benny exclaimed, pointing at the TVs with a near-unrestrained glee. Both agents frowned at the back of the guard's head as he laughed like a kid watching a Sunday matinee.

Sullivan's gaze returned to the monitors and saw Hunt draw his weapon and then pull a small walkie-talkie to his mouth. Sullivan could almost see the terror on the young man's face as he stood there in the quiet hallway, could almost feel the tension as he waited alone. A reply must have come back, because Hunt suddenly sprinted out of the picture the way he had come, one hand still clutching his gun and the other pumping at his side as he ran. The picture remained that way for another thirty seconds, and then flipped to a current feed of the massive holding area.

Benny spun around in his chair and shrugged at the two agents, who stood in front of him. "That's all we've got, guys. Sorry we don't have more. I watched from the time Alvarez was put into solitary to what you just watched, and there's nothing."

"Don't you have a better angle? Closer to the door or actually within the cell?" Stevens asked.

Benny shook his head. "No. The cameras were installed almost ten years ago down there and no new ones have been added, so all we have is footage of the hallway."

Sullivan glanced at Barry, and then back at the overweight guard. "Benny, we'll need you to copy the portion of the video from when Alvarez is transferred into the cell until our crime-scene team arrived. You can do that?"

"Oh, no problem. I'll do it digitally, and I'll copy a file to a disk as well as email," Benny said, his head twitching back and forth between the two men, as if he were a dog that had accomplished a trick.

After giving Benny their email addresses, Sullivan and Barry exited the surveillance room and stood in the empty hall. Barry ran a hand through his thinning hair and leaned against the wall. Sullivan stretched his back and stifled a yawn that crept up out of nowhere.

"Dead end," Barry said, his voice echoing down the empty hallway.

"Yeah. Although I didn't expect a solution delivered on high-res digital, all neat and wrapped up for us."

Barry smiled. "No, I didn't either."

"I don't know about you, but I'm starving. Want to get some food before we talk to Hunt?" Sullivan asked.

"Absolutely," Barry said, slapping his stomach. "Gotta keep my strength up."

"Is that what you're calling it now?" Sullivan said over his shoulder as he started walking toward the stairway.

"You know, Sully, I always suspected, but now I know. You're jealous of my physique."

Sullivan chuckled and was about to throw another remark at his friend when Everett Mooring stepped onto the landing at the top of the stairs, blocking their path. The man's pants were soaking wet from the knees down and droplets of water fell onto the floor around his feet. His eyes shifted between Sullivan and Barry, a silent rage thrumming just behind them. He stood with his body cocked toward them, one foot in front, the other braced behind. He looked like a man preparing for a fight.

"Officer Mooring, we were just looking for you. Could you—" Sullivan was cut off as the guard spoke in even tones of anger and distaste.

"You were supposed to wait until I escorted you up here."

"You're right, Warden Andrews mentioned it, but we thought we'd take initiative and find our way—"

"This isn't some crime scene you can waltz into and take over. This is a prison. You're out of your element here. Don't go wandering off again."

Mooring turned and disappeared down the stairs, his wet boots squeaking as he went. Sullivan waited until the footsteps faded altogether before he turned back to Barry, who looked as if he'd swallowed sandpaper followed by a lemon.

"Seriously, what the fuck is up with that guy?" Sullivan asked. He noticed his hands were balled into fists and he unclenched them, leaving little half-moons where his fingernails dug into his palms.

"Screw him," Barry said and began heading for the stairs again. "Guy's got a problem with us being on his turf. Fucking weird, if you ask me. I wouldn't claim this place if I got the deed signed over to me in gold ink."

The two agents turned toward the stairwell, and Sullivan paused at the top before descending. He stood stock-still until Barry noticed that he wasn't following and looked imploringly at him from the stairwell landing.

"What?" Barry asked.

Sullivan shook his head and continued down the steps. "Nothing," he replied. But in the back of his mind he kept replaying the sound he had heard in the hallway just as they were leaving it: the sound of a door quietly clicking shut.

==

The sausage and eggs from the prison kitchen were so greasy that Sullivan had to keep wiping his mouth on the stiff paper napkin the cook provided near the end of the chow line.

He and Barry sat at a low table that seemed to stretch the entire length of the prison's commons. Two dozen multicolored round stools were attached to the table with steel bars, and a joint every so often in the table's surface indicated that, if need be, it would fold up to a quarter of its original length. The room itself was half the size of the main holding area, but still maintained an impressive air. The ceiling matched those of the rest of the prison, and expanded above them to well beyond the second story. A walkway was positioned on either side of second-floor level for the guards to pace as prisoners ate below. A panel of steel doors lined the far side of the room; the doors were up revealing the kitchen beyond. Table after table sat in rows on the floor, designed to hold a quarter of the facility's population at a time. A bank of windows rested high in the north wall, revealing a grimy sky that matched the walls perfectly. Rain still fell outside in silver streaks, and every so often lightning etched a pattern through the unmoving clouds.

Sullivan chewed his breakfast slowly, wondering if the scrambled eggs were actual eggs and what animal the sausage really came from.

"Okay, let's outline this thing," Barry said from across the table, as he sipped at a juice box displaying an orange on the front. "We have a dead guy alone in a cell, torn apart and supposedly shoved down a tiny heating vent. We have no witnesses and no video, since this fucking place is still on *Shawshank* time. We have a warden who wants our help, a head officer who wants us out, an IT guy who wants to blow us, and no leads. Does that about sum it up?"

Sullivan laughed and pushed his spotless plate away across the table. "Yeah, that's about it."

"I thought so," Barry said, dropping his fork onto his unfinished eggs. "I don't know how you ate that shit," he said, jabbing his finger at the remaining food.

"Gotta keep my strength up," Sullivan said, smiling.

"Smart-ass."

"This coming from a guy that devours gas-station burritos by the pound."

Barry responded by flipping up his middle finger.

The commons was eerily quiet. Sullivan wondered if it was being in an empty space made for many people or if it was something more. The rain, the storms, the murder, Mooring, the incongruence of the prison, it all weighed on him. He had seen his share of horrors; there was no way of escaping them in this line of work. But something in the back of his mind kept setting off alarms. Something treaded there, disturbing the calm he normally felt while working cases.

"Okay," Sullivan finally said. "Let's talk to Hunt. I don't care how tired he is, we need to get a statement out of him about what happened. Then we go to see this Fairbend. I'm still guessing this ties in to Alvarez's upcoming trial date. We just have to figure out who got at him and who let them in the cell, agreed?"

"Agreed."

"Let's go."

Both men stood and returned their plates to the proper station at the food windows. The cook solemnly watched them as he toiled beside the ticking ovens, cutting vegetables and opening cans big enough to fit a man's head inside.

When they stepped into the main holding area, it was not Hunt's young face that met them but a different guard wearing a well-trimmed goatee and blue baseball hat with the Singleton insignia on the front.

"We were wondering if Officer Hunt was available to answer a few questions," Sullivan said to the new guard behind the desk. The guard gazed at the two agents, and then scanned the prison floor behind them in a nonchalant way that made Sullivan want to leap the desk and flip the other man out of his chair onto the hard cement.

"He just got off shift," the guard said.

"Where can we catch up with him?" Sullivan asked, his voice rising with the anger that began to boil within his stomach.

The officer stretched and lazily laced his hands behind his head as he leaned back in his seat. "He's going home, so he might already be gone. He was getting boated to the other side, far as I know."

Sullivan turned and strode to the security door and was buzzed through with Barry trailing behind. The main entrance doors were opaque with rain, and thunder drowned out the last words of the guard in the main holding area. As the two men swept across the lobby and through the doors outside, a wave of heat ran over both of them. The storm hadn't subsided a bit while they'd been within the building. If anything, it had increased. The grass around the prison walls was flat under the constant moisture, and the trees surrounding the facility swayed in the slow dance of the storm. Sullivan squinted through the slanting rain and spotted two figures past the perimeter fence, one sitting in the rear of a small boat and the other making its way toward the edge of the water, which looked closer than it was when he and Barry had arrived earlier.

Sullivan sprinted out from beneath the canopy and into the rain. He heard Barry yell something behind him, but he didn't pause or turn. He needed to catch Hunt before he got away. He couldn't let the young man leave his sight.

Somewhere deep inside he knew, if he did, he would never see Hunt again.

"Stop!" Sullivan yelled as he reached the fence and punched a red control button attached to the nearest post.

His voice must have carried, because the closest figure stopped at the edge of the water and turned toward him. Sullivan could just make out Hunt's young, drawn face beneath the hood of the poncho he wore. The gate rolled back and Sullivan hurried past it, jogging the rest of the way to where the boat rested on the blacktop. Hunt's eyes were red-rimmed and sagging, but there was also fear there. Sullivan saw it as he pulled up short and stopped a few feet from the guard.

"Officer Hunt, we need to speak with you before you go home. Are you able to do that?"

Hunt's shoulders sagged with the agent's words. Sullivan could see how tired the younger man was. Stress weighed on him and fatigue had settled in shortly thereafter. Sullivan knew he needed sleep and quiet, a chance to relax, but there was no time for that. There were questions to be asked and answered, and right now, Hunt was their best bet at finding out what had happened in that cell.

"He needs to go home and rest. Don't you people have any concern for fellow officers, or are we just shit you step on while you wade through a case?" Officer Mooring raised his head enough for Sullivan to make out his features in the dim light. Everett's eyes were shadowed further by his eyebrows, which were drawn down so far Sullivan wondered how the other man could see anything at the moment.

"I'm not going to argue with you," Sullivan said, biting his tongue at the insults he wished to throw at the man in the back of the boat. "We have a murder investigation going on here, if you haven't noticed, and Officer Hunt needs to be interviewed. Now, do I need to hold on to the goddamned boat until Warden Andrews comes down here and gives you an order to comply, or are you gonna play ball?"

Sullivan watched Mooring's jaw tighten and strain beneath the hood. Mooring's hand moved toward the starter button on the motor and Sullivan felt himself instinctually reaching for his HK45—muscle memory at its best. His fingers brushed the hard polymer and wet steel in the holster.

Hunt seemed to be caught in a churning riptide. His right hand rested on the bow of the boat, but his head was still turned toward Sullivan. His body swayed in time with the trees and he looked ready either to jump over the side of the boat or fall onto his ass; neither would have surprised Sullivan.

Hunt finally let go of the boat and began walking toward the prison. "I'll go back inside. I'm super-tired, but I'll tell you what I can." His eyes searched Sullivan's as he approached, and the agent felt his anger vanish at the sight of how distraught the young guard was. He looked like he was made of clay and was close to crumbling. "Then, can I go home? I'd just like to go home."

Sullivan nodded and brushed back his soaking hair with one hand. "We just need to talk for a little while, then you can go get some rest."

Hunt pulled his poncho around him tighter and set off up the hill, toward the prison. Sullivan watched him go, then glanced at Barry, who had caught up and looked at him questioningly. Sullivan turned and glared at Mooring, who was already starting the outboard.

"Fuck off," Sullivan muttered as the boat scraped off the blacktop and churned backward until Mooring spun it in a tight circle and sped out of sight around a grouping of pine trees.

Without another look back, Sullivan followed Barry and Hunt up the rain-soaked road to the waiting mouth of Singleton.

Chapter 4

Hunt wrapped his fingers around the steaming cup of coffee when Sullivan placed it in front of him, his eyes peering down into the black liquid as if there might be something important there. Sullivan sat down on the opposite side of the table in the interview room, feeling the unpleasant squishing of his clothes, as they pressed close to his body, while a fresh patter of rainwater dripped onto the floor.

Barry shut the door and sat down beside Sullivan. "We're very sorry to keep you, but you understand how important this is?" Barry said. Hunt nodded and tried to smile, but it fell flat and his mouth went back to its original half-open state. "You don't mind if we record this, do you?" Barry asked, placing his phone onto the table near Hunt's coffee cup.

"No, not at all," the officer said.

"So, Nathan—can I call you Nathan?" Sullivan asked, looking imploringly at the younger man.

"Sure … Nate's fine, actually."

"Good. You can call me Sully. Nate, tell us about your time here so far. How'd you become a prison officer?"

Nate's lips worked soundlessly for a moment. Perhaps he hadn't expected such a friendly question to begin the interview. Sullivan smiled and wrinkled his brow, trying to get his left eye to open fully.

"My dad, I guess. He got me the job. He's a prosecutor in Aitkin County. He went to school with Warden Andrews. They play golf together sometimes. I did two years of law-enforcement training up north, and then started here last week." Nate rolled his head on his neck and blinked several times.

"You okay, Nate?" Sullivan asked.

"Yeah, just really tired. I haven't been sleeping well."

"We'll try to keep this short. How do you like it here?"

Nate chuckled. "So far, it sucks. I have the shittiest shifts available, which I expected, but the other thing is, it's a little cliquey here."

"'Cliquey'?" Sullivan said.

"Yeah, you know. Nobody's been real friendly, except the warden, and I've only seen him a few times, since my shifts are at night normally. I don't know, maybe it's just a hazing thing, but sometimes, I walk into a room and some of the other guards are at a table talking and they stop and look at me when I come in."

Hunt shrugged. "And then last night." The young officer shook his head and closed his eyes. "We saw a few films in school—car accidents and gunshot victims. I watched *Faces of Death* when I was younger." Hunt's eyes opened and he stared at the two agents in turn. "I've never seen anything like that before."

"Let's run through last night, okay?" Sullivan said. "How'd it start?"

Hunt breathed out and seemed to deflate an inch lower into the chair. His hands gripped the mug before him, but he made no attempt to drink. "I came on shift at eight in the evening. It'd been raining all day and Mooring boated me in. My car's actually stuck here, so I got a lift from a friend to the edge of the water. I punched in, checked my report sheet for incidents during the last shift, and saw there'd been a fight between inmates."

"Alvarez and Fairbend," Sullivan said.

"Yeah. I read the report. It was short. Just said Alvarez became irritated and started screaming something at Fairbend. Then he attacked him, and the guards on duty pulled him off and brought him down to solitary."

"What time was that?" Sullivan asked.

"I think it said about six p.m. in the report. I didn't think much of it. In fact, to be honest, I was a little disappointed that I'd missed some action. Nights are fucking boring around here, pardon my French."

"Pardoned," Sullivan said, smiling a little.

"So the shift went just like the last week had. I made rounds on the floor, checked in with the front desk, played with my phone for a while, until about midnight. That's when I first started hearing the noises." Hunt looked around the room and glanced over the agents' shoulders, as if searching for an eavesdropper. His eyes took on the glint of fear that Sullivan had seen earlier.

Sullivan reached out to touch the young man's hand. "Nate, we're not going to tell anyone else what you heard. You can be honest. This is for the case, nothing else."

Nate swallowed and nodded, but Sullivan still saw doubt in his face.

"You ever heard a shipyard at night?" Nate said.

"A shipyard?" Sullivan asked, tilting his head to one side.

"Yeah, like the docks over on Superior when some of the big ore boats come in and spend the night." Sullivan shook his head and Stevens did the same. "The hulls of the ships groan with the change in weight and pressure when they're unloaded, and it sounds like whales sometimes, deep underwater, talking to each other." Nate paused, squinting at the memory he was, no doubt, examining. "That's what it sounded like last night."

"And you heard this from where? Your desk?" Sullivan asked.

"Yeah. At first I couldn't tell where it was coming from, it sounded like it was all around me, but then it was farther away and I narrowed it down. It was coming from the solitary level."

Sullivan nodded and rubbed the scar over his left eye. Perhaps the kid had cracked a little with the lack of sleep and the trauma of seeing what was left of Alvarez. Maybe he should have let him get a few hours of rest before asking him to recall details that might be a bit blurry at the moment.

"I'm not losing it, if that's what you're thinking," Nate said, seemingly reading Sullivan's thoughts.

"I know you're not, Nate. Tell me what happened next."

"I followed it. The sound. The prisoners either didn't hear it or they were pretending not to. None of them even got up from their bunks. When I got to the top flight of the stairs, I heard something else. Screaming." Nate stared down at the table, next to his coffee cup, and ran a fingernail along a crack in its surface. "You guys ever heard a man scream? I mean, really scream? Like he's dying?"

Both agents shared a glance before looking back at the man across the table from them, who now didn't look like a boy much past his teens. He had regressed before their eyes. "Yes, I have,"

Sullivan finally said, and held Hunt's stare when the younger man tried to see if he was lying.

Satisfied, Nate nodded and went back to scraping his thumbnail on the table. "It was horrible. I kept hearing it all day. I can still hear him. I shouldn't have been surprised when I looked into the cell and saw what I did."

"We saw the tape of the corridor when you found Alvarez. Where'd you go after that?"

"I ran. I ran up to the second level and right out to the front desk. I was radioing Shelly all the way, but she didn't answer. I don't know if it was the storm messing with the walkies or what. The rain had been coming down harder and most of the rest of the guards were outside stacking sandbags, so when I got to the lobby, I told Shelly what I'd seen. Then I called the local sheriff, told him we needed help. Maybe I shouldn't have, but I was panicking."

"Did you see anything else unusual down in the solitary hall? Anyone else?"

Nate jerked his head back and forth. "No, no one. When I got to the door of the cell, he'd stopped making noise and all that was left was his head on the floor."

Sullivan shifted uncomfortably in his chair, trying to find a position in which his wet clothes didn't pull at his skin so much, and then stopped and leaned forward. "Nate, where was his head when you looked through the window?"

The guard squirmed in his chair and swallowed. "It was on the fucking floor, in the middle of the room."

"You mean, in the vent at the corner of the room, right?" Sullivan said, letting his right eyelid drop so that it matched his other one.

"No, not near the vent. In the middle of the floor. His fucking eyes were still open, for Christ's sake. I won't forget that till the day I die." Nate was becoming unstable. His hands shook as he tried to grip the cold coffee cup. His shoulders hitched as if sobs were merely a few seconds away.

"Nate, did you see the crime scene after you initially discovered it?" Sullivan asked, willing the guard's fragile state to hold for just a few more minutes.

"N-n-no," Nate finally stammered. "I couldn't fucking go back in there. The closest I got was when I brought you down there this morning. Can we be done? Please?" The young man's voice began to quaver.

Sullivan nodded. "Yes, we can be done. You did great, Nate. Go get some rest." Sullivan said.

Nate stood, nearly knocking the cup of coffee over in his haste. Barry rose and opened the door for him as he neared it, but Sullivan grasped the guard's damp sleeve in a gentle grip, turning him back toward the table.

"You're going to be just fine, Nate. You hear me? Just fine."

Nate's eyes finally teared up and a few drops slid down his sallow cheeks. He didn't make a move to wipe them away. Instead, he swallowed and looked into Sullivan's face, as if really seeing him for the first time.

"Not everybody freaks out like this, do they? There's something wrong with me, isn't there?"

The kid's naked emotion and battered demeanor nearly broke Sullivan's heart. He waited only a beat, and then shook his head. "There's nothing wrong with you, Nate. Every one of us goes through something like this. You're just fine."

Nate waited for a moment on the threshold, and then seemed to accept Sullivan's words. He slowly turned and gave a halfhearted smile to Barry, who still held the door. Sullivan listened to the fading footsteps of the guard, until Barry shut the door and sealed them in relative silence. The faint boom of thunder could be heard every so often, but it was muffled and somehow comforting. Perhaps it was knowing that the real world was still out there, carrying on as it always had despite what happened between the walls in which they now sat.

Barry leaned on the table and looked at Sullivan, his eyes like pinpoints. "Did you get what I did out of all that?" he finally asked and sat on the table's edge, facing his friend.

Sullivan stared off through the glass walls of his mind, already debating the logic and probabilities of what the young guard's testimony meant. After nearly a full minute of silence, he sat back, squeezing more water out of his shirt onto the floor, and gazed at Barry, his left eye barely visible beneath his sagging brow.

"Yeah. It means the killer was still in the cell when Nate looked through that window."

==

Sullivan listened to the dull buzzing in the earpiece of his cell phone and was about to hang up when Hacking's gravelly voice finally answered.

"Hacking."

"Hey, boss. Just thought I'd touch base with you on what we've got so far," Sullivan said, leaning against the lobby entrance. He glanced over his shoulder and watched Barry discussing what they'd decided in the interview room with the guard at the front desk. Barry leaned over the desk and pointed animatedly at something, and the female guard motioned to the warden's door, across the room.

"Good, I was just about to call you anyway," Hacking said. He sounded better, Sullivan thought, happier. Although, in over two years of working with the man, he supposed he'd never really seen him happy. Not really. "Lee woke up this morning. I just got off the phone with his wife."

Relief swam through Sullivan's midsection, and for a moment he didn't even feel the harsh pull and uncomfortable dampness of his clothes. "Good. Christ, I was still worried, even after what the doctor said."

"He's going to make a full recovery. He'll be back in a few months, I'm sure. Now, what are we dealing with over there?"

Sullivan laid out the facts, or as much as he knew of them. Yes, Alvarez had been killed in the cell. No, there was nothing apparent yet. Yes, they'd already interviewed the first person on the scene. No, the crime-scene team hadn't come up yet.

Sullivan listened to the low murmur of voices and the occasional phone ringing on Hacking's end. The office sounded good right then. Warm, dry clothes, a cup of coffee, and some simple paperwork.

"So what do you think?" Hacking finally asked.

"I don't know. I'm waiting on Don to finish up in there, and then maybe we'll have something."

"That kid wasn't lying?"

"That kid was scared out of his mind, boss. He couldn't have lied if his life depended on it."

Hacking grunted. "Okay, keep me posted, and hopefully something'll turn up. The weather looks like it's not going to cooperate, so you'll have to make due with limited resources for the time being."

"Sounds good. We'll have someone boat us across tonight if things run their course. Find a motel or something close by, maybe meet up with the sheriff in the morning."

"Okay, be safe."

"Thanks, sir." Sullivan hung the phone up and mentally filed Hacking's beef with him as over. Lee's recovery had seen to that.

Barry finished speaking with the guard at the front desk and began walking toward him. When he was a few feet away, he held out a manila folder.

"Reports from yesterday's disturbance between Alvarez and Fairbend. An Officer Bundy was working that shift, same asshole with the goatee who took over for Hunt. The whole thing's there. After a little reluctance, she also agreed to have our friend Benny send us the footage of the fight via email."

"Why'd she give you grief? You weren't hitting on her, were you? You shouldn't be doing that while we're working, Jenny will not be impressed." Sullivan cocked his head at his friend and moved deftly away when the other man threw a mock punch at him.

"No, I wasn't hitting on her. I told her you wanted her number."

"That's not even a good comeback, my friend. Fail."

Barry smiled and shook his head. "Not sure why she didn't want to give up the footage. Maybe she just didn't want to do the legwork. She kept saying the warden would have to approve it first. I politely informed her that this was our case now, and the warden was giving us full access to the prison information. Everyone here got up on the wrong side of the fucking bed this morning, if you ask me."

"Especially Alvarez," Sullivan quipped. "Maybe it's the beautiful weather."

"Either way, she's having it sent to each of our emails, we can watch it on our phones."

"Good. Did you find out which way the infirmary was?" Sullivan asked.

"Yeah, it's off the main holding area to the right."

Sullivan began walking in that direction and Barry followed. "Let's go have a sit-down with Fairbend. See why his cellmate suddenly decided to try to kill him last night."

==

The infirmary was behind a door that led off the main holding area prior to the commons. It was a square room with wide windows set high in one wall, the glass interlaced with steel mesh. Several humming fluorescents shone down on the immaculately white tile floor. A few locked cabinets stood against the right wall, and a desk, decorated with strewn papers, held a position beneath the windows across the room. A lone guard sat in a chair just inside the doorway, his head tilted back against the wall behind him, his mouth open to the world. Soft snores issued from his nose every few seconds. Sullivan narrowed his eyes at the guard as he stepped into the infirmary, and saw Barry motioning if he should wake him. Sullivan shook his head. *Let him sleep, we're not here to see him.*

Instead, they proceeded across the tile to the two medical beds that hugged the left wall. The closer of the two was unoccupied, with blankets stacked neatly in its center. The other held a skinny dark-haired man with a sheet drawn up just below his scruffy chin. He had blue eyes and they followed the two agents as Sullivan and Barry made their way closer. Fairbend was slender, almost alarmingly thin, as if he were battling something worse than bruises and minor abrasions. Sullivan stopped beside the bed and smiled as he pulled out his wallet and flipped open his ID.

"I'm Special Agent Shale with the Bureau of Criminal Apprehension, and this is Agent Stevens. Are you Mr. Fairbend?"

The supine man's eyes squinted at Sullivan, and after a moment Fairbend's head nodded slightly.

"We'd like to speak with you about what happened concerning Mr. Alvarez, if that's okay with you." Sullivan watched the skinny man lick his lips and then strain to swallow.

"Choked the fuck outta me, that's what happened." Fairbend's voice sounded like sandpaper on a concrete floor, and gradually the prisoner drew the sheet down below his neck, revealing a collection of mottled bruises ranging from purple to green.

Sullivan could make out individual finger marks on the edges of the mass. Fairbend had been accurate; Alvarez had choked the fuck out of him. "I see that. Looks really painful. Could you tell me what happened, maybe why Alvarez decided to do this to you?"

Fairbend shrugged, which caused the bruises in his neck to ripple like a black-and-purple pond in a breeze. "Crazy Mexican."

Sullivan ran his tongue over his front teeth and turned to look at Barry who made a face that said, *well, isn't that something.* Sullivan looked back at Fairbend and leaned in closer to the man. He noticed a scent as he neared him. Something organic. Not really human waste, but close to it. Sullivan grimaced but didn't relinquish his hold on the edge of the bed as he closed the distance between his and Fairbend's faces.

"Listen, bud, I'm not new to this and neither are you, so let's just cut the shit, shall we? I want to know what happened in that cell. I want to know what Alvarez said and what you said in return to make him want to squeeze the life out of you. I don't know if you've heard yet, being in the state that you're in, but your cellmate got torn apart last night. There wasn't much left of him. I'm guessing you already knew that, but what I want is a name."

Fairbend remained unmoved by Sullivan's speech, and his eyelids had even drifted closed while Sullivan spoke. The thin man shifted in the bed and steel clinked just below Sullivan's grip. When he looked down, he saw that Fairbend's hand was cuffed to the bed's rail.

"Ain't gonna get me to talk no matter what you throw at me, buddy. He was a crazy spic and no one's gonna miss him. So just trot along and leave me to heal up."

Sullivan resisted the urge to reach out and grasp the other man's throat where Alvarez had less than a day ago. He was about to try another angle on the prisoner when he heard the door open and close behind them and a voice speak with authority that woke the sleeping guard.

"What do you think you're doing?"

Sullivan turned and saw that the voice belonged to a woman striding across the floor toward the beds. Sullivan guessed her age to be within a year of his own and he noticed that she walked confidently; this room seemed to be her territory. She wore a white coat over blue scrubs and her auburn hair flowed out behind her, held up by a black band. The brown eyes, which normally would have been appealing, were half lidded in fury. Her face was angular, with high cheekbones, and as she came closer Sullivan couldn't see any hint of lipstick. He quickly decided she would have been attractive if the anger that currently contorted her face would have been absent. The resident doctor, he presumed.

Sullivan and Barry both smiled and Barry beat him to an introduction as the older agent stepped forward and stuck out his hand. "Hello, I'm Senior Special Agent Stevens, and this is Special Agent Shale. We're here investigating the homicide."

"I don't care if the president was killed last night, you can't come in here and question an injured patient. This man almost died, you need to give him some time to rest. And who told you it was okay to come barging in anyway?"

A revelation bloomed in her dark eyes and she turned to the guard, who hovered behind her, his face locked in an accusatory glare, but nowhere near the vehemence of the doctor's.

A finger shot out toward the guard and suddenly the doctor's rage was turned to him. "Did you let them in?"

"I ... no ... I was just over there and—" the guard stammered.

"You were sleeping, weren't you?" she asked in awe. Her finger dropped to her side and she turned back to the agents. "Gentlemen, if I could ask you to exit the infirmary so that I can attend to my patient here, that would be great." She smiled without warmth and pointed toward the door.

Sullivan rubbed his brow. "Doctor?" She nodded impatiently and resumed glaring at him. "A man was killed here last night. He won't be able to sit in one of your cozy beds in this nice, sterile room. What's left of him is going to be dissected and examined in a morgue of some kind. Our job right now is to find out who killed him, because whoever it was is running free, most likely somewhere nearby."

The doctor's face softened somewhat and she glanced over at Fairbend, who was watching the exchange with interest. Finally, her eyes blinked and she nodded. "I'm sorry, it's just been crazy for the last twelve hours. I've been up for quite a while. I apologize. My name is Dr. Amanda Erling." She reached out and Barry shook with her. When Sullivan grasped her hand, he felt how cold her flesh was. It was like shaking with a bag of ice.

"No problem, we understand. We just wanted to ask Mr. Fairbend a few questions, but I suppose he does need his rest," Sullivan said as he looked at the prisoner. Fairbend's eyes met his for a moment and then slid away to examine a patch of wall at the other end of the room. Sullivan thought he saw something, just a fleeting look of victory and then gone.

"Perhaps later this evening you could stop by when he's more rested?" Dr. Erling asked.

Sullivan nodded. "Of course."

The group moved away from the bed and Sullivan looked one last time at Fairbend. The prisoner yawned and rolled onto his side. Sullivan blinked and stopped as the others walked toward the door. It had looked like the inside of Fairbend's mouth was coated in a grayish hue. Sullivan stared at the man for a beat, waiting for a convulsion or the onset of a seizure. Fairbend merely closed his eyes and seemed to fall asleep.

"Sully? You coming?" Barry asked from the doorway. The group watched him from the hall outside the room.

"Yeah," Sullivan said. Without another look back, he followed them into the hallway and shut the door behind him.

"I think maybe you should stand instead of sit out here, what do you think?" Dr. Erling said to the uniformed guard. The guard merely nodded and stepped back to the side of the door, his hands clasped behind him. The doctor motioned toward the lobby and began walking.

Sullivan and Barry fell into stride behind her. Amanda walked at a brisk pace until they'd cleared the security doors and stepped into the open space of the lobby. Sullivan glanced at the front entrance and saw nothing but a sheet of falling rain outside.

Amanda turned to both of them and sighed. "I want to apologize again. I'm just not myself today. I shouldn't have interrupted your investigation, but thank you for complying."

"It's not a problem, Doctor. We just need to ask Mr. Fairbend a few questions to clear some things up about the altercation last night," Sullivan said.

Amanda's eyes darkened and she looked at the floor. "Is it as bad as they're saying? Was he ... was he beaten to death?"

"We're really not at liberty to say at the moment, I'm sure you understand," Sullivan replied, glancing at Barry.

"Of course. Well, if there's any assistance that I can provide, please let me know."

Both agents nodded and watched as the doctor walked away. Sullivan noted the slight swing of her hips as she moved and the way her hair contrasted with her white coat. As the door slammed shut behind her, Barry backhanded Sullivan's shoulder with a loud slap.

"The fuck was that for?" Sullivan said, rubbing the spot through his shirt and glaring at his friend.

Barry grinned slyly. "Really? I've never seen you look at a woman that way before."

Sullivan blew air noisily between his lips and shoved Barry as he walked by. "You don't know me as well as you think you do, buddy."

"Oh, yeah, whatever. Tell me I'm wrong."

"You're wrong."

"You're lying," Barry goaded as he followed Sullivan across the floor toward the front doors. "When's the last time you were on a date?"

Sullivan stopped, and for a moment all he could see were red tablecloths and candles in crystal holders. A fireplace blazed somewhere nearby, and he felt a ring between his fingers, the sharp edges of the diamond cutting into his skin but feeling so right. He could smell steak and wine and he could taste something on his lips. He could taste her.

"Sully?" Barry gripped his shoulder, and the vaulted ceiling along with the hard floors beneath his feet came rushing back. Sullivan breathed deeply and rubbed his face. "You okay, man?" Barry asked.

Sullivan dropped his hand from his cheek and swallowed the faint taste of Cabernet Sauvignon. "Yeah, just fine." He feigned a weak smile before walking toward the front doors again. When he stopped at the double glass and peered out into the downpour, he noticed the line of the scar above his eyebrow glowing in the reflection. Soon, Barry was standing behind him, rummaging nervously in his pockets.

"I'm sorry, man. I didn't mean to bring anything up."

"I know," Sullivan said. "It's not your fault."

Lightning flashed just outside the canopy of the prison entrance, followed almost immediately by thunder that vibrated the windows and doors in their frames.

The entrance to the main holding area buzzed open, and when the agents turned they saw Don Anderson leading the rest of the crime-scene team into the room. Even from a distance Sullivan could see Don's face was beyond haggard. His normally merry eyes drooped behind his glasses. One of the other techs carried a black evidence bag in one hand. The bag bulged near the bottom, as if a rotted cantaloupe sat in its recesses. Don spotted them by the door and walked over, his head down and chin tucked tight to his chest like a prizefighter.

"Hey, guys," Don said as he approached.

"Hey, yourself," Barry answered. "You look tired, my friend."

"Yeah," Don said.

"So what did we come up with?" Sullivan asked.

Don pinched his nose between a thumb and forefinger, which pushed his glasses onto his blank forehead. When he settled them back into place, Sullivan saw something he had never seen on the examiner's face before: disquiet.

"Not that this is something to talk about over lunch, but I'm starving and so are my guys. Can we eat?" Don said.

Sullivan glanced at Barry, and both agents agreed that they also could use something in their stomachs.

"Good," Don said, as he turned and began walking toward his two waiting techs. "Nothing like a good murder scene to get your appetite up."

Chapter 5

The commons was much busier than when Sullivan and Barry had eaten earlier that morning. Close to a hundred prisoners sat at the long tables, shoulders and heads hunched down over their trays of meatloaf, mashed potatoes, and gravy. Only a handful of prisoners looked up from their lunch when the five men entered the room and gathered food from the lunch line. The techs had stored the evidence bag containing Alvarez's remains in a guard locker beside the interview rooms. When Sullivan asked Don why the bag looked so light, the older man waved the question off, his eyes saying, *Not here, not now*

Several armed guards stood watch on the main floor, and Sullivan counted three more above them looking down with disinterest from the wraparound balcony. The group picked a vacant table in the farthest corner and sat at the very end so that their conversation couldn't be overheard. Again Sullivan was struck by how quiet the room was, as he settled down with his tray of steaming mush that did not resemble any type of meatloaf he had ever laid eyes upon.

Don scooped a heaping pile of the stuff with a spoon and shoved it into his mouth hungrily. After chewing for a few seconds, he tilted his head to one side and shrugged. "I could get used to this."

"Jesus," Barry muttered as he picked at a dissolving heap of mashed potatoes.

Sullivan took a sip of water and looked across the table at the forensic head. "Spill it, Don. We're at a slight loss here without your expertise."

The balding man chewed another mouthful of the meatloaf, and then sat forward a little, his voice lowered. "Weirdest fucking thing I've ever seen, boys. And this ain't my first rodeo."

"You sound like the sheriff," Sullivan said.

"Yeah, well, he and I are on level ground, then."

"So you found the rest of him in the pipe? Shoved down there like you thought?" Barry asked.

Don merely closed his eyes and shook his head.

"You're kidding," Sullivan said, the surprise evident on his face as he fought to control the volume of his voice.

"We extracted the head from the drain, and I was hopeful since there was some blood and tissue in the pipe when we shined a light in there. But when I looked further, there wasn't anything substantial. It looked to me like the blood stopped after a few feet."

"That's not possible," Barry said. His tray was shoved into the middle of the table and he looked to be avoiding eye contact with it.

"Like I said, guys, never seen anything like it in my career," Don said, resuming his meal.

"Could someone have washed the pieces down the drain?" Sullivan said.

Don considered it for a moment. "Yes, I suppose if the chunks were small enough and the suspect had enough water pressure. Sure, it's possible."

"I didn't see any fire hoses in that cell, did you?" Barry said.

"No, just throwing out ideas," Sullivan answered. The table fell silent and the only sounds in the spacious room were the occasional clank of silverware and the connection of a plastic cup with a tabletop. Sullivan closed his eyes and reviewed the cell in his mind. He turned in a circle, as if studying the layout of the room in a 3-D rendering on a screen. The head in the drain, blood everywhere, bits of bone and flesh clinging to the walls like a psychotic's interpretation of a Pollock.

"Murder weapon?" Sullivan asked finally.

"Not sure on that either yet, but I'll say this, a cutting instrument was used, and not just one."

"How many? Two? Three?" Barry asked.

"I'd say closer to thirty."

Both agents squinted at the forensic specialist for a moment, and Sullivan wondered if Don was actually having fun with them. But when the older man merely looked back and forth without smiling, Sullivan spoke.

"Thirty? You're joking? Thirty different knives?"

Don held up a hand. "I didn't say knives, just instruments. And yes, at least that many different weapons were used."

Barry's brow furrowed in disbelief. "How can you be sure?"

"From the lacerations in the flesh of the victim. Each wound was fairly unique and the pieces of tissue that were on the floor and walls also held definitive incision patterns. Whoever did this also bashed him hard against the walls, like we thought earlier. I haven't determined if he was cut first or bludgeoned."

Sullivan shook his head. "We have a real psycho here, fellas." Suddenly the interview with Nathan rose in his memory, and he explained the details to Don, hoping that something would click with the older man.

But after a few minutes of thinking, Don unfolded his arms and leaned his elbows on the table. "That doesn't make sense either. You say the guard saw Alvarez's eyes?"

Sullivan and Barry nodded.

"Well, then my only hypothesis is this: the killer either must have been still in the room when Hunt looked in or was very nearby. As soon as the kid leaves, the killer cuts the remains to ribbons and batters the head down into the hole with some type of blunt tool, then makes his escape before Hunt comes back with reinforcements."

"That's a ballsy play, if you ask me," Barry said.

"Yeah, but it's the only one that makes sense, right?" Sullivan asked. "So what does it mean? The guy's already dead, why go back into the cell or spend any more time trying to shove his head down a drain?" Sullivan stared around the table at the watching faces. "To send a message, that's why. That's the only reason the suspect would take a chance like that. He wanted to make a statement, loud and clear to everyone."

"And what is it?" Don asked.

Sullivan shrugged. "Fuck if I know." Don and Barry huffed laughter and the two techs just stared. "But we'll find out."

Don finished eating and wiped his mouth with a napkin. Sullivan wished he could have eaten something, but the food and the quiet in the vast room were so unsettling, he really didn't feel hungry.

"What's next on the agenda?" Barry asked, pushing his tray even farther across the table.

"Well," Don said, as he rose and his two techs stood with him. "I believe it's time to unravel the mystery of Mr. Alvarez and cut what's left of him open."

Barry made a clicking sound in his throat as he swallowed and threw a disdainful look in Don's direction.

Sullivan just smiled wickedly and reached across the table to slap Barry on the arm. "Since leaving right now's not a good option, I think I know just the place."

==

The day was cooler compared to the last time they'd been outside, and Sullivan squinted at the hovering clouds, trying to discern if they were breaking apart or only amassing for another attack. The rain had dispelled somewhat, and now only a mist enshrouded the wet grounds as Sullivan led the group out from the canopy near the front doors. Barry followed close behind, his thinning hair already beginning to stick to his scalp. Don and his team came next, the last tech carrying the black bag containing Alvarez's remains. Dr. Erling trudged after them, bundled in one of the customary prison-issue ponchos, her head tilted toward the ground and her expression unreadable. Last came Mooring, his eyes burning holes in anything and everything he looked at as he stalked several paces behind the doctor.

Barry quickened his step and fell even with Sullivan, and he nudged his friend in the side. "How the hell did you know that the mental facility would have a better medical ward?"

Sullivan's mouth twisted up at one end in the semblance of a smile, the mist coating his face in a light sheen. "My grandfather worked at a state mental facility for a while. My dad used to tell me stories of when he would visit him at work. Dad mentioned a couple times how terrible the sick room smelled, like formaldehyde and shit all mixed together. But even back then, he said it was big, with lots of beds and equipment. I suppose there's more injuries and attacks at mental facilities than at prisons. Just a guess."

"Did the warden seem irritated that we asked to use the room at New Haven?" Barry asked.

"Maybe a little. I think he sent his golden boy back there with us just to make sure we don't walk off with some gauze and Q-tips."

Barry smiled. "And the good doctor?"

"I think she's just curious," Sullivan said. Then he snorted. "Morbid, if you ask me."

Barry barked laughter, which died in the suffocating mist around them. They followed a trail that had been concrete for a while but soon gave way to gravel, which in turn became mud that they all tried to avoid without much efficiency. The trail led down the side of the prison and away from its rear, into a copse of hardwoods. Sullivan could hear drops of water snapping from leaf to leaf as it made its way to the ground, searching for a river or stream that would eventually carry it back to its mother sea. Off to the right the cleared yard fell away, and Sullivan could make out a drive of sorts, or what he assumed was a drive. Water had stretched up from the nearby swamp and reclaimed the area for its own, and all that remained was a cleared path through the trees that twisted and turned around several corners. A few boulders poked above the surface of the water and an unseen bird called a lonesome cry that sounded like it was in pain.

The trail curved through the overhanging trees, and after one last bend to the left, a chainlink gate came into view. Razor wire adorned the entrance and Sullivan could see the corner of a building through an opening a few hundred yards on the other side of the fence.

Sullivan's phone chimed at almost the same instant Barry's did. Without looking, he reached down and pulled the slim device from his pocket. "Benny must have come through with those videos."

The words had barely left his mouth when he felt the phone slide from his grip. The black case pirouetted once in the dim light and then landed face-down in a large puddle.

"Fuck!" Sullivan cursed and bent to retrieve the phone. When he picked it up, he already knew it was too late. Water coursed out of the bottom connection point and he could see moisture beading beneath the screen. In his peripheral vision

Sullivan saw Barry shaking his head and wagging his own phone back and forth.

"Good thing one of us played college ball. Never dropped a pass," Barry said.

"Fuck your college hands," Sullivan said as good-naturedly as he could, but the irritation of ruining his phone was maddening. He pushed the on button a few times, and when nothing happened, he slid the wet paperweight back into his pocket.

Mooring had caught up with them by then, and he walked by, shooting daggers at both agents. Without a pause, the officer strode up to the control box on their side and slid an electronic keycard through a slit in the device. A motor hummed nearby and the gate slid open before them like a starving man's mouth accommodating a large bite.

Mooring waited for the group to clear the gate before closing it with the matching control panel on the opposite side. Sullivan tried to read the man's face as he watched the steel fence slide shut. Pronounced frown lines hung on the outside of Mooring's mouth, and Sullivan noticed the officer's gaze glazed over when he thought no one was looking. The gate snapped closed and Mooring glanced up, into Sullivan's probing eyes. A look of surprise surfaced and submerged on the guard's face.

"Something in my teeth?" Mooring sneered.

Sullivan shook his head, smiling. "Not that I could tell."

Mooring scowled even more deeply as Sullivan began walking toward the opening in the trees. Amanda fell in step beside Sullivan and he looked over at her. Her face was covered by the edge of the poncho, with just the tip of her nose poking out into the afternoon mist. A strand of her hair drifted in the breeze.

"How long have you been here?" Sullivan asked after a moment.

He saw the poncho tilt a little and then face back toward the building ahead. "Three years this fall. I did my residency at the Mayo and came up here after that."

"Why so far north?"

"I like it here. It's slower and more peaceful. I never liked the city life. I got tired of the people coming and going," Amanda said.

"Not sure if you're in the right profession if you don't like people."

She glanced at him again, and when he looked at her, he could see a glint of humor in her eyes. The change in her expression brought a light to her pretty features and he had to force himself to look away.

Stop it, he thought. *Keep professional and cold.* She could be a suspect for all he knew.

"I like patients, just not the general public. I like being able to help. I have ever since I was a kid patching up my brother when he got a scrape on his knee or a bump on the head." She smiled, and Sullivan had to look away again when he began to admire how white and even her teeth were.

Ahead, New Haven came into full view like a ship appearing out of a fog. The building was three stories, with at least four wings. Like Singleton, it was also composed of brick, but here and there the architects who designed the structure had added subtle hints of flat stonework and rounded doorways. There was a multitude of windows on the first and second floors, while the third was abysmal, unbroken brick. The road he had seen trailing through the woods appeared out of the water and wound to the front of the building, ending under a green cloth awning. Stark-white letters spelled out the facility's name beside the entrance doors made entirely of sliding glass. It seemed the creators had thought *New Haven* sounded wonderful, making the letters nearly two feet tall, while *Psychiatric Facility and Care Center* was printed in gray below, as though the actual function of the building was inappropriate and should be overlooked.

"Whoa," Sullivan said and slowed to a stop. Amanda stepped up beside him and also gazed at the building.

"Holds a certain ominous quality, doesn't it?" she asked.

"This coming from a prison doctor," Sullivan said without looking at her. "It looks like a pretty old place." He could see her hood nodding.

"Yeah. I thought I heard it was built in the late fifties, but I could be wrong. It's one of the last psychiatric facilities still operating in the state."

"Jesus. I've never heard of a prison being so close to a mental hospital before," Sullivan said.

"That's because of the location. The area is basically swamp for miles and miles around. You saw how desolate the country is on the way in, I'm assuming. That's why they picked this place. If an inmate or patient managed to escape and was able to get over the fence without being cut to shreds, there would be miles of uninhabitable swamp, water, and bugs to contend with. Not to mention the nearest form of civilization is over ten miles away."

Sullivan caught movement out of the corner of his eye and looked to the far end of the nearest wall. A steel door opened and two men dressed in white nurse scrubs appeared, their laughter barely carrying through the mist. One orderly pulled a pack of cigarettes out from his pocket and handed one to his co-worker. Both men lit up and a white plume of smoke formed above them, like a miniature storm cloud.

The rest of the group gathered behind Sullivan and Amanda while they discussed the facility. Barry stared at the walls of the massive building for several seconds before speaking.

"How many people are held here?"

"I think around two hundred at any given time, but there could be more," Amanda answered.

"Well, let's get out of the rain before we all catch pneumonia, shall we?" Don said, and made his way across the lawn of the facility.

Sullivan eyed the third story for another few seconds, and then followed the rest of the group toward the front doors.

==

The interior of New Haven was cool and blessedly dry. White tiled floor ran the length of the spacious lobby and ended at walls painted a tranquil green-gray. A waiting area sat to the right, with four overstuffed chairs in front of a sprawling fireplace, and against the wall a bookshelf stood solemnly, holding multiple paperback volumes. A mirrored ceiling vaulted above them like a tidal wave of glass, and a massive mahogany desk awaited them as they stepped through the door. A dark-haired receptionist in a white blouse sat behind the counter, smiling politely as they approached. Amanda asked a few questions in a low voice, and soon Sullivan saw the woman behind the desk point to a bank of elevators lined against the left wall.

The elevators were spacious. Large enough, Sullivan deducted, that two or three orderlies along with a full hospital bed between them could fit inside. The dull humming and claustrophobic confines within the elevator reminded Sullivan of the solitary cell in the lower level at the prison. His eyes roamed absently until they came to rest on the bulging bag in the tech's hands. As soon as he realized what he was looking at he immediately examined a booger pressed into a gap in the metal walls. Sullivan dropped his eyes to his muddy shoes, until he heard an electronic ding and the doors slide open.

The medical ward was on the third floor, in the west wing of the facility. Having only seen the lobby, Sullivan didn't know what to expect when he stepped off the elevator, but somehow he really wasn't surprised.

A wide hallway stretched away from them and, almost fifty yards away, turned ninety degrees. Steel doors stood in the walls on either side every ten feet. A small observance window reinforced with steel mesh was recessed into each door, much the same as all the glass in its sister building only a short walk away. Sullivan led the way down the hall, trying to discern exactly which direction he was traveling in. After a moment, he deduced that the left wall was south and the right wall north. South faced into the building's innards, north faced onto the grounds. *Left side—garden view, right side—ocean,* his mind intoned. He shook his head in annoyance and rubbed his scar.

"We follow the hallway to the very end," Amanda said, walking a few steps behind Sullivan. Her hood was down letting her hair fall onto her shoulders. Even under the fluorescents she was undoubtedly pretty.

A door ahead on the right opened and a large male nurse with a graying beard entered the hall. If the ragtag group coming toward him was a surprise, he hid it well. Without giving them another look, he reached into the confines of the room he'd exited and pulled an aging man in a gray straitjacket out into the open. The restrained man had a scalp so devoid of hair, the light above glared from it. His eyes were wide and watery blue, and his mouth quivered as though he were a fish recently plucked from the water.

The patient's gaze met Sullivan's as the group neared and funneled to the far side of the hallway. Sullivan stared at him, his eyes narrowing. The man had focused on him. Like a sniper aiming at a target in a crowd of people through a scope, the man had singled Sullivan out, and when he spoke, Sullivan wasn't surprised that the words were directed at him.

"You're government? FBI? CIA?"

Every ounce of Sullivan's being told him to keep walking and just smile, but something from deep within him pushed an answer out of his mouth and into the open air. "BCA."

The man nodded fiercely, as if he had expected as much. "Bureau of Criminal Apprehension. Who's the SAIC now? Hacking, isn't it? Yeah, Hacking. How is he? Fair?"

"Okay, Jason. Let's go get you something to eat," the large nurse said. "He loves state and federal agencies."

Sullivan halted and the rest of the group waited a few feet down the hallway. Jason stood grinning and nodding. Suddenly, he leapt across the distance of the hall and pressed the hard plastic buckles and straps of the straitjacket against Sullivan's chest. The nurse leaned back and then lunged forward, his arms out and face pulled into an almost comic representation of horror. Sullivan saw this all as he was slammed into the drywall behind him, feeling the mental patient's breath flow over his exposed throat. He felt his hand going automatically to the butt of the forty-five on his hip. He started to draw the weapon, and then realized Jason had turned his body just a little, pressing his left elbow over the top of the gun, preventing Sullivan from pulling it fully from the holster.

The patient's lips sprayed spittle across Sullivan's earlobe, yet he only whispered the words that he finally spoke. "Don't drink the water."

The nurse yanked Jason off Sullivan and hurled the restrained man across the hall, into the opposite wall, with enough force to rattle the ceiling tiles above them.

"What's the matter with you, Jason? You don't treat people like that! You're supposed to be nice to guests," the nurse yelled as he grabbed the stunned patient by the back of the jacket and shook him with more than a little urgency.

"It's okay," Sullivan said, as he locked the gun back into his holster. "No harm done. He's okay."

The shine in Jason's eyes hadn't diminished, and he stared almost through Sullivan and into the next room. He nodded imperceptibly, and then he was gone, being shoved down the hallway by the bearded nurse.

Sullivan watched the two men walk away and nearly grabbed for his gun again, when Barry touched his shoulder.

"You okay?"

"Yeah, fine."

Barry wrinkled his brow and leaned forward, as if to say, *You sure?* Sullivan nodded and squeezed his friend's hand. "I'm good, let's go."

A desk manned by an orderly gazing at a crossword sat just before a door marked "Infirmary" at the end of the corridor. Amanda spoke to him briefly, and after eyeing the group and the black bag in the tech's hand, he punched in a code and the door clicked open before them.

A short entry opened up into a wide room, with beds lining the walls on either side. Stainless-steel cabinets and locked drawers shone in the light from banks of overhead fluorescents. At the far end of the room Sullivan saw a makeshift operating theatre, partially obscured by a curtain hanging from a track in the ceiling. No one else occupied the room, and their squeaking footsteps were the only sound besides the muttering of the receding storm outside. Another doorway sat at the far end of the room, and it was through this that Amanda led them.

The smell reached Sullivan before he stepped fully into the small morgue. Scents of formaldehyde buried beneath an odor of stale death permeated the room. The floors and walls were a matching white tile, which refracted the cold light from above. A stainless-steel table occupied the center of the room and it drew Sullivan's attention. There was no mistaking the pipes and faucet at one end and the gaping mouth of the drain at the other.

"This will work splendidly," Don said, gazing around the room. "I appreciate the accommodations, Doctor."

Amanda smiled. "Happy to help. I'm sure Dr. Rabbers won't mind us using his space."

Don motioned to the tech holding the black bag. The man stepped forward and placed the remains in the middle of the autopsy table with a flat thump.

"I would have waited until we made it back to our lab, but with the weather and the unusual urgency of the crime, pertinent findings are very important." Don said the last words while looking over the top of his glasses at Sullivan. "Bob, Gene? Let's get dressed for the occasion."

Sullivan and Barry stood near the door while Don and his team located protective gowns, masks, and gloves from a nearby cabinet. Amanda offered to help, but Don politely declined. Mooring stood silent, brooding in the far corner, his soaked hat pulled down just above his eyes.

Don flipped on a powerful light that hung just above head height, directly over the table. Its beam spotlighted the black bag, making it glow darkly on the stage of shining steel. One of the techs produced a small digital recorder and placed it on the edge of the table to Don's left and hit a button.

"June second, two thousand twelve, approximately two fifteen p.m. Don Anderson acting as forensic pathologist. Attendants include Gene Wilson and Bob Englund, forensic technicians, Agents Sullivan Shale and Barry Stevens of the BCA, as well as Dr. Amanda Erling and Officer Everett Mooring." Don breathed out, and to Sullivan it sounded like a sigh. Don opened the black bag in front of him, the plastic crackling like static on a dying radio.

Sullivan felt a moment of disgust and anticipation as Alvarez's remains were drawn into the light. The head was as misshapen as he remembered and even more battered. The upper part of the man's face was distinguishable, but below the nose the flesh and bone had been warped by the crushing confines of the drain. Alvarez's lips were puckered in something that resembled a kiss, and Sullivan could see bloodied teeth buried in the darkness of the mouth.

Don lifted the head carefully, and then set it onto the table after one of the techs pulled the bag clear. The head stared straight up at the ceiling, and now Sullivan could see the trauma incurred on the neck.

Large gouges and wide slashes were everywhere in the skin just below the head's jaw line. Pieces of flesh had been ripped free and striations of muscle hung like red and gray party favors from the stump of spinal cord protruding obscenely from the severed neck. Sullivan could see places where the killer or killers had hacked insanely at the man's flesh as it was separated from the rest of the body. Don's voice startled Sullivan out of his examination and he blinked, coming back to his surroundings.

"Autopsy proceedings are based on the remains of Victor Alvarez, Mexican male, age thirty-four, hair color black." Don reached over and slid a shriveled eyelid up to expose a dark pupil that stared at the ceiling. "Eye color is brown." Don leaned in and tilted the neck up into the light. "Remains are limited to disembodied head, beginning just above the C5 vertebra."

A scale hung above one end of the table, and Don placed the head in the tray. Sullivan watched the scale's needle jump and then stop at the ten-pound mark.

"Big melon," Barry whispered, leaning close to Sullivan. Sullivan shook his head in mock annoyance as Don continued.

"Remains weigh in at ten pounds, three ounces. Victim appears to have died from numerous lacerations and severe blunt-force trauma."

Don motioned to the nearest tech, and both men began to wash the head beneath the faucet that extended over the table. Blood and gore rinsed free and flowed in a grisly river, disappearing in the drain. Gray-tinged flesh became clear as Alvarez's head was cleaned, and when Don was satisfied, the remains looked both more and less human. The abject countenance gained distinct features: a smashed nose, puckered eyelids over sunken eyes, and grizzled cheeks ending in broken jawbones.

Don set the wet remains back in the center of the table. "Earlier examination presented no residue of external contaminates. No fingernail marks or hair follicles were retrieved from the victim's wounds." He picked up a tool that resembled a flat chisel with a narrow grip from the edge of the table. The tip of the wicked-looking instrument ended in a thin blade, which Don used to poke and probe the wounds on Alvarez's neck. "Skin and flesh at severe trauma point have been lacerated multiple times." Don moved closer, and Sullivan could see the man's eyes narrowing as he focused. "Wounds are indicative of edged weapons varying in lengths and widths. Extreme wound on victim's right side indicates a drilling mechanism—flesh is curled outward, and in this area missing completely."

Sullivan and Barry exchanged looks, and even Mooring raised his head to gaze at what was left of the cadaver.

Don brought the edged tool to Alvarez's lips and began to work the steel between the head's teeth. Sullivan had to mentally restrain himself from plugging his ears as the sound of steel on enamel filled the room. Slowly, the misshapen lower jaw sagged open, and even from where he stood Sullivan saw that there was something inside the mouth. The white end of the object stuck out like a bleached tongue, and when Sullivan glanced up, he saw the same surprise he felt on Don's face.

"Foreign object inside victim's mouth. It looks to be lodged in the back of the throat." Don looked around at the expectant faces of the group before picking up a forceps in one hand. The steel tongs gripped the object on either side, and after a few agonizing seconds of tugging, Don pulled it free with a wet pop. Sullivan watched as the thing slid free of Alvarez's throat and dragged across his gaping lips.

The object was nearly five inches long, by Sullivan's estimate, and viciously pointed at the opposite end of where the forceps gripped it. Jagged edges spiraled down its length and faded into a smooth surface, where it raggedly ended in what appeared to be soft tissue. Don held the object up just below the powerful overhead light and squinted at it, his mouth agape.

"What the fuck is that thing?" Mooring asked from the corner. His face was twisted into a mask of disgust, and to Sullivan it looked like he was about to lose whatever lunch he had consumed earlier.

"Everett," Amanda said in a chiding tone as she tilted her head toward the recording device on the table.

"Don't worry, Doctor," Don said without taking his eyes from the thing in the forceps. "I was wondering the same thing myself." Don motioned again to one of the techs and the younger man placed a sterile sheet of paper on the surface of the table. Don set the object down carefully, and then peered at it again as he rolled it back and forth with the tool in his hand.

"Foreign object retrieved from victim's mouth and throat. Approximately five and a half inches long, white in color. Surface is dense and hard, almost bone-like. Sharp protrusions line the length and there are multiple grooves on the exterior. Opposing end is fleshy and soft, ending in a jagged tear. Small amount of unidentified fluid is gathered at terminating end." Don reached over and tapped the recorder with his forefinger, and stepped back from the table, his hands on his hips. The pathologist remained silent until Sullivan cleared his throat, breaking the older man from his reverie.

"Sorry, never seen anything like it," Don said.

Sullivan walked around the table and bent close to the object on the paper. The smell of blood was stronger here and he swallowed the revulsion he felt. The thing on the paper looked like a bone-white seashell he had seen before. An auger shell? Was that what they were called? He looked closer and could see bits of tissue clinging to the spiny edges lining the thing's length. It looked dangerous and *organic*. He could almost feel those tiny blades cutting into his skin. How would it have felt in his mouth?

Sullivan straightened up and stepped away from the table. "What do you think, Don?"

The pathologist shook his head. "I have no idea, but it looks almost like bone here," he said, gesturing to the pointed end. "Then it transitions to something cartilaginous, and finishes in some kind of meat."

"Meat?" Barry echoed from across the table.

Don shrugged. "Looks like lobster or crabmeat to me."

Mooring laughed in the corner and his head dropped forward, obscuring his face. Sullivan frowned at the officer, and then looked back to Don. "What's it doing in our guy's mouth?"

"Not sure of that either. To me it looks like it was shoved in and twisted around. Then maybe Alvarez bit it off?"

Sullivan looked at the head with its mouth open lying on the table. He didn't have to look inside to imagine the carnage the thing would have created in the soft tissue.

Don touched the recorder again and resumed his position. With gentle hands he began to explore the mouth and throat. "Examining the interior damage of the victim's mouth, assumedly caused by unknown object found within. Gums and rear of the throat have extensive tr—*aaahhh!*"

Don's words were lost in a bellow of pain as he stood straight up, his eyes bulging behind his glasses. The cry caught everyone by surprise, and Sullivan saw each person react. He and

Barry stepped forward, while Amanda flew backward with her own short scream. Mooring only flinched. Both techs may as well have been statues, as little as they moved. When Sullivan looked down at the table and saw what had caused the pathologist to cry out, it took a moment for him to process what he was seeing. When the scene finally registered in his mind, he nearly screamed himself.

The head's jaws had clamped down and were biting through Don's first two fingers on his right hand.

Don lurched back and pressed his free hand against Alvarez's face. Sullivan heard a distinct snapping sound, and he watched as the disembodied head and Don both fell to the floor. The head rolled under the autopsy table, and the aging pathologist fell against the cabinets behind him and slithered down to a sitting position, his left hand cupped protectively around his right.

Sullivan and Barry hurried to Don's side and crouched next to him, both men's guns drawn, although they didn't really know in which direction to aim them. Amanda emitted a few choked sobs and pressed a whitened hand to her mouth. Mooring leaned over and stared under the table with narrowed eyes, his own sidearm not yet out.

"What the fuck was that?" Sullivan asked, gazing down at Don's injured hand. Don was breathing heavy and pinching his index and middle fingers tightly with his left hand, staunching the blood flow, which nevertheless still leaked out from the severed stumps. Sullivan saw the white edge of bone glisten in the bright lights and his stomach lurched involuntarily.

"Should have known. My fault, my fault. I'm okay. Cadaveric spasm." Don uttered the last statement as if it should explain everything.

"You two, get some gauze and a clamp over here," Barry yelled at the two stunned technicians. The men rifled through the nearby drawers for the supplies, as Sullivan focused again on Don, whose face had paled further.

"What are you talking about?" Sullivan asked as he shot a glance under the autopsy table. He could see the outline of the head lying there. Thankfully the face was turned away toward the far side of the room.

Don blinked and heaved in a great breath like a man treading in deep water. "It happens sometimes. Bodies, their muscles spasm and stiffen when they die in an extreme bout of physical anguish. That's what happened. God, I think I'm going to be sick."

Sullivan saw Don's eyes flutter, and in a matter of seconds the pathologist's hand fell away from his wounded fingers as he passed out. Fresh blood flew out of the amputated stumps and splashed down onto the white tile of the floor in brilliant red streams. Sullivan grabbed Don's bleeding fingers and pressed them tight in a grip he feared might actually snap the already traumatized bones. After a moment, Bob and Gene knelt next to him, and then Amanda was there too, seemingly having shaken off the shock, her doctor's instincts taking over. Sullivan released his hold on Don's hand and watched as the two techs, directed by Amanda, clamped off the injuries with a thick elastic band, followed by a dose of antiseptic and a tight wrapping of sterile gauze.

Sullivan and Barry backed away and circled the table. Reluctantly Sullivan holstered his .45, and knelt as he stared into the shadow cast by the steel platform above. His gorge rose in his throat as Barry and Mooring leaned closer to him and took in the sight that he wished he could run away from. Alvarez's head lay on its left cheek. Its eyes were still mercifully shut, but that wasn't what abhorred Sullivan to the point of sickness.

The muscles in its jaw were still clenching, the teeth partially visible in the mouth as the head bit again and again on Don's fingers.

Chapter 6

"Fuck me sideways."

Barry fell into the chair to Sullivan's left and placed his face in his hands. The two sat side by side in the interview room off the prison's lobby. Everything had become a blur after Amanda and the two techs successfully stopped the bleeding. Don woke in a bleary daze and threw up violently on the floor, the vomit mixing hideously with his drying blood. Sullivan and Barry had offered to try to retrieve the fingers from Alvarez's mouth, but Don merely shook his head and replied that he didn't want them back after where they'd been. Dr. Rabbers was notified and a report had been filed. Afterward, Mooring left for Singleton and returned with the ATV he'd been driving earlier that day. Don rode back in comfort, cradling his right hand and grimacing whenever the vehicle went over a bump. Officer Bundy had pulled the prison's boat around, and Gene, Bob, and Don were all loaded inside and whisked away down the watery roadway, back to the crime-scene van. The last thing Sullivan saw as he stood on the bank below the fence was Don's attempt at a smile, which looked more like a scowl, fading in the waning light of the evening, and then they were gone around the bend.

Barry sat back in his chair and looked over at Sullivan. "Have you ever. In your life. Seen anything. Like that before?"

Sullivan rubbed his face and turned toward his friend. "Have I ever seen a decapitated head bite off someone's fingers? No, not that I can recall." Sullivan's guts churned, but for some reason he felt laughter tightening his stomach, and he shook his head as the first chuckles fell from his mouth. Barry glanced over at him and made a gagging sound, and Sullivan realized the other man was trying to keep from laughing also. Tears sprang to Sullivan's eyes as he bit down on his lower lip to keep the insane giggles from spilling out, but it was no use. Soon, he and Barry were slumped back in their chairs, twisting and turning under the thumb of the hideous humor that gripped them. It was minutes before the laughter eased off and Sullivan was able to look through the glass walls to make sure they were still alone in the interview area.

"Jesus, what are we laughing about?" Barry said as a few remaining giggles slipped out.

"It's this day, my friend. This is by far the strangest shit I've ever been witness to, and I think it's just an overload."

"Must be, because I nearly puked just now thinking about what happened back there in that room, and laughing only made it worse."

Sullivan nodded in agreement. Visualizing Alvarez's head biting down on Don's fingers and the sound it had made—the cracking of bone being sheared through, the smell of blood—was enough to sober him once again. Sullivan shifted and felt something poke him through the material of his slacks. He reached into his pocket and pulled out an evidence bag that contained the object that had been removed from Alvarez's mouth. In the haste and panic that followed Don's injury, he'd put the bag in his pocket and simply forgotten about it.

Now, he stared through the thick plastic at the object. If it had been found somewhere besides in a dead man's mouth, the spiraling teeth and slender shape might have been beautiful. Were the sharp points teeth? Not teeth, just jagged tips. He looked closer at the ivory coloring of the thing. Slight variations like layers could be seen as swirls on its surface. They resembled the lines in agates he used to hunt for as a child. The more lines, the cooler the rock. When he flipped the bag over to look at the object's base, he could see the likeness Don described earlier. The material hanging out of the hard shell was light in color and striated. A few flaps dangled raggedly from the edge, assumedly where Alvarez had bitten through it. The head clamping down on Don's fingers now made sense—the victim had died biting through the murder weapon.

"What do you think that is?" Barry asked, startling Sullivan.

"Not sure, but I think forensics will match some of the wounds on Alvarez to this thing. Might be from some kind of sea animal. Looks marine anyway."

"Someone stabbed him to death with a crab claw?"

"Looks that way, smart-ass. You'll be pissed when that's exactly what it turns out to be," Sullivan said as he tucked the bag into his pocket.

Footsteps outside the room caused them to turn their heads, and the lanky form of the warden filled the doorway. "Hello, gentlemen, how are you?"

"Just fine, sir. Thank you," Sullivan said.

Andrews's face pulled in on itself as he frowned at the floor. "I'm very sorry to hear that a member of your team was injured. Freakish, isn't it?"

Sullivan nodded. "Yes, really strange, but Don's going to be okay."

"Good, good." Andrews reached into the pocket of the light jacket he wore, pulled out two small pieces of plastic, and handed them to the agents. "These are electronic keys to the prison's security doors. I thought they would be of use, so you can come and go a little more freely, but please keep them on your person at all times. They won't unlock the prison cells or the armory, but they'll get you into most any other room on the premises. Take care of them well."

Sullivan was reminded of a grandfather handing a grandson his first slingshot and a pocketful of taconite pellets. "Thank you, Warden. We'll keep them safe."

Andrews waved his hands before him. "Please, call me David. Now, what's next for you gentlemen? Anything else I can do for you?"

Sullivan looked at Barry and then back at the older man. "We'd like to interview Officer Bundy when he gets back from dropping our crime-scene team off."

"Very well, I think he's just returned, actually. Anything else?"

"Only a ride back to our vehicle when we've finished, if that works. We'll stay in Brighton tonight and come back as early as we can," Sullivan said.

The warden's lips pursed as if tasting something sour. "I think it might be a better idea for you to stay here tonight. Have you looked outside in the last twenty minutes?"

Both men shook their heads. The warden motioned for them to follow him, and led them to the lobby.

"Unbelievable," Sullivan muttered as he stepped close to the glass doors and peered out at the yard.

The approaching storm had worsened since their return to the prison. Rain fell sideways in sheets thick enough to obscure the fence outside, carried on winds that tossed the nearby forest into a frenzy of falling leaves and whipping branches. A slight abatement in the gusts provided a view of the water level near the front gate. Unbelievably, it looked higher than when he'd last seen it.

"Shit," Barry said beside him. "You're sure no one can bring us across?" he asked Andrews, who stood behind both men.

The warden's eyes squinted out at the elements. "Gentlemen, I'd love to, but I don't think it holds much sense to endanger one of my staff, or yourselves, on a night like this. Like I said, I'd be happy to arrange a room for you both tonight. They're quite comfortable and they lack the bars the other guests have to put up with."

Sullivan looked at Andrews and saw that the older man had just a hint of a smile playing at the corners of his mouth. All at once, the warden grimaced and grabbed his left bicep with his right hand, as if someone had struck him. Pain flashed like the lightning outside across his face, and Sullivan reached out to steady Andrews as he wavered on his feet.

"You okay, sir?" Sullivan asked.

The warden opened his eyes and Sullivan saw an accumulation of tears there. Andrews nodded and tried to smile again. "Arthritis." He motioned to the doors. "This damp weather always sets it off. I won't be right until a week after it's dried up and blown away."

Sullivan dropped his hand to his side and nodded, unconvinced. Andrews smiled again and turned toward the main desk. "So you'll stay tonight?"

Both agents followed him, and Barry just shrugged when Sullivan tried to read his expression. "I suppose that's best. I don't want to put one of your men at risk," Sullivan said.

Andrews stopped and leaned on the desk, and Sullivan noticed that the tall man wasn't just idly resting; the counter looked to be holding him upright. "Good, good. I'll send Officer Bundy to you gentlemen as soon as I locate him," Andrews said.

Sullivan and Barry thanked him and headed for the interview rooms once again. As soon as they were inside, Barry withdrew his cell phone and began punching it with a fingertip. Out of habit, Sullivan withdrew his own, and was momentarily confused when the usual display didn't light up. He then recalled the phone's version of a swan dive into the puddle outside, and cursed as he tucked the useless thing away.

"Who're you calling?" Sullivan asked, sitting on one side of the table.

Barry's face was scrunched up in concentration as he brought the phone to his ear. "Sheriff Jaan," he said. After a few moments, he pulled the device away from his head and frowned at it. "No answer."

"Cell number?"

"Yeah, that's all he gave me. We'll have to look up the landline when we finish the interview."

"Did you think of something to ask him?"

Barry sat in the chair beside Sullivan and sighed. "No, I just don't want to stay in this fucking place tonight."

"Why?"

Barry looked at Sullivan and just shook his head. "Not sure. I just don't."

Sullivan was about to agree and suggest that they simply commandeer the prison's boat when the slouched form of Officer Bundy appeared in the doorway. The man stroked at his goatee and knocked on the door frame before entering.

"Come on in," Sullivan said, gesturing toward a seat on the opposite side of the table. The dislike he felt at seeing Bundy's lackadaisical manner and movement surfaced again like heartburn.

The officer slumped into the chair and looked back and forth at the two agents. "Whatcha guys need?"

Sullivan felt his left eyebrow slouch down as he studied the guard. "We need to ask you a few questions, if that's okay with you."

The guard tilted his head to the right and smoothed his facial hair again. Sullivan had the urge to reach across the desk and pull out a chunk of the pitiful beard, but managed to remain seated. "Whatcha want to know?"

Barry, sensing Sullivan's anger, leaned forward. "We'd like to know what exactly happened last night while you were on shift. Can you run us through that?"

"Well, I clocked in at the regular time and got briefed on the prior shift. Myself and four other guards were scheduled to go out and keep sandbagging. I would say we stayed out until midnight, and then we were called in by the front desk. Told us that one of the inmates was dead. We all came scramblin' in and accompanied Hunt down to solitary." Bundy raised his hands in front of him, as if to say, *you know the rest.*

"Did you see anything out of the ordinary on your way down to the crime scene?" Sullivan asked.

"Other than Hunt shitting his pants? Nope," Bundy said, chuckling through his goatee.

"Does this whole situation strike you as funny, Officer?" Sullivan asked. The tone of his voice was like a bullwhip snapping in the room.

Bundy quit laughing and scowled instead, his tongue pressed into the space of his bottom lip. "No," he said after a brief pause.

"Good, because I don't know if you looked real close down there, or maybe it was too dark, but that man was literally torn to pieces and battered to death. Someone tried to shove his head down a drain. To me that says crazy, but what the hell do I know, right? I'm just a dumb special agent stomping around in your territory."

"Sully," Barry said out of the side of his mouth.

"I don't really care to be talked to like this," Bundy said and began to stand.

"Sit down," Sullivan growled. Something in his voice must have registered with the guard, because Bundy sat and blinked at Sullivan, as if he had just become aware of him. Sullivan could feel his pulse beginning to slam inside his chest, not necessarily fast but *hard.* The adrenaline-laced blood coasted through his veins, asking for release.

Barry placed his hands flat on the table. "Look, we just need to know if there was anything out of the ordinary during your shift before Hunt came and told you what he'd found. Any visitors that day or disturbances other than what landed Alvarez in solitary?"

Bundy looked like he wasn't going to answer, but then shook his head. "No, nothing strange. Just like you said, the fight that started this whole mess."

"Do you know of any internal gang problems? Maybe someone that had it in for Alvarez prior to yesterday?" Sullivan asked. He could feel his pulse calming, but the compulsion to unleash his anger on the man across the desk still burned.

"No, nothing like that. Everyone usually gets along just fine here," Bundy said, and Sullivan detected a hint of a smile, then it was gone.

Sullivan glanced at Barry and the other agent shrugged. "Thanks for your help," Sullivan said.

Bundy rose from his chair, gave one contemptuous look over his shoulder, and went out into the hallway. Barry shut the door and sat down in the chair Bundy had vacated. Sullivan studied his friend. Barry's thin hair was disheveled and there were dark bags hanging beneath his eyes.

"You look tired," Sullivan said.

"You look like shit," Barry answered, rubbing his eyes. "What do you think?"

"I think we should watch the videos that our friend Benny sent us."

Barry pulled his phone from his pocket and queued up the attachment in the email. Sullivan leaned over the table and watched as the dark screen came to life. The video was the one they had watched before in the surveillance room, but this time it was hours earlier when Alvarez had been locked away initially. Barry fast forwarded through the video, watching for any movement in the hall. There was nothing until Nathan entered the scene. Sullivan stared as Hunt came into view and cautiously made his way to the door. Hunt stumbled back, aghast, and ran from the picture. They watched for a flicker of movement or a gap in the video that would signify a manipulation of the content. The digital feed rolled on uninterrupted until a host of shadows came into view and half a dozen male and female guards followed at a fast walk. Nathan trailed after the pack as they closed in on the door, and stopped a dozen feet away, just as he had that morning when he'd escorted them to the crime scene. Sullivan could see Bundy among the guards as the door was thrown open and the group stared into the blood-drenched cell. None of the figures moved for several seconds, and then Bundy's head turned toward Hunt, and he motioned to one of the female officers. She broke off from the group and gripped Nathan's arm as she led him away from the scene. Bundy turned back and stared into the chamber.

Barry stopped the video and darkness flooded the small screen in his palm.

Sullivan sat back in his chair and massaged his left temple, felt the scar tissue there and stopped. "That's unbelievable. Nothing, fucking nothing. No one came in or out. How the hell is that possible?" Sullivan went over the video in his mind again and looked up at Barry. "Can you tell me something?"

Barry's brow wrinkled as he looked up from the phone. "What?"

"Why in God's name would trained prison officers not have their weapons drawn when responding to a murder scene?"

Barry blinked and seemed to chew on an imaginary piece of gum. "You're right. They were acting—"

"Like they already knew," Sullivan finished. The quiet of the room flooded over them. It was the sound of something unsaid cementing into place, being mortared in their minds.

"Shit," Barry said.

"Double shit," Sullivan said. He sat forward and pointed to the phone. "Let's watch the other one with Alvarez and Fairbend."

Barry fiddled with the device for a moment, and after a few seconds, the next video began to play.

The shot was centered on three cells in the main holding area. The camera seemed to be mounted beneath the second-floor catwalk, and when Sullivan thought about it, he recalled seeing a few small black spheres positioned there every twenty yards or so. Two guards came into view, each gripping an arm of an inmate that Sullivan recognized as Fairbend. The guards opened the cell door and Alvarez appeared in the innermost confines, leaning casually against the wall. Fairbend entered and the door slid shut. Both guards exited the frame and all was still within the cell. Alvarez remained against the back wall and Fairbend faced the camera, staring out into the corridor. Sullivan could see Fairbend's lips moving between the bars and his head tilting from side to side as he spoke. It looked as if he was speaking to Alvarez, but neither man acknowledged the other in any way. Fairbend finished talking and Sullivan watched as Alvarez stepped away from the wall, as if he'd been shocked. Fairbend smiled and turned toward Alvarez. There was a beat and then Alvarez launched himself across the cell's short width and began to choke Fairbend. Sullivan could see the dead man's fingers wrapped tightly around the other man's throat, and then, as suddenly as he'd attacked, Alvarez fell away like he'd been shocked by the other man's skin. Fairbend recovered and began to stalk into the depth of the cell, chasing Alvarez. There were flailing arms and legs, and then both men came back into view. Fairbend fell and landed on his back, while Alvarez pounced on top of him. Again, the dead man began to choke his cellmate, but he was interrupted as a flurry of guards came running onto the screen. After a few seconds, the door was opened and Alvarez came out, swinging his fists wildly in sweeping arcs at his captors. A guard on the left drew a black gun-like object from his belt, and a moment later Alvarez fell to the floor, his legs and arms locked tight by the current coursing through his body. The video ended there, the screen once again turning black.

"Well, now we know Fairbend's lying too," Sullivan said.

"Yep, he definitely said something that pissed that poor fucker off," Barry said. "And now we're stranded here tonight unless I can persuade the sheriff to come get us. Stranded at a creepy fucking prison in the middle of nowhere with one staff member, maybe more, that could be involved in the murder. And I was looking forward to bed."

"Yeah, we're in a bad spot. Let's get Hacking on the line and tell him what's what. Let him know we might need some extra help here in the morning. If we stay here tonight, I'd feel better if one of us keeps an eye open while the other one sleeps." Sullivan stood and stretched his back, each adjustment popping like corn in a hot skillet.

"But how could it be Bundy? He was outside when the murder took place, he's got half a dozen witnesses, along with video evidence," Barry said.

Sullivan made his way around the table and clapped his friend on the shoulder as they walked to the door. "If I know one thing, buddy, it's this: don't ever trust someone that shares a name with a serial killer."

==

Sullivan chewed the remaining bits of his cold turkey sandwich and sipped ice water to wash it down. The prison food actually wasn't that bad. Don had been right. *Don.* He hoped the pathologist was home with his family, nursing his wounded hand, warm and dry with a good shot of liquid painkiller in a tall glass. Sullivan looked around at the rest of the commons, which was eerily silent. The cooks had told him the prisoners ate early, usually by five and never later than five thirty. Now, there was only a cluster of guards seated at the far end of the room. Every so often a head would swivel in Sullivan's direction, only to turn away when he tried to make eye contact.

Barry appeared from the nearby hallway, holding his phone, looking as if he'd like to take a bite out of it. The older agent dropped onto the seat across from Sullivan and tossed his phone onto the table with disdain.

"I don't know what the fuck is wrong with that thing. Got ahold of Hacking, but it kept cutting out. I think he got the gist of what was going on and where we're staying tonight." Barry uttered the last words as he gave a cursory glance around the room.

"So no luck with the sheriff?"

"No, not even a ring this time, it just went to voicemail. The call dropped before anyone picked up at his office too. You done?" Barry gestured at Sullivan's empty plate and his own sandwich that he'd barely touched.

"Yeah. Let's find our lodgings for the night and get some shut eye."

They dumped their plates off at the kitchen and made their way back out toward the warden's office. As they approached the oak door with the brass nameplate, it swung open and Andrews stepped out like he'd been waiting for their approach.

"Done for the day, gentlemen?" Andrews asked.

"Yes. We were wondering if you could show us the room we'll be staying in," Sullivan said.

"Of course. Follow me."

Andrews walked toward the door Mooring had disappeared behind earlier that day. The warden flashed his own keycard across an electronic eye mounted in the wall and the door clicked open. A hallway extended out and branched off at the end in a T. Andrews took a left and began climbing a switchback of stairs to the second level. Their footsteps echoed off the concrete walls and came back to them, their passage sounding like fifty men instead of three. Sullivan heard the warden panting ahead of him, his breath coming in short, heaving gasps. At the top of the stairs, the thunder that had been muted until then made itself heard once more. Sullivan followed Andrews as he made his way down another hallway lined with doors on both sides. The doors were old and made of heavy steel. Some were intricately paneled, their designs bordering upon art. The paint was scratched here and there, and Sullivan realized this was a very old part of the prison. While the rest of the building had undergone face-lifts and updates in recent years, this portion appeared untouched.

Andrews stopped at a door at the end of the hall, the corridor continuing further into the wing to the left, to more dormitory rooms, Sullivan assumed. The door was unlocked, and when the warden pushed it open and flipped on the single overhead light, Sullivan thought Andrews's comparison to the inmates' dwellings hadn't been much of a joke.

The room was Spartan at best. Two sets of cast-iron bunk beds were positioned on either side, with a short-legged table nestled between them. A lavatory barely big enough to turn around in was to the left. Other than that, the room had no defining features save an imitation of a window less than eight inches wide, which sat ten feet off the floor. The small gap in the wall revealed a roiling torrent of clouds the color of a river bottom.

"I know it's not much, but for now it's all I can offer you," Andrews said. The older man's face scrunched with what looked like real regret, and Sullivan felt himself like the warden a little more.

"It's just fine, David. Thank you. We'll come see you in the morning bright and early," Sullivan said as he stepped inside the room.

"Excellent. You can find me at the far end of the hall if you should need anything in the night. The shower room is the only door on the right, if you're so inclined."

"Perfect, thanks again," Sullivan said as the warden turned and raised a hand in parting, then shuffled down the hallway. Sullivan watched him go, sure that a man no older than sixty shouldn't move like that. Barry stepped inside and shut the door. It made a satisfying clank that spoke of security and strength.

Barry gave the room a once-over, then sat heavily onto the lower right bunk. "Well, here we are."

"Yeah, here we are," Sullivan said. He turned and sat on the left bunk, his hand running over the rough wool blanket covering the lumpy mattress. "Wanna take a shower?" He couldn't resist the grin that spread across his face at seeing Barry's eyebrows rise in unison.

"Did you just ask me to shower with you in a prison? Really?"

"I'm sure they have a nice setup, soap on short ropes and all."

Barry groaned and bent to untie his shoes. "How 'bout never in your wildest dreams?"

Sullivan laughed and pried his own dress shoes off. The bottoms were encrusted with mud, as were the laces. He'd have to buy new ones when they got back to civilization. The thought of his house, on its own quiet street, the windows dark and a few cold beers waiting in the fridge, gave him a bout of homesickness so strong he had the urge to leave the confines of the prison and swim back to the car, just so he could sleep in his own bed tonight. The foolishness of the idea made him snort. Two miles of water stood between him and the Trailblazer. He was a strong swimmer, but not that strong.

Barry ran his fingers inside his mouth and rubbed his teeth before smacking his lips in disgust. "Don't even have a toothbrush."

"Well if you go to get yours, could you bring mine back too? Try not to get it wet, though. I heard these old prisons have kind of archaic sewer systems. No telling what's floating out in that swamp."

Sullivan watched as Barry's face deepened with comic revulsion. "Jesus, you're sick sometimes."

Sullivan chuckled as he lay back on the bunk and undid the top three buttons on his shirt. "Did you call your wife yet?"

"Yeah, left a message earlier, but I should try again now."

Sullivan watched as Barry dialed and listened for a few moments until his face lit up at the sound of his wife's voice on the other end. The senior agent stood and ambled over to the door, his words low and soothing. Sullivan listened. Not to what was actually being said but to what the words sounded like. Assurances. That's what cops and agents made when they called home. They calmed and made bold statements of safety to their families. *Yes, I'm okay. Yes, I'll be coming home soon. No, not dangerous at all, just routine stuff. Let's talk about your day.* How many conversations just like that had he had with Rachel? A hundred? Two? But it was more than telling her he was safe. It had been checking up to make sure *she* was okay. Making sure that she would answer and there would be some semblance of sobriety in her voice. He could always tell if she'd been drinking. She would slur her *S*s, turning them into *Z*s instead. He would finish work on a case and feel the relief wash over him, only to have a new fear step in to take its place. The fear that she wouldn't answer. That she'd panicked for too long and that now she was three drinks deep in a bottle of Glenfiddich. His heart would stutter when she finally answered; even if her *S*s sounded like *Z*s, he would be relieved. At least he could talk to her, tell her that he would be home soon and that they could make things "flatten out," as he always put it. The panic attacks were mountains and valleys, and all she'd ever wanted was a straight line. She'd told him as much when they first started dating. She'd wanted evenness in her life and he'd thought he'd be able to provide it. Something his father used to say came back to him whenever he remembered his ambitions for fixing her. *Even fools have dreams,* his dad would say. Yeah, that was about right.

Barry ended his call and stared at the phone for a few seconds before he turned and came back to his bunk.

"Everything good at home?" Sullivan asked.

Barry raised his head and smiled. "Yeah, lucky I got through. Jen's already got Josie and Darrin in bed. They were scared of the storm, so she had to sit with them for a while." Barry's eyes grew distant for a few seconds. "I usually do that for them."

The quiet between them said all that needed to be said, and it wasn't long before Sullivan stood and walked soundlessly to the door, locked the heavy bolt home, and flipped the light off.

It was sometime later when Barry spoke in the darkness. "I'm sorry for earlier today."

Sullivan frowned and turned his head toward the other man's bunk. "For what?"

Barry was silent for a long time. "For making the cracks about the doctor. I can't imagine what you went through with Rachel, and here I am making dumb jokes."

Sullivan blinked at the mention of her name, but smiled a little. "It's okay, buddy. I know you didn't mean anything by it." Sullivan paused and turned his head so that he stared up at the bottom of the bunk above him. "It's just hard to think of anyone else that way. It feels like she's still here. Like she'll be waiting for me when I get home."

Sullivan heard Barry breathe deeply. The other man had never even met Sullivan's dead wife, but the compassion that resided within Barry Stevens was something almost immeasurable. Sullivan had never known another person more empathetic in their line of work.

"I'm sorry, man. I'm so sorry. I can't even imagine," Barry repeated.

"It's okay. It is what it is, as they say."

"Yeah."

Lightning clawed its way into the room and outlined their cramped quarters in strobe flashes. Thunder answered after a moment, and to Sullivan it felt like a freight train passing a few yards outside the room.

"Think we need to sleep in shifts?" Barry asked.

"No, not after seeing that door and the big fucking dead bolt on it," Sullivan said. "I'm thinking we'll be safe."

"Good. I think I can sleep now."

"Good night."

"Good night."

The room lit up again in a cavalcade of dancing negative images as Sullivan curled onto his side, pulled the pillow close to his head and fell asleep before he heard the thunder.

==

He chased her again.

She ran away from him on a broken landscape of rock and volcanic glass. Her feet bled and he could see the red mixed with the black and gray of the ground. As he ran he looked around at the place they were in and absently wondered where exactly they were.

The air smoked with the smell of sulfur and something else. A stench, almost like rotting meat in the sun. The sun. He glanced overhead and saw what looked like a large star in the distant sky. It did not fully light the ground that they ran upon but gave the entire surrounding an ambivalent illumination. Shadows were everywhere, thrown from mountainous rock formations with protruding jagged edges shaped like blown glass. In the distance he could see an openness in the air that suggested they were traveling toward a cliff of extreme height. Beyond that, the land was pockmarked with holes wide and deep enough to house entire cities.

Rachel ran.

He tried to call out to her, but every breath was choked and he barely could keep his legs pumping beneath him. He could not gain on her. Her bloody feet pelted the shards beneath them, even as his own plodded to keep up. A vibration of a sort he had never felt before thudded through his chest and he looked overhead to be sure a storm wasn't upon them.

A storm. A storm. So much water.

But there was no water here, or anything that resembled it. Dust spun up in ghosts across the land and twirled in dances unknown to him. He tucked his head and leaned forward as another vibration racked his internal organs. A sound now audible became clear. A groaning so deep it dwarfed any lighthouse's horn came from nearby, and he looked around, afterimages of rock ledges and serrated buttes coating his vision.

Rachel neared the cliff's edge, an abyss of such depth he couldn't fathom it. Her dress billowed out behind her, and if he could just reach out and snag it, he could stop her, because there was no iron railing on the cliff's edge for her to pause at. She could tumble off into the nothingness and fall forever. Maybe this time he would follow her over. It would be a relief to do so. To just fall along with her and hold her and tell her soon it would all be okay.

She reached the edge and stopped without any real effort, her hair falling against her back and her dress settling around her like a cloud ready to disperse. He cried out to her, this time to tell her to wait, instead of to stop. He would go with her now without any reservation. He belonged with her; the meager strings of purpose that held him within life were weak and worthless in her absence.

Her head turned and she looked at him, her face wreathed in the confines of her hair, and she smiled. Such a sad smile with so much possibility. He screamed for her to wait, the dust and toxic air saturating his lungs and making it hard to speak, let alone fuel the need of his burning muscles. He waited for the tipping of her body that seemed so familiar. He waited but she didn't move. Instead, something else emerged from the drop a few feet from where she stood. He could see the winding shapes of rope and coils that moved like dozens of snakes. Two hard points punctured the dead ground and found enough purchase to heave the thing's bulk into view. Its eyes were black holes that killed light and exuded despair. He felt lost as he ran on toward them, hopeless. Even if he reached her, there would be no escape from that which pulled itself free of the chasm beyond.

He received an impression of an articulation of legs and a maw opening that defied anything he could relate to. Not teeth. No, but something far worse yawned to accept Rachel as she smiled and leaned into the thing's open mouth.

==

A stifled scream bled out of Sullivan as he rolled over the side of the bed and thought he might be sick on the floor. He put a hand to his teeth and bit down on the skin of a knuckle, as he felt the first tears squeeze loose and stream down his face. He tried to breathe, but there was a hand deep inside him, constricting his diaphragm in a steel grip. Instead, he leaned back onto the bed and forced his eyes shut as he listened to rain batter the roof above him. A dream. Just a dream. The same but different somehow. He felt winded, as if he'd been running for a long distance without rest, and now that his body was still, the sensation of movement twirled within him like an amusement-park ride.

He reached up and rubbed the side of his face and ran both hands through his tangled hair. He'd seen her falling again, he was sure of it, but there was something else. Something new in the dream. He hadn't been in their apartment in Minneapolis. They had been somewhere else. He could almost taste the foul air on his tongue … or maybe it was from not brushing his teeth the night before. The flavor made him grimace. Lightning lit up the room in a short flicker and he recalled where he was. The prison. Alvarez. Don and his fingers. The storm.

Sullivan licked his lips and spun his body until his feet touched the cold tile of the floor. His head hung toward his chest and he felt the weakness of sleep leaving his muscles. He needed to pee and he was thirsty. God, he was thirsty. He'd never felt his throat so dry in his life. As he stood the back of his head connected solidly with the overhead bunk, and he immediately sat back down, cursing under his breath and rubbing the growing egg on his scalp. He blinked and thought his vision had flashed with the blow, but it was only lightning again. But what he saw in the brief illumination stopped him cold and made his guts shrivel.

The door to their room was open several inches.

And Barry's bed was empty.

Chapter 7

Sullivan froze on the edge of the bed, telling himself he hadn't seen what he'd seen. The door's intricate steel plates must have caused an illusion and Barry's tangled sheets and blanket thrown back were actually hiding his sleeping form. He waited for another pulse of light and tried to determine what time it was. It felt like early morning, but with the storm outside he couldn't be entirely sure. He felt somewhat rested, as if he'd slept more than a few hours. While the seconds of darkness lingered with only the sound of rain and his own heartbeat to keep him company, he discarded the simple hope that Barry had gone to the bathroom. *He would have turned on the light,* Sullivan thought. But there was no illumination coming from where the bathroom was positioned, only the constant dancing darkness.

Light bloomed outside the narrow window, but not as bright as before, indicating the storm was perhaps moving away, and his stomach dropped as he confirmed that Barry was gone and the door was indeed open at least five inches. Instincts began to take over as Sullivan scooped his handgun and holster off the bed behind him, where he'd placed them the night before. After attaching the holster firmly to his belt, he slid his feet in a tight circle until they encountered his shoes.

He rose, and after a second of hesitation, drew his handgun and pointed it at the doorway. It felt good and solid in his grip, a promise of protection should he need it. He stepped closer to the door and flipped on the overhead light. The room flooded in a pale glow and, after merely glancing in the direction of the cramped bathroom, he saw that he was truly alone.

Sullivan took a deep breath and opened the door unto the deserted hallway, his mind already running through scenarios that would explain why his partner had left the locked room in the middle of the night. None satisfied him.

He swung to the left and pointed his weapon at the head of the empty stairway, the feeble light seeping in from the high windows did almost nothing to alleviate the blackness. He listened above the throbbing in his eardrums and couldn't hear any other sounds. He turned to the right and followed the hallway, which ended a few dozen steps from his room. Two doors branched off on the left wall and, only one sat opposite. He took the one on the right, the door being propped open, and after two steps found himself in the entry to the shower room that Andrews mentioned the day before. Only a few lights were on, casting long shadows of the shower stalls on the floor. A fan overhead hummed, pumping air out, while a vent near the door blew fresh oxygen in.

"Barry?" The word came back to him immediately, like someone else had spoken it. He swallowed and listened for a sound other than his own breathing, but there was nothing. He turned and walked back into the hall and examined the door that he assumed led to the warden's quarters. It was shut and no light seeped from the gap at its bottom.

A scraping sound pulled Sullivan's head around toward the stairway, and he flinched, bringing the .45 to bear in its general direction. He waited for it to repeat, and when it did, he began to walk toward it, arms straight out, one foot in front of the other, heel to toe.

The noise came from the bottom of the stairwell on the first floor, which was well lit compared to the where Sullivan stood looking down over the rail. He saw no movement, and heard no voices, only the soft scrape of something sliding on the tiled floor. He wanted to call out for Barry again, but all his senses screamed for him to be quiet. He felt the urge to return to the room, lock the dead bolt behind him, and wait with the handgun on his lap until full light came. But he couldn't do it. Not with his friend wandering the prison with a suspect capable of the carnage he'd witnessed yesterday on the loose.

He moved sideways down the stairs, his eyes never leaving the lit hallway at the bottom. The gun's barrel remained steady, and as he moved he wished he had something more appropriate on his feet. The dress shoes didn't make much noise, but to Sullivan it sounded as if he wore diving flippers. He pivoted at the landing and kept moving at a steady pace; his pulse had revved up and he could feel the thrum of it in his temples and wrists.

The hollow boom of a door closing made him stop three stairs from the main level. Someone had just left the hallway and stepped into the lobby. Sullivan crept down the last few stairs and leaned against the wall before peering around the corner, his arms tucked close to his chest, the rear sight of his gun pressed against his right shoulder.

The hallway was empty.

Sullivan stepped out into the open, ready to jog to the door at the far end when a sound came from behind him. Before he could turn, something hit him solidly in the back and drove him headfirst toward the opposite wall. He tried to maintain his hold on the gun, but the concrete swiftly coming to meet him made his hand slacken enough to try to catch himself. He heard the Heckler & Koch hit the floor somewhere to his right as he was crushed against the unforgiving wall. He managed to deaden some of the blow with his hands and arms, but the side of his head still bounced painfully off the cinderblock, spraying stars across his vision. His assailant yanked him away from the wall and slung him in the opposite direction, trying to trip him with a foot in the process, but Sullivan stepped high and widened his stance as he braced for the collision he knew was coming. This time the wall didn't hit so hard, and he managed to twist in the attacker's embrace. His elbow flew around in a short arc, and he felt it connect with what he hoped was a temple. There was a grunt of pain and the arms around his midsection loosened. Sullivan spun and slipped his right arm through the hold the man had on him while he reached over the assailant's shoulder with the other. He locked his grip behind the man's back and threw all his weight to his left as he yanked his right arm up.

The attacker's grip broke as Sullivan felt the man's feet leave the ground. He twisted and slammed him to the hard floor, the vibration of the impact shuddering through his own body. Until then he hadn't gotten a look at the man's face, but now as Sullivan postured up and pinned him to the ground with one leg and a hand at his throat, he blinked with surprise.

Henry Fairbend lay beneath him.

The inmate's thin form felt like a live wire as he strained and tried to flip Sullivan off him. The man's eyes were closed and his mouth hung open like a forgotten door.

"Henry, stop it!" Sullivan yelled, but the prisoner continued to struggle. Sullivan increased his grip on Henry's throat, but yanked his hand back when he felt the flesh *move* beneath his palm. "What the fuck?" Sullivan said.

Henry's throat convulsed and bulged. It looked like the man had tried to swallow an entire sandwich whole and it had gotten stuck. A soft hissing issued from Henry's mouth and Sullivan sat back farther, a thought blossoming like a poisonous flower in his mind.

Whatever was in the man's throat wasn't being swallowed—it was trying to get out.

Henry opened a pair of eyes that were the color of old lead. There were no pupils to break the static flatness of the inmate's stare, although as Sullivan stood and backed away he knew the other man saw him. He could feel the gaze prodding at him, pushing him back as his feet obeyed.

Henry sat up and something flickered in the confines of his mouth. It reminded Sullivan of an air hose he had seen spring a leak. The tube had swung and gyrated like it was alive, which was exactly what the thing in the prisoner's mouth was doing. Soon there were more of them there, all twisting and turning as if they were lost and in search of a way out. It wasn't long until they found it.

Sullivan felt a scream well up in him as the first tendril snaked free of the inmate's lips. It was the same gray as the eyes above it, and less than an inch wide. Its tip looked fairly sharp from where Sullivan stood, and he took another step back as the second tendril joined the first. The ends were slightly different shades, and as more of them emerged, Sullivan saw that they were curved and pointed like gray daggers and fishhooks. Soon, Henry's face was engulfed by a writhing mass of the things. They whipped and danced around each other like cobras looking for a charmer to strike.

"Jesus," Sullivan whispered. He was incapable of screaming or moving, or of anything besides staring at the snake-like things that pointed and stabbed at the open air.

Henry pushed himself into a standing position, and Sullivan noticed his head was tilted back at an odd angle, his mouth open wide to accommodate its occupants. Henry started toward Sullivan, the gray eyes searching between the swinging tendrils. Sullivan looked past the prisoner and spotted his gun lying a few yards down the hall. His eyes shifted back to the walking nightmare, and then he made his move.

With one motion he lunged forward and kicked out. Henry tried to spin to the left, the tentacles snapping angrily in the air, but wasn't fast enough. Sullivan's shoe caught the prisoner solidly in the solar plexus. He heard the air whoosh past the tendrils as his attacker flew backward and connected with the wall. Henry's skull cracked audibly against the concrete, but Sullivan didn't hesitate to see if the injury would drop him to the ground. He took two steps and dove for his handgun, catching it and rolling back lightly to his haunches in a crouch.

Henry was coming at him full bore, arms outstretched, multiple tongues finally stilled, their points all directed at Sullivan. He fired twice. The gunshots in the enclosed hallway were louder than anything he'd ever heard before. He saw two holes open in the man's chest and matter fly out the back of Henry's jumpsuit. The impact of the hollow-point slugs didn't throw the prisoner backward but only stopped his forward movement. Henry stood up straight, his feet sliding together as his featureless eyes gazed at Sullivan.

Through the smoke that still curled from the barrel of the gun, Sullivan watched the prisoner topple to the side, like an ancient tree finally succumbing to gravity. Henry's body hit the floor with a sound like a wet sack being dropped. Without taking his eyes off of the man or the things that were beginning to recede into his mouth, Sullivan stepped closer. He trained the muzzle on Henry's head and resisted the impulse to pull the trigger again. The last few inches of the mouth-snakes retreated out of sight and Henry's jaw closed as his eyelids slid shut over the silver eyes. One last hiss of breath, or whatever resided within the man's body, and Henry was gone.

Sullivan felt his muscles pull excruciatingly tight and then loosen. He let out the stale breath he'd been holding since firing the shots, and saw edges of black eat at his vision before swimming away.

"Oh God," he gasped and leaned against the wall. He turned and looked down the empty hallway. Where was everyone? Certainly they'd heard the shots. Why wasn't an army of guards descending upon him from up above? Slowly he calmed his breathing, and made his way to the far end of the hall. After jamming on the locked handle of the door, he jerked the keycard from his pants pocket with a shaking hand, and saw the light below the reader flip from red to green. He exploded out of the hallway and ran toward the main desk.

A young officer with his hat pulled down over his eyes dozed in a chair, his feet propped on something beneath the counter.

"Hey!" Sullivan yelled, and had the presence of mind to holster his weapon as he approached. The guard started and batted his hat up his forehead. "I need help, I just shot a prisoner in the hallway!" Sullivan skidded to a stop, his hands grasping the corners of the large kiosk.

"What?" The guard looked at him dumbly, as if he'd never seen another person before, much less heard one speak.

"I was attacked by a prisoner in the hallway and I shot him!" Sullivan waited for something to register behind the younger man's eyes, and when he made no move for the phone near his right hand, Sullivan reached across the desk and gripped him by the collar of his uniform. "I just killed a man in the hallway!" he yelled into the guard's face. This got the young officer moving, and he dropped the phone twice before bringing up to his head while dialing furiously with the other hand.

Sullivan turned away from the desk as he heard the guard begin stammering into the phone for help. The clatter of feet running on the other side of the main holding door could be heard, and soon it opened, spewing out a crowd of prison officers into the lobby. Sullivan waved them toward the door on the far side of the room and walked in the same direction. His heart sank when he saw Mooring among them. Sullivan stopped just outside the door and watched as several guards filed through, their guns drawn and their eyes darting left and right. Mooring stopped a few feet from the entrance and made no move to follow the rest of the officers.

"What's going on?" Mooring asked.

"I was attacked by Henry Fairbend and was forced to shoot him in the hallway. There was something—" *Inside of him,* Sullivan almost finished. Mooring raised his eyebrows under the bill of his ever-present hat. "There was something wrong with him," Sullivan said instead. "I woke up a few minutes ago and agent Stevens was missing from our room. When I went to look for him, Fairbend attacked me."

"So you shot him? You couldn't just restrain him? Yell and wait for help?" Mooring's eyes darkened. Sullivan detected no compassion on his face. In fact, he saw suspicion rising.

"Yell for help? No one heard the two fucking shots I fired, and I should have yelled for help?" Sullivan imagined his face becoming a warming burner on a stove, his anger twisting a knob inside him to high.

"I'm gonna need your weapon," Mooring said, holding out a palm.

"Fuck off," Sullivan replied. The words were automatic, as a snapshot of Fairbend's mouth straining open to accommodate whatever had been inside him flashed through Sullivan's mind. *Still* inside him. Sullivan's eyes widened. He had to warn the guards. He made a sudden move toward the door, groping for his keycard, and saw Mooring pull his own sidearm free. Sullivan stopped short and was about to tell the guard that the rest of his team was in trouble when the door burst open from the other side.

The guards walked back out into the lobby, their narrowed eyes taking in the scene before them. Sullivan stood grasping the plastic card, while Mooring's handgun pointed directly at his head a few feet away. The last person to step through the door was a bleary-eyed David Andrews. The warden wore a plain blue pair of pajama pants, with a threadbare robe tied loosely around his narrow chest and shoulders. To Sullivan, the man looked ten years older than the night before.

"What's the meaning of this? Jesus, Agent Shale. What happened to your head?" Andrews asked.

Only then did Sullivan feel the warm wetness coursing down from the left side of his head and onto his shoulder. As if in a dream, he reached up and touched the spot where he'd been driven into the wall. When he looked at his fingers, they were slick with blood.

"When Fairbend tackled me, I hit my head," Sullivan said, rubbing his fingers on his slacks.

Now, it was Andrews's turn to squint at him. The warden blinked a few times and then motioned to Mooring, who was still keenly training his weapon on Sullivan. "Did you say Henry Fairbend attacked you?" Andrews asked.

Sullivan nodded. "Agent Stevens is missing and when I went to look for him, Fairbend hit me in the hallway."

The guards formed a circle around Andrews and Sullivan, and now they were exchanging glances, their hands hovering close to the weapons on their belts.

"I'm sorry, Sullivan, but that's really not possible. Henry Fairbend died late last night from an epileptic seizure. The doctor thinks it was brought on by his prior injuries."

The words were like a string that would not thread through the eye of a needle. As Sullivan tried to make sense of them, they slid away from him, the writhing mass in the prisoner's mouth taking precedence until he pressed a palm to his left eye, which came away bloody. "Dead? Can't be."

"I'm afraid so. Son, maybe you should sit down," Andrews said and pointed toward a wooden bench against the nearest wall.

Sullivan shook his head and licked his lips, realizing he still desperately needed to pee. "If he's dead, then who's lying in that hallway?"

Andrews shared a look with Mooring, and then turned his gaze back at Sullivan. "Son, there's no one in the hallway."

==

He didn't remember brushing past the guards who tried to hold him back or scanning the key against the reader. The impossibly empty hallway became everything. He walked numbly to the spot where Fairbend attacked him. The red smear where his head had hit the wall was there, as well as two gleaming shell casings that lay a few feet apart. The smell of gunfire was still in the air too, a tangy scent that illuminated memories within him without effort, the cordite acting as an olfactory photo album. But none of this concerned Sullivan. What did concern him was the absence of the body he'd left lying in a gathering pool of blood.

He stared at the area where Fairbend had fallen. There was some blood there, but not much. Not enough for a full-grown man to have lain there after being shot twice in the solar plexus. His mind convulsed as it coughed up images of the tendrils poking from Fairbend's mouth. The way they'd whipped around and searched him out. He closed his eyes and nearly cried out when a hand came to rest on his shoulder. He turned and found Andrews looking at him, concern evident in the creases beside his mouth and the furrows in his brow.

"I don't know where he went. He was right here. He had something—"

"Sir, don't you think we need do something about this?" Mooring interrupted from over the warden's shoulder.

The older man stared at Sullivan as he spoke to the guard. "We will, Everett. Let's get him to medical, he's losing color. All of it's on his shirt."

Sullivan blinked and touched his brow again, which was still alarmingly wet. He began to say that he was all right, but stopped when the floor tilted like the deck of a ship beneath his feet.

"But sir, don't you think he should be contained? Can't we—"

"Everett, we need to get him to Amanda. Grab his arm." Despite Andrews's frail appearance, the man had steel in his voice, and after a moment Mooring came to Sullivan's side and slung the agent's arm around his shoulders. Andrews gripped Sullivan's left bicep, and they began to walk.

The distance between the hallway and the infirmary became a blur.

Sullivan sagged at times, and kept blinking as encouraging words filtered into his ear from the warden's side. Then, he was being laid on a bed and the ceiling came into view. Amanda's pretty face hovered over him and a flashlight glared into his eyes. The world dimmed a little and he felt a floating sensation, as if the bed beneath him was rolling across an oiled floor. The prick of a needle brought him racing back to himself, and for a moment he wondered if he was lying in the same bed Fairbend had been in earlier. The thought was enough to clear the rest of his senses, and he tried to sit up while nausea did a two-step in his stomach.

"Whoa, big guy. Let's just lie back for a minute, shall we?" Amanda put her hands onto his bare shoulders and pressed firmly. Sullivan looked around the room, his eyes wide, but he allowed himself to be pushed back onto a soft pillow. Amanda leaned over him, surgical gloves encasing her delicate hands.

"Did I pass out?" Sullivan asked.

"I think you flickered for a second," Amanda said. A hint of a smile played at her lips as she rattled something on a steel tray to his left. "You lost quite a bit of blood. Your temporal artery was open, and I think your black shirt hid a lot of the blood." Her hand came back into view, holding a pair of hemostat pliers, which in turn grasped a wickedly curved needle. A length of thread hung from the dull end of the needle, and as Amanda smiled, he realized he would be feeling a little more pain before the day truly dawned.

The stitches didn't hurt as much as he'd feared, and while Amanda cleaned up the mess of bandages and supplies beside his bed, he rubbed the area around the wound. It still felt numb and enormous, partly from the swelling, he supposed, and partly from whatever agent she had injected him with.

"Thank you," he said, dropping his hand onto the bed.

Amanda smiled crookedly and continued putting away the unused instruments. "There's some water on the table," she said, motioning toward a plastic pitcher and stacked cups.

Although Sullivan's throat burned with thirst, his bladder was currently winning the battle for his attention. "I'm going to use the bathroom," he said, sliding off the bed and onto his bare feet. Someone had removed his shoes and socks. He glanced around the room to make sure no other guards lingered nearby. His vision doubled, and then steadied while he paused, balancing as if he were standing on a narrow beam.

"Let me help you," Amanda said, stripping off her gloves.

"I'm good. Just needed to get my bearings," he said, and muscled himself toward the open bathroom door to the right. Slowly, his legs began to feel like his own and the slight nausea receded.

After closing the door and releasing what felt like two gallons of blazing urine, he bent before the sink and splashed cold water onto his face. After drying off, he stared at his reflection in the harsh light of the single fluorescent. The cut on the left side of his skull was crisscrossed with fine black thread. The white scar just beneath it looked like a longer twin dressed in white. He fingered both wounds, one old, one new. What was the old comic he used to read when he was a kid? *Spy vs. Spy*? One long-faced bird-looking character dressed in black, and his counterpart in white. Now he had something akin to them on the side of his head. Scar vs. Scar.

He laughed under his breath and walked back out into the room. Amanda had finished cleaning up and was at her desk against the far wall. He stopped next to the bed and watched her. He liked the way she leaned over her work and how she braced her forehead with her left hand while her right scratched down notes on a tablet. A length of hair had fallen free of her ponytail, and he had the sudden urge to cross the room and gently tuck it back behind her ear.

Amanda paused her writing and glanced over at him. He averted his gaze to the brightening windows above her and had a sudden bout of self-consciousness as he realized he was still shirtless. Amanda must have read his mind, because she gestured toward a gray T-shirt hanging from a chair near the bed.

"One of the guys brought you a clean shirt."

He nodded and moved to the chair. Had she noticed him looking at her? Had a smile been playing at her lips as she spoke? He unfolded the shirt, which looked a size too small. He confirmed the assumption as he struggled to pull it down over his head.

"Fit okay?"

Her words came from very close by. He finally won the battle with the shirt and managed to yank it down past his eyes. Amanda stood a few feet away, smiling openly at his efforts. He grinned as he smoothed out the taut material over his chest and stomach. "Yeah, just fine. Thanks."

"Let's sit back down on the bed and check you out one more time," Amanda said.

Sullivan obeyed without complaint, looking at the flashlight she held up to dilate his pupils and following her finger while she dragged it back and forth across his field of vision.

"I think you're going to be just fine," she said as she stepped to the side and leaned against the bed frame. "No signs of concussion and you seem to have all other cognitive functions."

"You're giving me too much credit," he replied.

She laughed. "Feeling better?"

"Yeah, still a little groggy, but better." Sullivan brushed back the tide of unruly hair on top of his head and looked up at the doctor as if he had been struck with a whip. "Did they find Barry … Agent Stevens?" he asked.

Amanda pursed her lips and barely shook her head. "Sorry. From what I understand, they've been searching the whole time you've been in here."

"And how long has that been?"

Amanda shrugged, glancing at the clock on the wall. "Probably an hour and a half, give or take."

Sullivan felt his stomach drop and tighten. Barry was officially missing. There was no reasonable explanation. He hadn't gotten turned around on a midnight stroll through the facility or gone to follow up on an idea for the case. If Barry knew that Sullivan had been involved in a shooting this morning, he would be standing a few feet away, the concerned look Sullivan had seen a hundred times before wrinkling his face.

"I need to call my SAIC," Sullivan said as he began to slide off the bed. Amanda put a hand on his shoulder and pushed him back to a seated position.

"You need to relax. You might still be dizzy, and I don't want you running off down the hallway only to fall and reopen the hard work I just did. How about some water?" Amanda crossed to the pitcher beside the bed and poured a stream of icy water into one of the cups.

Sullivan stopped her with a hand on her arm before she turned to hand him the glass. "Do you have any orange juice? I think that would give me a boost."

Amanda paused, giving him a strange look, and then nodded. "Sure, I've got a bottle in the fridge."

She moved to the small refrigerator beside her desk and retrieved a bottle of Tropicana from within. After opening it, Sullivan guzzled the contents almost without stopping, the tangy bite of the juice sluicing through the accumulated spit and phlegm in his throat. He repressed a massive belch as he finished and glanced at Amanda.

"Sorry," he said, setting the drained bottle onto the bedside table.

"No, that's good. It should help with the blood loss, actually," she replied.

A silence fell between them, and when he looked up to say that he thought he could make it to the warden's office under his own power, he noticed she was studying the side of his head. He assumed she was inspecting her work, making sure all the threads in his stitches were holding.

Amanda reached out and touched not the most recent cut but the one below it. The one he had carried for years, its presence holding so much more than the irritating droop of his eyebrow.

"How did this happen?" she asked, brushing the puckered skin with a touch that sent goose bumps trailing down his arms. Sullivan bowed his head, and Amanda pulled her hand back and leaned toward him. "I'm sorry, I didn't mean—"

"It's okay," he said, stopping her apology. "It's just not a nice memory."

"I'm sorry," she repeated, stepping back and giving him polite space. But as she did, he realized he didn't want her to move farther away.

"I was a cop in Minneapolis before I became an agent," he said, looking up at her. "I was off-duty one night and I ran to a grocery store to get a few things. On my way, a guy stepped out from an alley and pulled a knife." *A broken wineglass, not a knife,* the voice in his head intoned from somewhere far away. The lie was so accustomed and polished that it flowed off his tongue like it had actually happened. "I just reacted instead of listening to what he had to say," he continued. *She was so angry that night. You remember how she'd screamed at you, how disjointed and erratic her mind had become. You remember.* He blinked and paused, forcing the voice to stop, to relent for just a moment so he could finish. "He went for my face and I got lucky. The knife went in and slid along my skull but didn't cut any major arteries. Now, it's just irritating, because if I don't do strengthening exercises, my eyebrow droops because of how the tissue was cut there." *You remember how she lunged at you, the hatred on her face so deep and penetrating that it hurt more to look at her than the actual cut did.* He breathed out and silenced the voice. This was why he avoided telling people about the scar. It was the wounds inside that flared up and hurt like they'd just been opened that caused the real pain.

Amanda stared at him, her eyes running over every inch of his face, and he wondered if she suspected he hadn't told her the truth.

Finally, she tilted her head to the side, a smile playing across her lips. "Scars are our closest memories, my dad used to say. Sometimes they're good and sometimes not, but they remind us of who we are."

Sullivan nodded and returned her smile the best he could. At times, he thought, it was better to forget.

Chapter 8

Filtered sunlight coated the lobby as Sullivan strode across it. It seemed the storm had moved on, its overbearing presence having forged ahead to soak other places out of sight and earshot. A smudge of gray clouds still besmirched the otherwise pleasant-looking day, and as Sullivan knocked on the brass-plated door, he wondered if the improving weather was an omen of better things to come. While he waited for an answer, his eyes stole to the doorway at the far end of the large room and his thoughts slid back to the morning and what he'd seen come out of Fairbend's mouth. He shuddered as he imagined the darting tendrils reaching for him, and examined the possibility that his sanity was slipping. Fairbend had died the night before. Amanda confirmed this before he left the infirmary. She said she'd been unable to do a thing as the man convulsed in the throes of a seizure so powerful he had hemorrhaged internally. So who, or what, had he shot in the hallway? And more importantly, where was it now?

The door opened, startling him, and Andrews's kind face appeared in the opening, wrinkled with a smile. "Agent Shale, come in, come in."

The warden ushered him inside and closed the door behind them. The office looked more distinguished in the brighter sunlight, and Sullivan felt the strain of the past day's uncertainties weigh upon him in the neat and orderly room.

"Please sit," Andrews said, motioning to the same chair Sullivan sat in the day before. The other was blaringly empty.

Sullivan cleared his throat while the warden busied himself with two cups of coffee. "Agent Stevens hasn't been located yet?"

Andrews glanced over his shoulder and shook his head before he turned and brought Sullivan a steaming cup, then made his way behind the large desk. "I'm afraid not," the older man said, and Sullivan heard a pained grunt as he settled into his chair. "My officers have been scouring the prison ever since this morning, and there's been no sign of him."

Sullivan set the coffee down and scooted forward in his seat. "Sir, I need to call my senior agent in charge and notify him of what happened. My cell phone is …" Sullivan paused. "… not working correctly."

Andrews sighed and sat forward as he leaned his elbows upon his desk. Deep hollows were carved beneath each of the man's eyes, and after a moment of inspection, Sullivan came to the conclusion that the warden also hadn't slept much the night before. "That's where we're in a bit of a pickle, Sullivan. Can I call you Sullivan?" Sullivan nodded. "We lost our landlines late last night, about the time Henry died, I'm suspecting. It's this damn rain. I just heard on the weather radio that there's more coming, this is just a lull. They're saying we'll be getting another three to five inches by this afternoon. Hopefully our power will hold, and if it doesn't we have our backup generators, but I'm afraid we'll have to start planning for an eventual evacuation to New Haven." The warden turned in his chair and stared out of one of the high windows. The deep lines on his face became canyons in the harsher light, and Sullivan wondered again if he'd been wrong presuming the man's age. "I think some of the main junction boxes must have washed out in the night, and now there's nothing," Andrews said, gesturing toward the impassive phone on his desk.

"How about cell phones? I could borrow yours or someone else's—" Sullivan broke off as he watched Andrews bow his head and shake it again.

"Cells are out too. All I can figure is the surrounding towers must've either toppled with the softened ground combined with the wind or we had one hell of a lightning strike." Andrew dug in his pocket, and then slid a small flip phone across the desk. When Sullivan opened the device, he saw that the other man told the truth. A "No Service" message blinked at the top of the square screen and no matter which direction he turned, no bars appeared. Sullivan snapped the phone shut in anger and pushed it back to the warden.

"Do you have a shortwave radio?" Sullivan asked.

"No, I'm sorry. Before this bout of storms, we never saw a need to have an emergency backup."

"How about the hospital? Do they have separate lines or better service?"

Again, the warden had a pained look on his face. "No, I checked with them this morning."

A revelation struck him that was so simple, Sullivan barely restrained himself from smacking his forehead. "The boat. We can use the boat now that the storm's passed." Sullivan heard the hope in the pitch of his own voice, and then felt the creeping sense of disquiet when Andrews bit his lower lip and wrinkled his brow. The older man's eyes looked right at him, through him, pinning him to the chair.

"That's something else I wanted to speak to you about," Andrews finally said. "There's been a development that I haven't made you aware of, and I knew you'd be upset by it, so I wanted to tell you in private."

Sullivan's unease deepened and he reached out to grasp the arms of the chair. "What is it?"

"The prison boat was found this morning, half sunk where it had been tied up last night. Officer Bundy was on his way to town to report our phone outage and to radio the necessary authorities about Agent Stevens, as well as your, um, incident this morning, when he found it."

"Sunk," Sullivan repeated. "Sunk how? The storm swamped it?"

"That's what we initially thought, but then we found this nearby on the ground where the boat was beached." Andrews opened a drawer in his desk and pulled out an evidence bag. A black handgun poked at the confines of the sack, and Sullivan leaned back in his chair, the strength going out of his arms and legs.

"There were also a few spent casings on the ground, and after further inspection we saw that the hull had been shot several times, along with the motor," Andrews continued. He set the bag with the gun onto the top of his desk, and the sound it made filled up the entire room like an echo in a tomb. "I'm gauging from your reaction that you recognize it?"

Sullivan barely comprehended the warden's words. As he stared, the rest of the room dimmed, with the darker clouds outside closing in over the sun or the implications of what rested within the plastic, he didn't know. All he could do was look at the gun on the desk.

Barry's gun.

Sullivan licked his lips, which had somehow become numb in the last few minutes, and glanced up at Andrews, whose fingers were steepled before him.

"Sir, I know Agent Stevens personally, and he would never do anything like this, I assure you," Sullivan said, finally finding his voice.

Andrews seemed to consider the words for a moment before turning toward the windows again. "And how do you know this?"

The question caught Sullivan off-guard. "I know him. He's a good man with a family. To be honest, sir, he wanted to leave the prison as soon as possible."

Andrews flapped a hand in Sullivan's direction. "It's David, enough with the *sir* shit. Makes me feel old. So what do you make of this?" he said, motioning at the gun.

Sullivan looked at the weapon on the desk. He searched for something that would signify it wasn't Barry's gun, but he saw nothing but familiarity. How many times had he given Barry a hard time about carrying a 1911-style pistol? Several references to the *Untouchables* had been made at the office, and Barry merely laughed them off, claiming the weapon was a flawless piece of machined death. Sullivan could almost hear his friend chuckling at the jokes and see him tucking the heavy handgun into his leather holster.

"I don't know," Sullivan managed at last. There seemed to be no explanation for the evidence except what the warden was implying. He could find no reason that would justify Barry destroying their only transportation from this place. Sullivan reached out and picked up the bag, studying the weapon more closely. Bringing the bag nearer did nothing to alleviate the accusations. Instead, it only strengthened them. He dropped the gun on the desktop with a thud and sank back into the embrace of the chair.

"A full-scale manhunt is underway, and the staff at New Haven has been notified to keep watch for Agent Stevens," Andrews said with apparent regret.

"There must be some misunderstanding or other explanation," Sullivan offered, his mind doubling its effort to pair some connection with Barry's alleged actions.

"I surely hope so," Andrews said. "We have enough problems right now without worrying about a rogue agent."

Sullivan let the comment pass and stood from his chair, his coffee sitting untouched and cooling nearby. "I'd like to take a look at the boat myself. See if I can glean any ideas or reasons why Barry would do such a thing."

The warden stared through the space between them, and finally nodded, gesturing for the door. "The boat's lying near the groundskeeping shed at the north end of the perimeter. See what you can see and let me know what you find." Sullivan noticed sadness in the older man's voice, as he turned and moved toward the doorway. It seemed as if Andrews knew something fresh and terrible was barreling toward them, and he was only waiting for its eventual arrival to mourn.

"Sullivan?"

Andrews's word stopped him as he grasped the doorknob with a sweating palm, and he turned back to gaze at the prematurely aged man behind the desk.

"We'll need to speak more of Henry Fairbend later, after you've returned," the warden said.

Sullivan stared at the older man, trying to read his expression, but Andrews remained stoic, his hands resting in his lap and his eyes two motionless holes.

Sullivan nodded, opened the door, and slid out of the office, glad to be free of the warden's gaze.

==

By the time Sullivan reached the drowned boat, new clouds were already filling the sky. Their bloated underbodies bulged with a heaviness that could only mean another downpour. Not for the first time Sullivan wondered how long the storms would last. As he rounded the corner of the shed he assumed housed weed whippers and riding lawn mowers, he remembered a weatherman saying the storms were unprecedented and potentially devastating. He tried to recall another time in his life that it had rained so vehemently, but could not.

Sullivan slowed as he approached the aluminum boat he'd last seen cruising out of sight around the bend the night before. It had been pulled up on dry land, but now the licking tongue of water was almost halfway up its sides. The brackish liquid spoke in deep tones as it sloshed against the sunken vessel. Sullivan stepped to its side and ran his hand along the gunwale. His eyes searched the inside of the boat, taking in the coffee-colored water that filled its bottom, along with a few floating pieces of plastic. He studied these, and when he looked up and saw the outboard's engine cowling shattered from apparent gunshots, he knew where they'd come from.

"Shit, Barry," Sullivan muttered under his breath. Why would the man do such a thing? He'd talked to his wife hours before doing this? It made no sense, and the unknown reasons were so much more frightening than the actual deed.

Sullivan looked around the surrounding grounds, which grew darker beneath the wet blanket of clouds on the horizon. The forest outside of the fence was already black, its branches and leaves beckoning, fingers waving with promises to the answers he sought. He closed his eyes, forcing the disturbing thoughts away, and when he opened them, a darker spot just below the water's edge within the boat snagged his attention. He moved around the side, being careful to avoid the water's ever-growing hold on the muddy land. Leaning inside the boat, he reached down, dipping his fingers into the water to inspect the dark eye. He was surprised at how cold the water felt when compared to the muggy air above it, but was distracted as his fingers found the mark, and then went through it.

Sullivan paused, feeling the rim of the bullet hole. The hole his friend had shot in their only hope of leaving this place. Sullivan carefully ran his fingertips over the sharp points of aluminum that twisted and tore free when the slug from Barry's gun ripped through it. Sullivan poked his finger farther into the hole, and then stood. He remained motionless, like the looming prison to his back, as thoughts whirred through his mind on a broken reel. Without taking his gaze from the boat, he slid his own handgun from its holster and released the magazine. His thumb found the top cartridge and stripped it from its home. After replacing the magazine and tucking his weapon safely away, he leaned into the boat again, this time with the bullet pinched between his fingers. Slowly he submerged his hand, moved the tip of the round into position, and tried to push it through the hole in the aluminum. It went in a bit and then lodged. Sullivan pushed harder, but the bullet wouldn't fit through the hole.

A swooping sense of elation filled his stomach, but immediatly changed into a heavy ball of dread. His and Barry's guns were the same caliber. They fired the same round and they could easily interchange ammunition. The hole in the boat was smaller than their ammo.

Barry hadn't shot the boat at all.

Sullivan stood and dried off the round on his T-shirt, glancing over his shoulder as he did. His mind tried to compute the size difference between his bullet and the hole. The rounds that sunk the boat and destroyed the motor were smaller, but not by a lot. Perhaps a forty caliber? He stopped polishing the cartridge, his hands beginning to shake. Forty caliber was what most of the prison officers carried. He had noticed the detail at dinner the night before while inspecting the table of guards in the commons.

Instead of putting the round back into his mag, he dropped it into the pocket of his slacks. Its weight and pressure there would be a reminder, a voice urging him to be on his guard now that he knew he and his partner were being set up.

Sullivan turned in a circle, making sure he was still alone. When he was certain no one lurked nearby, he did an inventory of the options he had. He could play along with whoever was doing this and hope someone else would come looking for them. That could take days, since he and Barry checked in with Hacking only yesterday. He could go back to the warden and fill him in on his discovery; he didn't feel that Andrews was in on it, whatever *it* was, and perhaps they could confront the people responsible. Sullivan saw Bundy's and Mooring's faces float within his mind before anger shunted them away. His last choice would be to try to hike out alone, over the perimeter fence and through the surrounding swamp. He could already feel the cold touch of the water soaking hungrily through his clothes and leeching his warmth. How far could he swim, and would he be able to navigate the thick folds of brush, trees, and grass to find the way back to his vehicle?

Sullivan sighed and turned away from the boat. The prison's stout outline greeted him, and without warning the memory of the things protruding from Fairbend's mouth fell upon him. Now he knew why Alvarez had similarly shrunk away from and attacked his cell mate. He grimaced and gritted his teeth, and imagined the sharp points burrowing into his flesh, trying to make his body their home. The man must have had some sort of infestation. The things had looked parasitic.

His stomach flopped and a chilled snake of nausea wriggled through his guts. What the hell had been inside that man? And if it hadn't been Fairbend, then whom had he shot? Sullivan's mind veered away from these questions, for the fabric that held together the sane, waking world was not tailored to encompass them.

He took a step on the sodden ground, but instead of heading toward the massive building to his right, he veered left, his feet taking him away from one institution and in the direction of another.

==

Sullivan hunched his shoulders and quickened his pace. He would need all the daylight he could get if he was to succeed in his plans. The gate set in the perimeter fence clanged shut behind him and he thanked God that his passkey still worked at the barrier. Now that he was committed to the plan in his mind, he felt a sense of disbelief mingled with fear settling over him. There was no other choice but to try to hike out. He supposed he felt the same way a bungee jumper or a skydiver did when stepping to the edge of an impossible drop, but he saw no alternative. An agent was missing, possibly dead. He'd shot and killed a man who had been infected with some sort of bizarre parasite. And not to mention a murderer was still walking free, most likely a member of the prison staff.

"Plus, this place blows," Sullivan grumbled as the edge of the mental facility came into view. He slowed his stride and turned to the thick undergrowth beside the well-groomed path. With a few frustrated pulls, he managed to clear enough room in the bushes to squeeze himself through. He was struck by how green everything had become with the rain. While people cursed the water as it washed away vital roads and destroyed groomed landscapes, the wild thrived. He could almost feel the presence of something ancient relishing the water in the swell of nature.

After crouching beneath a few low-hanging evergreen branches, Sullivan was able to stand to his full height and began walking again. Here the ground was fairly level, with only a few curved ferns and rotten logs dotting the landscape between massive white pines that towered above all else. It was darker, and already he could feel moisture seeping through the thin leather of his shoes, but he felt better passing the mental facility without being seen. Snippets of voices floated to him and he smelled a ghost of cigarette smoke on the breeze. As quietly as he could, he traveled until he could no longer hear the nurses' conversation.

He stopped to check his bearings and was immediately engulfed by a swarm of mosquitoes. Sullivan slapped and swung his arms against their numbers, but they kept coming, just another force standing in the way of his escape.

"Christ!" he swore under his breath and set off once again.

Soon the ground began to slope away and several black boulders poked their heads up from the earth to watch his progress. Sullivan realized coming this way was the right choice. The land was much higher here, and the longer he could walk before having to wade and then swim, the better. As he made his way over a fallen oak that looked too strong to have been toppled by anything other than the recent storm's touch, New Haven's fence came into view.

Razor wire glinted in the sick light, and Sullivan was already imagining its cold bite, when he saw that one of the fallen oak's massive branches stretched over the fence, mashing the pointed wire flat. Finally, some luck. A sound stopped him in his tracks before he could begin to climb the tree. He turned his head and listened. After a few seconds it came again, and he dropped into a crouch, pulling his weapon as he knelt. It sounded as if someone was rooting around in the underbrush on the other side of the fence line. He waited, ignoring the thousand bugs that needled his flesh, sweat rolling down the center of his back like rain. He blinked and sighted down the H&K's barrel at a spot where a thick bush began to tremble. Its leaves shook, and then swayed for a moment before becoming still. Sullivan waited for a squirrel to emerge, and he swore if it did he would take a shot at it just for making him feel like an idiot. After several more minutes, which extended into eternity with the mosquitoes' attentions, he stood and took a few tentative steps closer to the fence. Nothing moved and he heard no rodent-like scurrying flee his presence.

"Fucking rats," he said, holstering his gun. His eyes ran up and down the steel mesh of the fence as he stepped onto the downed tree and scrambled up its trunk. When he neared the branch stretching over the fence, Sullivan steadied himself and edged out over the wire until the wood beneath his feet began to bend and sway. He looked one last time at the drop and jumped.

The fall was shorter than he anticipated, and the ground punched the soles of his feet without warning. He felt his legs give way and he fell roughly onto his back, landing in a shallow puddle that immediately soaked into his ill-fitting T-shirt.

"Fuck," he said and rolled onto his side. As he stood, he gazed around at the new terrain before him and his heart sank. The relative dryness of the land ceased a few yards from where he stood. Tufts of humped grass grew out of the ground like cancerous nodules and black patches of water gleamed between them. Farther out, the flood began in earnest. He spotted a few downed trees lying in the water, their spiny branches reaching toward the sky, as if their last dying thought had been of the sun. Live trees, both deciduous and coniferous, grew out of the flooded swamp, creating an eerie forest without visibly solid ground to hold them. The sight of their trunks jutting up out of the deluge was so strange, Sullivan merely stared for a time. Coming back to himself, he stepped onto the hillocks, balancing on their soft backs as they sank beneath his weight. The landscape continued to drop away, and soon he was left with no choice but to step into the water and commit fully to what he intended to do.

The water shocked him with its icy embrace as he settled one foot and then the other onto the spongy surface below the water. His feet sank several inches and the water crept almost to his knees, as visions of becoming lodged in the bottom spiraled through his mind. Sullivan pulled one shoe free and placed it down again, surprised by how fast the bottom sloped away.

A splash straight ahead pulled his eyes up from the next step and he stood still, searching for any ripples or waves on the otherwise calm surface. After a moment he saw some rings emanating from the hump of a massive tree trunk partially submerged a dozen yards away. The tree's remaining bark was pitch-black and scaly looking, like the skin of a cedar, only darker. Several sharp-looking branches were broken off a few inches above the trunk, and Sullivan began to dread the thought of trying to climb over them, since the tree was directly in his path. It looked like nature's version of the fence behind him. A frog must have jumped from the tree's back, causing the noise and the subsequent waves.

Sullivan turned his attention to the surrounding forest. His sense of direction had always been acute, but now, with the looming sentries of trees guarding the swampland beyond, he felt disarmed. What if he did get stuck somewhere between here and the road to the prison? What if he broke an ankle or leg climbing through the downed mire of trees? The answer was simple: he'd die.

Sullivan took a breath, checked his bearings once again, and was about to take a tentative step when he heard another splashing sound. He looked up, expecting to see another wavy circle expanding out from near the fallen tree ahead, but he did a double take as he realized the tree was gone.

His eyes scrambled across the rippling surface, searching for the black branches, but found nothing. He turned a few degrees, thinking he must have gotten confused and that the tree was to his left instead. Only blank water met his gaze. He felt his pulse speed up. Somewhere deep inside him an instinct dormant but for those few occasions when the primal need of survival kicked in and cried out. Before he even really new why, he was backpedaling, his feet slipping and sinking into the mud. *Runrunrun* something within his blood chanted, a feeling of terror so thick, he felt it drenching him, weighing him down as he moved away from the deeper water before him. With an effort he pulled his right foot free of the sludge and stepped back onto one of the grass mounds behind him. His hand moved to his gun, and just as he was about to pull it free, the water a few yards before him surged and several of the black spikes he'd originally thought were broken branches pierced the air.

Sullivan ran.

He charged back through the sopping vegetation, insanely thankful for the feeling of semidry ground beneath his feet. Water flew from his soaked pants legs and a squishing sound that would have been comical any other time came from his shoes. Whatever was behind him launched itself out of the water, and he heard it sink into the spongy earth. *It's heavy,* he thought as he pelted through bushes and over logs. He could see the fence coming up and he knew he would never have time to climb and make it over without the thing behind him plucking him off it like a ripe fruit from a low-hanging branch. Instead, he turned right, slapping leaves out of his way as he heard the crack of what sounded like a small tree breaking behind him. His legs pumped and he nearly fell as he swung up and over a downed tree. His hands brushed the ground and he kept going. The fence scrolled past to his left and he followed it as closely as he could, the clearing around it giving him a rough path to run on.

A deep resonance vibrated, first through his chest, then flowed down into his feet. It was like being hit by the bass in front of an immense speaker. It felt as if his organs were shaking loose from their moorings, and his hurried breath caught in his chest as his lungs constricted with the force. Thunder seemed to answer the sound, and rolled out ahead of him in the sky, as a few drops of rain found his streaking form through the gaps in the canopy.

An errant stick flew up with his passage and hit him in the face, and pain spread out from his left cheek into his eye socket. He barely registered it as the vibration came again. The urge to turn and see how close the thing was nearly overpowered him, but he managed to continue on. A pine bough scratched the top of his head, leaving hot furrows, while the fence jagged right and then continued on in a straight line. Faintly he registered a glimpse of a building through the trees to his left: New Haven. He was getting closer to Singleton. Something cut the air a few inches behind his head and he ducked instinctively. His hand strayed to his gun again, and he pulled it this time, his finger looping through the trigger guard.

An opening in the trees ahead drew his attention and he pushed his burning legs harder, knowing that reaching it might be his only chance. His mind tried to fathom what could be chasing him, but he batted the thoughts away. It was large and it wanted to hurt him, that was all he needed to know. Instead, he tried to calculate how many shots he had left. *Twelve in the magazine, one in the chamber.* He'd fired twice earlier that day and one round still sat in his pocket. That left ten shots available. He heard the hissing of the thing behind him drawing in air, and felt newly horrified at how close it sounded. He would have to make a stand.

Sullivan exploded into the clearing, and in a single movement he spun and slid to a stop, landing low on his stomach. He pushed his arms out before him, thrusting the barrel of the handgun toward whatever chased him.

The path behind him was empty.

He lay prone on the ground, moisture soaking the front of his shirt and pants, his breath forced in and out of him by lungs starved for oxygen. Rivulets of sweat and blood from the gouges on his scalp crept into his eyes and he tried to blink them away, unable to tear his gaze from the forest around him. Leaves snapped with the impact of each raindrop, creating a flurry of movement everywhere. He listened past the pounding of his blood and his labored breathing. Nothing moved.

Scrambling to his feet, he holstered his gun and grabbed the chainlink with both hands. His muscles burned as he pulled himself up in a furious pace until he reached the top. Without pausing, he swung a leg over and felt the wire bite into his skin, but the sensation was secondary to the sound coming from the nearby foliage. The thing was moving closer through the woods, branches breaking and leaves scraping against its body. Sullivan risked one glance as he threw himself over the top of the fence and saw jagged edges of black scales emerge into the clearing.

Pain, sharp and clear, bloomed in his right shoulder as he let go of the wire and fell to the other side of the fence. The impact was incredible and spangles of light exploded across his vision. He rolled and somehow found his feet. Fearing the thing was coming over the fence behind him, he turned and threw two quick shots in the general area where he'd crossed. He caught the impression of something dark and angular reaching up toward the razor wire, and then he was running again.

The forest blurred by in different shades of green and brown. The ground slipped beneath his feet and he stumbled as thunder spoke above him again, spurring him onward. Suddenly he was in the open and the storage shed and sunken boat were to his left. The sky was a deep, inky black and the clouds were jagged. *Like the thing behind you,* the voice in his head echoed.

Sullivan ran past the shed and toward the hunched form of the prison, the fear of hearing the fence collapsing in the woods driving him onward.

Chapter 9

He chased her again.

She laughed and looked back over her shoulder, dodging through the thick upright posts of the playground. She danced in and out of the moonbeams tunneling down from the sky. The sand was cool under his feet and the breeze kissed his skin. He laughed too, trying to catch up to her nimble form so that he could grab hold of her and pull her down on top of him. He wanted to feel her close and relish the touch of her lips on his skin. He wanted to pull the dress from her body and love her here in the sand beneath the moon, but he'd have to catch her first.

Her laughter echoed to him from beneath a darkened slide, and as he drew closer he could see a dim light there. Did she have a candle? He peered beneath the overhang where so many children whooped and cried out with joy in the daylight hours, but this was night and it was their time. So many possibilities lay beneath the slide with her in the sand and he wanted her more than anything ever before.

He saw her face come into view and she reached out to him, to draw him close. Her mouth parted, asking for a kiss, and her eyes closed. He pulled her toward him, breathed her in.

==

"Sullivan, stop."

The words forced his eyes open. Sullivan blinked and looked around the room. He was in the infirmary again, and Amanda stood over him. She was leaning away, and it was only then that he realized his hand was on the back of her neck, pulling her closer.

He released his grip and let his arm fall back to his side. Pain murmured in his shoulder, but it was dull and inconsequential.

What mattered was Rachel. She needed him and he had to go to her. He tried to sit up on the bed and Amanda's hand pressed him back flat.

"You need to rest a bit more," she said.

He blinked and nodded, the fog beginning to lift from his mind. Rachel was dead. He was in the prison. Barry was missing. Something had chased him.

Sullivan sat bolt upright, and when Amanda reached to push him back, he slapped her hand away.

"There's something out there, some kind of animal in the woods. We need to leave. It's gonna get in here!" Sullivan said, swinging his feet to the floor. The room oozed around him and the floor canted sickeningly. He reached out and gripped the edge of the bed, until his vision steadied and he was able to bring the doctor's face into focus again. Her pretty features were drawn down in dismay, and it was only then he realized he'd swatted at her. "I'm sorry," he whispered, leaning back on the bed. "What the hell happened to me?"

Amanda's expression relaxed, but she remained a few steps away. "The guard at the front desk heard you run into the lobby doors. When he went out to check, you were unconscious beneath the awning. They brought you here and you've been out for several hours."

Sullivan put a hand to his face and rubbed his eyes. A day's worth of stubble scratched his palm and he suddenly wished he could shower and shave. He wanted to cut away everything that had accumulated on him in the last day. He wanted to go home and sleep in his own bed. He wanted something normal and mundane, something that would make sense.

"Look, I know this is going to sound crazy, but there's something in the woods, some sort of predator. It chased me back to the prison and hit me on the shoulder." As he spoke, he recalled the attack and the lancing pain in his arm as he'd crested the fence. He searched his right shoulder and felt a thick bandage that covered the entire muscle there. He realized he was shirtless again, and saw a new white T-shirt hanging from the back of a chair a few yards away. He worked his arm in little circles, testing to see how badly injured he was.

"A predator? Like a bear?" Amanda asked.

"Yeah … no … I'm not sure. I really didn't get a good look at it." Sullivan closed his eyes and watched the dancing darkness behind his eyelids for a moment as he searched his memory. "It was bigger than a bear and its skin was strange."

"Strange? Strange how?"

Sullivan looked at Amanda, searching her face for disbelief but only finding concern, which was somehow more troubling. "I'm not seeing things," he managed finally, but it was just above a whisper. He shook his head as a short bout of dizziness overcame him. "What did you give me?"

"Just a low-grade sedative. It helped calm you while I cleaned the cuts on your legs and back." Amanda paused and motioned toward his shoulder. "That one was quite deep and needed a few sets of stitches."

Sullivan hung his head to his chest, and then sat back onto the bed, his shoulder throbbing dully with the exertion. "Do you have any more orange juice?" he asked.

Amanda laughed a little and went to the fridge. She returned holding another bottle of Tropicana and handed it to him. Sullivan gulped it down greedily and passed her the empty container. He could feel the beginnings of stability coming back to him, and wagered standing again. The floor remained solid beneath his feet, so he crossed to a chair, where his shoes rested between its legs.

As he tied the damp laces tight around his feet, he glanced up. Amanda was still watching him, her expression unreadable. He supposed she thought he was crazy. He'd been here twice in the last twelve hours, both times incoherent or unconscious, and now he'd physically lashed out at her while she'd only been trying to help.

"I'm sorry," he said. "I'm a little distraught about Agent Stevens. There haven't been any developments, have there?"

Amanda shook her head. "I'm afraid not, and the phones are still down. Warden Andrews said at noon that we would most likely be evacuating to New Haven by tomorrow if the rain doesn't clear up, and it doesn't look like it will." She motioned to the high windows, which were stained dark by the clouds outside. Water ran in crooked trails across their surfaces, and for a moment

Sullivan had the image of the building around them crying in the storm's embrace.

"I think I need to speak with him, if you'll let me go." Sullivan managed a halfhearted smile, and was relieved when Amanda returned it.

"Just don't go climbing any more fences, okay?" she said, turning from him as lightning slit the sky beyond the windows once again.

==

"Come in," a tired voice behind the door said before the echo of Sullivan's knocks faded from the lobby. He twisted the knob and stepped into Andrews's office for the second time that day. The warden sat behind the desk, his hands splayed out before him on its top. The older man's eyes were shadowed from beneath by the deepest bags Sullivan had ever seen. Andrews's hair was also disarrayed, giving Sullivan the impression it had been only seconds since the warden had run his hands through it.

"Sullivan, come in. Sit down."

Sullivan made his way to the chair and grimaced as he settled into it, the cuts and scratches on his legs and back making themselves heard over the soft glow of the fading sedative.

Andrews noticed his expression and sat forward. "Are you okay, son?"

Sullivan dipped his head once. "A little worse for wear but still moving." Now that the painkillers were leaving his system, Sullivan felt the shock and fear of the morning return to him: the flight for his life through the forest, his desperate climb over the fence and back into the grounds he'd tried to escape.

Andrews appraised him for a moment, the older man's eyes roaming over him in an inspection that went further than his physical state. "I'm told your injuries are a result of climbing the perimeter fence."

Sullivan licked his lips, deciding what direction to take with the warden. He liked the man, but knew he could lie sufficiently enough to fool him. He was sure no one had seen him disappear into the woods or return from them a while later. "Yes, they are," he said, deciding the truth wasn't his only option but currently the best one. But he didn't feel the need to tell the warden which way he was climbing when he sustained the injuries.

"And I suppose you thought you were going to slog your way out of here?" The older man's eyebrows rose expectantly.

Sullivan nodded again. "Yeah, I thought I could make it out, try to get some help since the phones were down."

"I'm not trying to sound admonishing, but that was dumber than dumb."

Sullivan sighed and placed a hand to his forehead, blocking the older man out completely. "Sir, I don't think I need to remind you that we have a murdered man, an injury to one of my forensic specialists, and my missing friend, and on top of that you've accused him of destroying our only contact with the outside world. Forgive me, but I thought at the time it was my only choice."

Andrews remained motionless behind the desk, and Sullivan began to think he wasn't going to respond when the warden exhaled and pursed his lips. "You're right, son. I'm sorry. If I were in your shoes, I would've done the same damn thing. I just feel like a wheel spinning in mud, working hard but not going anywhere."

"And Agent Stevens hasn't been found?"

Andrews continued to frown. "No. As of now, we've swept the entire compound, along with New Haven. There's been no sign of him."

An internal war raged within Sullivan, but finally his judgment of the man on the other side of the desk won out over instincts. He scooted forward on the chair's edge. "Sir, I have something disturbing to tell you, something I think you should be aware of, but first I need to ask you a question."

Andrews nodded and motioned with his hand. "Go ahead, can't get much worse than it is."

"Who brought you Agent Stevens's gun this morning?" Sullivan asked.

"Officer Bundy, why?"

A hovering puzzle piece sank into place within Sullivan's mind. "Sir, I think one or more of your staff is responsible for Agent Stevens's disappearance."

The warden couldn't have looked more surprised if Sullivan had suggested they simply carry the prison to higher ground. "Why would you think such a thing?"

"Because Agent Stevens carries a forty-five-caliber handgun. The rounds that were shot through the hull of the boat were smaller. Not by much, but a little."

The room fell silent except for the patter of rain upon the windows behind the warden's desk. Andrews leaned back into his chair as if he'd been struck. Sullivan supposed, in some ways, he had.

"I'm guessing the holes were closer to the caliber my officers carry?"

Sullivan breathed in. "Yes, sir. And may I ask why everyone here is armed? I was under the impression that most prisons were basically weapon free."

"It's one of the reasons we don't have as many problems here. I mandated that all of my officers must be armed at all times. It's been implemental in keeping order and respect," Andrews said waving away the question. His eyes darkened again as he studied Sullivan. "You're sure of the caliber? You do recall that you told me you'd shot a man this morning who was pronounced dead last night?"

Sullivan's gaze hardened. "Did you actually see Fairbend's body, sir?"

Andrews blinked. "Well, no, but Amanda—"

"Is Amanda someone you truly trust?" Sullivan said, cutting the older man off.

"Yes, she is. If she told me that Fairbend was dead, it was because she believed it. Really, the more rational explanation would be that you hallucinated seeing Henry at all."

"I did not hallucinate shooting that man!" Sullivan said, finally losing control of his voice. His breath was hot and he longed to stand, to move and release the anger he felt rolling off him in waves.

Andrews watched him for a moment and then nodded. "I believe you, son. It's just everything that's happened. I'm at a loss."

Sullivan felt his jaw unclench. He dipped his head in acknowledgment of the other man's apology.

Andrews stood and walked to a cabinet above the coffeemaker, near the door. He pulled a bottle of amber liquid from within, along with two glasses, as he glanced over his shoulder at Sullivan. "Like a drink, Sullivan?"

"I think I would."

Andrews poured the glasses almost full, and then handed one to Sullivan on his way back to the desk. Before he sat, he gestured at the far wall. "You see that man there, the first picture on the left?"

Sullivan turned his attention to the wall and squinted at the black-and-white eight-by-ten that hung beside several others containing color, which gradually got clearer and more defined as the row went on. The picture the warden indicated was of a handsome man in his mid-forties. The man's nose was knife-like and the eyes above it were equally sharp. They stared out of the photograph like the man had been studying the inner workings of the camera at the time of the picture.

"His name was Oliver Godring. He was the founder and first warden of this prison. He was a visionary. He drew up the plans for Singleton and New Haven in narrow times. He came up with the idea of establishing a penitentiary and a mental facility in proximity to one another to save funds. The state was tight back then, tighter than it is now, if you can believe it. They needed more space for inmates and psychiatric patients at the time, but didn't have a pot to piss in or a window to throw it out of. Godring came up with the solution by using the natural landscape as a barrier, keeping the facilities close enough to share resources. Brilliant man."

Andrews sat at his desk and sipped almost half the glass of whiskey down in a gulp. Sullivan tried his own drink and felt the liquor trace a burning path down his throat into his stomach. It tasted like bright honey.

"I guess I don't follow you, sir," Sullivan said after a minute of silence. Andrews looked up and seemed to notice Sullivan again.

"Each man is a measurement of what he does. I try to run this facility as well as I can, treat the inmates with dignity, befriend my officers, and what do I get? Betrayal and fucking rain." The warden motioned toward the high windows. "I've failed this place and the people within, is what I'm saying, Sullivan."

"Sir, the circumstances aren't exactly normal here. So—" Sullivan paused, watching a grimace of pain arc across the other man's features. Andrews leaned forward and set his glass down. Some of the whiskey slopped onto the desktop and pooled in puddles. "Are you okay?" Sullivan asked, beginning to rise to his feet.

The warden put up a hand, shook his head, and gradually opened his eyes. "Sorry, I'm …" The older man's hands fumbled in a drawer. Soon, they reappeared holding several pill bottles, which he dropped onto the desk. One bottle rolled through the spilt whiskey.

"Are you sure you're okay?" Sullivan asked again. The warden's posture was stiff and his hands clawed at the bottles with urgency.

"Yes, I'm fine. Shit, I didn't want to do this in front of anyone," Andrews finally said. His fingers found purchase on one of the lids and he poured out two white pills from inside the bottle. Without bothering to screw the top back on, he did the same with the other three containers. Sullivan watched as the older man cupped the handful of tablets and tossed them back into his mouth. A shaking hand brought the whiskey close, and after a quick swallow, Andrews sat back in the chair, his thin chest expanding and contracting.

"I'm sorry." The warden's voice was weak, but Sullivan could still hear him over the whisper of the rain. "Don't be alarmed, I take them with booze sometimes. I think it makes 'em work faster."

"What's wrong, sir?" Sullivan asked. He still felt as if he should call for help, but the older man looked to be calming. *No shit,* Sullivan thought. *He just washed down half a dozen pills with some Jameson. He should be calm.*

Andrews rubbed his face and finally opened his eyes. "Bone cancer. I have maybe five months left. The pills are experimental, but they're not doing shit. I can feel it."

Sullivan felt his stomach drop. "God, I'm sorry."

The warden nodded. "Me too. Didn't want to believe it when they told me last year. 'You've got fourteen, maybe fifteen months.' the doctor said. It's only been ten and I feel like dying. I can take the weakness and the nausea that comes and goes. It's the pain that kicks my feet out from under me. It shoots up out of nowhere and only one of these"—he motioned to the white bottles before him—"is an actual painkiller."

Sullivan swallowed a mouthful from the glass and felt warmth spread outward from his stomach, mellowing the pain in his shoulder and legs. "I don't blame you," Sullivan said. He watched the warden's eyes level with his and then blink, registering him again.

"For what?" Andrews asked.

"For mixing the booze in with them. My mother died of cancer and I think she would have liked a drink at the end."

Andrews nodded and stared down at the pills. Sullivan sipped from the glass again and relished the numbing sensation that made his vision fuzzy at the edges. *Strong stuff,* he thought as he watched Andrews fasten the caps back onto their respective bottles.

"Sometimes I feel like just chucking them in the garbage. I just want to be done with it. Let it take me and go down the road since my ride seems to be here. Sometimes I think all this"— Andrews motioned to the bottles again as he tossed them into the desk drawer—"is just spitting in the face of whatever awaits us."

Andrews turned and studied the rain that speckled the windows and ran down out of sight as more fell to take its place. "You married, Sullivan?"

Sullivan felt his gut clench and the room swim in vertigo. *Like falling,* his mind said, and he felt the press of nausea within his stomach. "No," he heard himself say. He set the empty glass down and rubbed his hand across the bleariness of his vision in an attempt to clear it. "I was, but not anymore."

Andrews studied him from the confines of his chair and took the last of his drink in one hand. He watched the whiskey glow in the light before finishing it off with a practiced toss of his head. He hissed and set the glass down on the desk. "Me too. I'm not anymore either. Maddy was the most careful driver I ever met, and she was killed in a car crash. Ironic, isn't it? Wasn't even her fault. She was sitting at a stop sign, waiting her turn, and a kid who was texting, of all things, never touched his brakes. The teenager was fine, but he took my Maddy from me that afternoon. Almost seven years ago this fall."

Andrews's watery eyes found Sullivan's and held them. "That's why sometimes I feel like this is all for naught. Everything I've done and accomplished has been wasted. Everything I've worked for is falling down around me. I'm alone, Sullivan. Alone and forgotten."

"Sir, we need to focus on what's happening now," Sullivan said, sitting up and trying to clear his vision of the whiskey. "I'm very sorry about everything, but my friend is missing, and he needs our help."

Andrews's head dropped lower and lower until his chin rested on his breastbone. He stayed that way for some time, and then looked up at Sullivan and nodded. "You're right, son. I didn't mean to lay anything on you. I apologize. I'm not sure what card to play next. If what you say is accurate, then one of my own is responsible."

"For the time being, let me poke around a little, don't let on that anything is off. We can't spook whoever's behind this."

Andrews nodded. "Let me know about anything out of the ordinary. I have a few people here I'd trust with my life, but I won't breath a word until you say so. The only problem is, we'll need to start organizing our evacuation very soon if this rain doesn't stop." Andrews twisted in his chair again and looked at the windows, then brought his gaze back to Sullivan. "Do you think it's letting up at all?"

Sullivan shifted his eyes up to the windows for a moment before meeting the older man's pleading gaze. Pity welled up from inside him like blood from a cut, and he did his best to smile. "I think so."

==

Sullivan shut the warden's door behind him and stared at the officer behind the main desk in the lobby. The man's eyes hovered just above the countertop, and then dropped back to the paperwork before him.

Sullivan walked to the door that led toward the guards' barracks and swiped his key against the reader. The door clicked and he slipped through. The hallway was barren and quiet. He paused, waiting for any sounds ahead. There were none. When he reached the top of the second floor, he realized where his body was leading him. The fatigue, paired with the soreness of his injuries, was pushing him toward bed without his consent. The whiskey had faded a little, its former power just a pleasant humming in his skull. Every instinct in his being cursed him as he opened the door to his and Barry's room. He wanted nothing more than to search the entire complex for Barry, but his muscles would have none of it. He knew that if he pushed himself now, he'd only end up a puddle on the floor in a few hours.

As he pushed the door shut behind him, he became aware that someone was in the room.

He smelled cigarettes and something else—peppermint? The hair on the back of his neck stiffened and his hand yanked the H&K from its holster. He spun and scanned the room with the barrel. His and Barry's beds were exactly as they had been. He crouched and peered beneath them. Without waiting, Sullivan lunged forward and kicked open the door of the small bathroom. He knew as soon as he did it that no one stood in the small space. After doing a thorough once-over of the room, he holstered the pistol and examined the small table between the beds. The drawer was open a quarter inch. Sullivan pulled it out the rest of the way, shutting it again after confirming it held nothing but a layer of dust.

After locking the dead bolt in the door, he returned to his bed and sat on the lower bunk. He sniffed the air, pulling in the scents again. He could barely register them now. Someone had been there only a few minutes before he came in. Maybe they'd even heard him ascending the stairs and ducked out just before he came into view.

He looked up at the window and realized he hadn't completely lied to Andrews. The rain looked to be letting up some, with only the occasional drop splattering against the glass. He glanced around the room one last time, waiting for one of the things he'd seen in the last twelve hours to come rushing out from the wall itself, as if the prison's flesh was alive with whatever malevolence resided here.

Sullivan felt himself lean toward the bed and his head settle into the pillow, as exhaustion pulled him completely under.

==

A pounding rebounded inside of his head as he awoke. For a moment, as he came to in the dark, he thought it was only the whiskey wreaking havoc with his senses, because he could feel his pulse thudding in the back of his skull. Then it came again, and he sat up, too quickly, his eyesight flashing with lightheadedness.

"Agent Shale? I thought maybe you'd like dinner. Warden Andrews sent me up with a plate." The voice from the corridor was a female's, and Sullivan thought he recognized it from the guard who'd checked them in the day before.

He rose from the bed, steadying himself for a moment before walking to the door. He wished in vain for a fisheye that he could peer out of, and instead, drew his weapon again. "Coming," he said more groggily than he felt. He drew the dead bolt back and felt the door bite into his wounded shoulder as it was kicked open from the other side. *Must've had the knob already turned,* he thought, as he fell onto his back and watched his handgun clatter out of sight beneath the bed.

Three guards rushed into the room. The first two were men he recognized from the group that came to investigate the lower hall that morning. The female guard from the day before was behind them, her sidearm drawn and pointing directly at his face.

"Grab him!" she yelled, and the two men in front of her dove at Sullivan.

He caught the first guard with an upward kick below the jaw. He heard the man's teeth clack together and a cry of pain as he stumbled sideways toward the bed. The other guard fell on top of Sullivan and rained two quick punches down, which rocked his head off the floor.

"Fucker broke my teeth!" the first guard cried, swinging a graceless kick into Sullivan's ribs. The wind flew from him, and he felt a blow from the man on top of him connect with his ear.

"Alive!" the female guard yelled, and Sullivan took the opportunity to breath. His lungs worked without catching on any broken ribs, although they felt tight enough to snap any second.

Hands encircled his biceps on both sides and hauled him to his feet.

"Piece of shit!" the first guard said, as he spit a piece of what Sullivan could only assume was his tooth at the side of his face.

"Cuff him."

"Got it."

Sullivan tried to resist, but both men forced his arms behind his back, and he felt the bite of cold steel against his wrists. He flexed his forearms as the guard behind him closed the cuffs tight, and was thankful when he felt the flexibility of a chain between the shackles.

"Walk," the guard that punched him said from behind, shoving him toward the open door.

"You guys could have just brought me dinner instead of taking me to it. Way easier, you know," Sullivan said.

The woman's pistol whipped across the side of his face, and leveled once more in his eyes as he opened them. Both men pushed him again, and he nearly fell as he stumbled into the hallway.

Only a few lights glowed outside the room, leaving the hallway dappled in shadows. Sullivan's heart rate accelerated as he felt the two male guards grab his biceps again and steer him toward the stairs.

"Where are you taking me?" Sullivan asked, working his jaw where the female guard had hit him.

"Somewhere special," the man on his left responded.

"The same place you took Agent Stevens?" Sullivan heard similar sniggers on either side of him, and anger began to override the fear he'd felt in the room. He heard the sound he was waiting for—the soft dragging of steel sliding into plastic—and knew that the woman had holstered her handgun. He tested the give in the handcuffs and pulled the chain tight across his lower back, calculating how much he'd have to stretch. "Jesus, you guys opened up the stitches in my shoulder. I think I'm gonna be sick."

"Who gives a fuck? Dave, do you care?" the guard on his right asked.

"Nope, how 'bout you, Shelly?" the man on his left said.

"Both of you shut up and hold on to him, it looks like he's passing out."

The head of the stairs neared and Sullivan mentally braced himself for what was to come. Before they could force him down the first step, he halted and leaned forward as if he were going to vomit. The grips on each of his arms tightened and both men moved out from behind him, closer to his sides. He breathed out once, and then in.

With a short lunging motion, Sullivan kicked the guard on the right in the knee, and felt the joint give. The man flailed and screamed as he lost his balance and tipped into the stairway. Without putting his foot down, Sullivan kicked back, hoping that Shelly was right where her voice had come from a moment ago. She was. He felt the heel of his foot sink into her generous stomach and heard air launch out of her lungs in a startled cry. The guard on his left finally reacted with a haymaker, which Sullivan partially blocked with his shoulder. He returned with a knee to the man's crotch, which doubled him over in agony. Sullivan threw himself into the guard and both men tumbled into the open space above the stairway.

The edges of the stairs sent flashes of pain throughout Sullivan's body as he and the guard bounced and rolled down them. The landing came up quickly and stopped their progress. He felt himself land on top of the guard he'd kicked in the knee. Immediately, Sullivan launched his hips into the air and tucked himself toward his legs. He pulled the handcuffs down and felt them slip beneath his buttocks, and then past his feet as he tightened himself into the fetal position.

Movement at the far end of the landing drew his attention and he scrambled to his feet as the guard he'd kneed stood shakily and pulled his handgun. Sullivan stepped forward and caught the man's wrist of his gun hand. In a twisting movement he wound the handcuff's chain tight around the small bones in the guard's hand and pulled straight up. He heard the man's wrist snap and pop, as ligaments and tendons shredded and broke. The gun fell to the floor and Sullivan drove his head forward, smashing the guard's nose flat and cutting off a scream.

A brush of air pushed at the back of his neck and chips of cement from the wall pelted his face. It was only then that he registered the sound of the shot. Shelly had recovered enough to point her pistol and fire at him, as he ducked down the second set of steps, snatching the dropped handgun as he fled.

Another shot sank into the stairs as he leapt to the main floor. Sullivan spun and slid to one knee, pointing the guard's weapon back the way he'd come. The seconds ticked by and sweat ran freely down the back of his scalp. He imagined he heard the pounding steps of reinforcements responding to the sound of the shots, but then the edge of Shelly's arm appeared at the top of the stairs, and Sullivan focused, drew a bead on the exposed flesh, and fired.

Shelly screamed and disappeared from sight. Sullivan got to his feet and ran low up the stairs, easing around the corner, gun-first. Shelly lay propped against the guard who'd fallen down the stairs initially. Sullivan glanced at him and noticed the odd angle of the guard's head and the dead stare in his eyes. Shelly's breathing came in ragged gasps, and Sullivan searched the floor until he spotted her weapon lying a few feet away from her open palm. Blood ran steadily from a hole just above her collarbone and stained the blue of her uniform black. He stepped forward and kept the sights of the handgun between the woman's staring eyes.

"Where's my friend?" Sullivan asked. His voice came out in a growl, his words garbled by adrenaline and rage.

Shelly breathed and blinked through tears streaming down her wide face. "You'll never find him. It's too late."

Sullivan moved closer, shoving gun into her upturned face. "It better not be. I'll bring this whole fucking place down if he's gone."

The guard's soft laughter shocked him and he lowered the muzzle a few inches. Her eyes were squeezed shut and her belly shook. When she looked at him again, only cold indifference resided in her eyes. "You'll see. Everyone will see. She's here and nothing can stop her."

Tendrils erupted from her mouth as she lunged for her handgun. Sullivan felt his finger twitch on the trigger and most of Shelly's head sprayed the dead guard and wall behind her as she slumped to her side.

He stepped back and tried to steady his shaking arms as he watched the twisting appendages slither back and forth across the hard floor. Gradually they receded back into what was left of the corpse's head.

Keeping his eyes on the dead body before him, he searched the unconscious guard's duty belt. At last his fingers found a small key, and he forced it awkwardly with one hand into the opposite handcuff.

A door opened somewhere above him and his head snapped up, stomach tightening into a hot ball. The handcuff sprang open, and as he turned and hurried down the stairs, Sullivan heard voices murmur above him, along with the scuff of shoes moving closer.

He unlocked the second handcuff just before he reached the lobby door, and dropped them in a jangling heap on the floor. Again he wished for a window in the door before him, some way to see if the lobby teemed with guards and if this was the end. He opened the door as softly as he could and peeked out.

The main desk was empty. Perhaps it was Shelly's shift here tonight. He hoped so. He pushed the door open the rest of the way and jogged across the silent lobby. The doors to the outside were black rectangles, and the lights overhead threw the entire room into an eerie shade of yellow.

He slid to a stop at Andrews's door and wrenched at the knob. It stayed immobile in his hand.

"Shit," Sullivan cursed. He needed to find the warden. He was the only one who could help him now. Sullivan pulled on the knob again, praying it would give so he could at least hide in the office until he figured out his next move. He let go after a moment, in exasperation, and ran in the opposite direction.

Miraculously his keycard was still operational, and he flung the door to the main holding area open, shoving the handgun into the back of his pants as he went. The guard desk on the other side of the door was as empty as the front desk had been. Sullivan searched the rows of cells and the portion of the second floor catwalk that he could see. He spied no uniforms in either area.

He tried to control his breathing as he walked at a brisk pace to the hallway that led to the cafeteria, scanning his key against the reader when he reached the locked door. The hallway was dark when he stepped inside, with only a fan of dim light creeping from beneath the infirmary door. Hope flared within his chest at the sight. Amanda could help him hide. She'd know a way out or somewhere safe.

The door to the infirmary clicked open and Sullivan cautiously pulled on the handle. Amanda sat at the small desk in the corner of the room, her hair pulled back in a ponytail and a pair of thin-framed glasses on her face. She looked up as he stepped inside.

"Sullivan? What's going on?"

He went to her as she rose from her chair, her eyes finding his as he neared. "Amanda, you have to listen to me very carefully. Something is horribly wrong here. There's some sort of parasite in the prison, in the people. A few guards attacked me in my room and tried taking me somewhere—"

"Wait, what?" Amanda asked. "Some of the guards tried to attack you?"

"Yes, and I'll explain everything, but there's no time now. I'm sure they'll be coming here any minute. Is there somewhere to hide?"

Amanda's face became a mask of confusion, and she backed toward her desk. Her eyes squinted and her blinking became more rapid.

Sullivan saw her shoulders go rigid, and raised his hands in front of him. "Look, I know this sounds crazy, but I'm telling the truth. Someone tried to frame Barry after he disappeared. They tried to make it look like he destroyed the boat."

Amanda stopped edging backward. "The boat's destroyed? What do you mean 'destroyed'? It won't work?"

"Someone shot it full of holes, but Barry didn't do it, one of the guards did. You have to trust me."

"I don't even know you, you're not making any sense," Amanda said. Her eyes ran over him as if she wasn't sure if he was dangerous, but her muscles relaxed and she stood her ground. "Maybe you should lie down for a while, I'll call the warden—"

"No, there's no time for that!" Sullivan said. Amanda winced and he breathed deeply, trying to calm himself. "I'm sorry," he continued in a lower voice. "But I really need your help."

Amanda stared at him, and he could see the indecision pulling at her, swaying her.

"Please," he said, his voice raw with emotion.

A beat and then her head tilted forward once. "There's a mechanical room off the cafeteria. The air ducts are pretty large. You might be able to fit in one. Follow me."

She moved to the door and opened it without a sound. Sullivan followed her closely. He could smell a faint whiff of her perfume, something sugary. Any other time it may have excited him, but now, stepping out into the darkened hall, all he felt were the pangs of fear streaking through his chest and stomach.

They walked fast through the black of the hall, and soon a pale light spilled into the space around them as Amanda opened the door to the cafeteria, which was blessedly devoid of life. Sullivan's hand rested on the butt of the handgun at his back, but he didn't draw it, in fear of alarming Amanda further. Only half of the overhead fluorescents were on, drowning the long tables in patches of gloom.

Amanda skirted the wall and moved into an alcove set off to the east side of the room, which Sullivan hadn't noticed before. There was a scraping of metal and then they were in a narrow room with a large electrical panel dominating one wall, a row of boxes and shelves lining the other. Sullivan heard the hum of electricity and the soft hiss of air escaping around the door Amanda shut behind them.

"Thank you," Sullivan said, turning toward her. Amanda nodded and pressed her lips together until they were nearly white.

"I'll probably lose my job over this," she said, as Sullivan began examining the far end of the room for an access panel that would accept his bulk.

"If I get out of here alive, I'll make sure you have a job," he replied.

"How did you know that it wasn't Barry's gun that destroyed the motor on the boat?"

Sullivan stopped walking toward the rear of the space, the gears of his mind grinding against one another. A stone dropped into the pit of his stomach, and as casually as he could, he said, "I don't think I ever said someone shot the motor."

He looked over his shoulder at the doctor and felt his stomach sink lower. A cruel smile sat on her lips, where only worry had been before.

"I'm just curious. You don't seem to be the sharpest knife in the drawer," Amanda said.

Sullivan turned and faced her. His nerves tingled, begging his muscles to fly into action, but he restrained them. "What's really going on here?" he asked.

Amanda laughed, and it was so cold, Sullivan thought the sound might freeze solid in his eardrums. "A revolution. Something so beautiful, you have to see it to believe it."

"What do you mean?"

"I mean, things are going to change in a big way and they'll never be the same."

"Where's Barry?" Sullivan asked. His right hand crept closer to his side, his fingers open and ready.

Amanda laughed again and Sullivan nearly winced at the sound. "Oh, he's serving a purpose more pure than any he ever had in his meager life before this. You should be happy for him, since you won't ever get the chance to do the same."

Amanda rushed across the space between them, her mouth open, revealing a squirming mass of tissue, wriggling to spill free. Sullivan reached for the gun and managed to draw it halfway out, before she hit him.

They fell to the floor in a heap, Amanda on top of him, the tentacles streaming from her mouth, reaching for him, the tips snapping back and forth. Sullivan brought the gun around and watched Amanda easily catch his arm in a firm grip. One of the tendrils lashed out and cut a wide swath in the skin of his wrist. The pain burned through his arm as if he'd reached into a furnace. His hand spasmed and the gun fell to the floor beside his head. Sullivan bucked his hips and tried to roll Amanda's slight form over, but she balanced upon him like a tightrope walker and countered his every move. Her free hand flashed to his throat, and he coughed as she began to squeeze, the blood in his face and temples pressurizing, pushing tears into his eyes.

Sullivan reached out with his left hand, searching for something within his reach to use as a weapon, but he only felt boxes and cold floor. He could see his pulse in his vision now, a bobbing that made him feel like he was driving fast over a rough road. Amanda leaned forward, bringing her face and the whipping feelers closer, and he pushed against her to no avail. A tendril paused above Sullivan, and he saw a strange serration along its edge. He had seen the ridges before, only larger, on the object extracted from Alvarez's head.

"This is the future, Sully. Isn't it beautiful?" Amanda's words were barely discernible through the coils in her mouth. Her eyes were silver and dead in her face, frozen steel in January.

A pistol appeared beside Amanda's head, bucking as a round blew through the side of her skull.

The sound was deafening, and Sullivan grimaced as he felt wet matter spray his face and hair. The iron-like grip on his neck slackened and fell away, as Amanda's body tipped off him and slumped to the floor. Sullivan sat up, retching and scooting away as fast as he could. He kicked at the corpse's legs until he was free of their touch. His eyes shot up to the figure that stood over him, and for a moment he didn't believe his senses.

Everett Mooring's hand shook as he tried to keep the gun trained on the body before him. He still wore his baseball cap, but Sullivan could see his squinting eyes were now wide and unblinking beneath its bill. Sullivan slid back another few feet, until his shoulders met the unyielding surface of a shelf. His chest heaved and his heart blasted against his ribs.

"What the fuck?" Mooring finally said, his eyes never leaving the doctor's corpse. He pushed the gun farther away from him, and Sullivan thought that he might fire again, until it gradually dropped to his side.

"Thank you," Sullivan said. His throat was full of gravel. Everett's eyes slid over to where Sullivan rested. The man was in shock. Sullivan gained his feet, grabbed the gun from the floor, and went to him. Everett remained motionless, and only looked up when Sullivan placed a hand on his shoulder.

"Are you okay?" Sullivan asked.

Everett blinked and nodded, his eyes creeping back to the spreading pool around Amanda's head. "I killed her."

"Yes, you did, and you saved my life. Everett, listen to me. Is there somewhere safe we can hide? There's more of them like this, and they'll be here soon."

Everett swallowed and looked at Sullivan, his eyes awash in a faraway stare. "More?"

Sullivan snapped his fingers a few inches in front of the guard's nose. Everett flinched, but his eyes cleared a little. "Yes, we need to hide, Everett. Where? Where can we go?"

Everett licked his lips and holstered his weapon after shooting the corpse on the floor one last look. "They won't find us in the shed. Follow me."

Chapter 10

Sullivan wiped away the last vestiges of gore from his cheek using the bottom edge of his T-shirt. He tipped his face up into the night sky, which was still dampened with a light mist, and reveled in the feeling of the moisture. He could smell the copper of Amanda's blood and it nearly gagged him. Hopefully the mist would help wash it away. Sullivan turned his head to either side as he followed Everett's footsteps across the quiet grounds, and halted a short distance behind the other man when they reached the toolshed beside the sunken boat. Everett worked for a few seconds in the dark, and Sullivan heard the rasping of steel on steel. The outline of the door opened toward them and Everett disappeared inside. Sullivan followed and eased the door shut.

The air in the shed was stale and smelled of iron and gasoline. Sullivan could tell the floor was concrete and that the wall to the right was close by, but other than that, his eyesight swam in the utter blackness of the building. A small LED lit up a few feet away and illuminated a portion of a large riding lawn mower and Everett's booted feet.

"This way," Everett said, and the light bobbed away toward the rear of the shed.

Sullivan followed, mimicking the guard's path and avoiding barking his shins on several sawhorses, steel canisters, and a dormant snow blower. The back wall of the structure was studded with shelves and pegs that held a number of hand tools and various containers. Everett paused and moved to the far left corner of the building, where a sheet of plywood leaned against the back wall. The guard set the flashlight down, which lit up the corner well enough for Sullivan to see the other man slide the wide board away from the wall, revealing a black square just large enough for a man to walk through bent over.

"Come on," Everett said, picking up the LED again and motioning to Sullivan.

"What is this?" Sullivan asked in a hushed voice, his vocal cords rusty from the abuse Amanda inflicted.

"Somewhere safe for now," the guard replied.

Sullivan felt apprehension rearing in his mind but shoved it aside. He had no other options. He ducked and stepped past Everett into a narrow room behind the rear wall of the shed. He moved a few feet in and tentatively stood, fearing the ceiling was low and he would hit his head. The air was open above him, and he scooted forward another step to accommodate Everett, as the guard moved in behind him and slid the plywood into place over the doorway. Everett turned and swung the flashlight's beam into the space, and Sullivan got his first look at their surroundings.

The room they stood in ran the entire length of the shed's back wall but was only three feet wide from Sullivan's estimation. A narrow cot sat at the far end of the room and a flimsy bench jutted out from the real rear wall. There were two cases of bottled water near Sullivan's feet, and a crooked pile of books sat near the entrance.

"Have a seat," Everett said, and positioned himself on the floor. Sullivan settled onto the edge of the bench, waiting for it to snap into kindling beneath him. Everett pushed one end of the flashlight and the little LED winked out. "Sorry, but you never know who might see a flash in the dark and come to investigate."

"What the hell is this place?" Sullivan asked, trying not to panic in the sudden wash of darkness.

"Just a safe place I set up awhile back. I come here when I need to. Jesus, I think I might throw up."

Sullivan waited for a moment, letting the other man calm down before he asked, "You built this?"

"No, the false wall was here. I noticed the inside proportions didn't match the outside one day and measured when no one was around. My father was an architect, so I know a little about buildings. Out of curiosity I cut a hole in the wall and found the space. I'm not sure if it was a mistake or purposely built. Thought it might come in handy, so I covered the hole with the plywood. No one knows about it but me."

Sullivan rubbed his eyes, and there was nearly no difference in his sight as he blocked out his vision. "Why? What's this place for?"

Everett sighed. "I guess you could call it my thinking room. I come here sometimes after shifts, sometimes during, and just sit and go over everything that's in my mind. My memory's kind of bad, so I write everything down in those journals over there."

Sullivan's head involuntarily turned toward the stack of books, although he couldn't make them out. "I don't understand. What do you write down?"

"Things that might help me."

"Help you do what?"

"Help me find my brother."

Silence hung between them, as thick as the darkness. The wheels of Sullivan's mind spun for a moment, and then caught. "Everett, what's going on here?"

He heard the other man shift on the floor, into what he could only guess was a more comfortable position. "My brother Alex—well, my half brother, I should say, same mother, different fathers—went missing here a year and a half ago. He was in corrections just like me. This was his first position. He got into the program about five years after I did. He was like that since we were young, always following me around, trying to do what I did. I thought he'd grow out of it, but—" Everett stopped. Sullivan couldn't tell if he was considering his thoughts or fighting to keep his voice steady.

"He was so proud when he got the call for the job here. We went out and celebrated. I was working at the state penitentiary in Iowa at the time. I got a call a month later from the local police, saying that Alex hadn't shown up for work one evening. That fuckup Jaan you met earlier said he must have run off on his own. I didn't buy it for a minute. Alex was dedicated, he got top marks in his graduating class. He loved being in corrections. He wouldn't just walk away from his first break for a woman or another opportunity, like everyone said. I knew him. Something happened to him and I had to find out. Have to find out." Everett's voice faded away and was replaced with the renewed tapping of rain on the metal roof above their heads.

"So you came looking for him," Sullivan said, waiting and listening to Everett's steady breathing.

"Yeah. We have different last names and no one knows me around here, so I used that as an advantage. I know his disappearance has something to do with this place, I felt it the moment I saw it for the first time. Something's wrong here."

"It's too quiet," Sullivan offered.

"Yes, and the guards themselves are strange. I've only met a few of them that acted really normal, and they were brand-new like me. The personnel are cliquey and closed off. The warden's the only one that's been truly honest and forthright with me. I had seniority when I transferred here, so I started higher than most others and became Andrews's right hand. Like I said before, any information I found concerning Alex I wrote down in my journals and kept them out here. The shed's close and relatively safe, so it doesn't raise any suspicions."

"Have you found any information about your brother's whereabouts?" Sullivan asked.

Everett shifted on the floor again. "No. Nothing. It's like he dropped off the face of the earth."

Sullivan shook his head, Barry's face flashing through his mind. "Have you done any research to see if this has happened before? Any other disappearances of employees or inmates?"

"Yes, I checked. One other guard vanished about five years ago, a woman named Susan James. Almost the same situation as Alex, and there's something else." Sullivan heard the guard fumble for something in the dark, and then the flashlight came back on, shielded by Everett's palm. "The top journal over there, there's a newspaper clipping inside of it."

Sullivan turned in the cramped space and pulled the uppermost journal from the pile. Inside the cover was a folded article from *USA Today*, dating four months earlier. A smiling picture of a balding middle-aged man in a dark suit hung above bold text that read *Nuclear physicist still missing*. Sullivan scanned the article below, which named the man in the picture as Dr. Arnold Bolt.

"He went missing from a US Department of Energy conference in Minneapolis four months ago. His hotel room had been broken into and he was gone."

Sullivan studied the article for a few moments in the dim light before tilting his face up to Everett's. "What does this have to do with what's happening now?"

"A few days after that article came out, I swear I saw two guards leading the man in that picture into the basement of the prison." Everett punctuated the end of the sentence by snapping the LED off again, leaving Sullivan to blink at the eclipsing darkness.

"You saw him?"

"I think so. I just caught a quick glimpse of him as Bundy and Johnson led him downstairs. For some reason his face rung a bell, and then I knew why. I'd seen it in that paper only a couple days before."

"Did you follow them, see where they put him?"

"Not right away. I realized who he was a few hours later, and when I went down to the solitary level, there was no one there."

Sullivan rubbed the newspaper between his fingers, the rasping sound barely audible above the constant patter above them.

Everett's voice came out of the dark again, startling Sullivan with its raw emotion. "I'm sorry, but I have to ask before I go completely nuts: what the fuck was inside Amanda? I mean, Jesus, I've never seen anything like that in my life, and I killed her. I shot her in the head."

Sullivan heard the panic rising in the other man's voice, hysteria begging to be set free. He knew the feeling well. The thoughts so clear as they played across the mind, over and over, faster and faster, until a person couldn't discern what had truly happened and what hadn't.

"Everett, listen to me. I don't know what that was, but I can assure you this: that was not the woman you knew in there. That was not human in any way. There's something inside of the staff, a parasite or something. It was inside Fairbend and Shelly too, and I think it's all connected to Alvarez's murder."

Sullivan listened to Everett's panicked breathing and hoped the calmness in his voice would help soothe the other man. He considered telling Everett about being chased through the woods outside the wire, but thought it might be too much for the guard to absorb at that moment. Sullivan remembered the bottled water nearby, and after a few seconds of feeling around blindly, he found the topmost case, which had an opening in the plastic wrapping. He pulled two bottles free, which were surprisingly cool, and turned back to Everett.

"Here, have some water," Sullivan said, holding one bottle out in the darkness. The guard reached for it and took it from his hand. Sullivan opened his bottle and tipped it to his lips, savoring the feeling of the liquid on his parched tongue. After a moment, he heard Everett break his seal and drink also.

"Better?" Sullivan asked.

"I think so," Everett finally answered. His voice was still shaky but had lost the edge of distress. "Christ, what's going on here? Are we both losing our minds?"

"I wish. I could have convinced myself earlier that I was, but now that you've seen the same thing, that theory doesn't hold up anymore."

"What do we do now? I just killed a woman, and we don't know who we can trust."

Sullivan drained the rest of his water and set the container on the floor. "We need to get help. Do you have a cell phone?"

"Dammit! No, I left it inside. Forgive me, but I'm not going back in to get it."

Sullivan snorted. "Don't blame you."

"This fucking rain!" Everett said.

Sullivan tried to sort all of the events of the past days into separate pieces and align them into a semblance of pattern or repetition. After straining against the unreality of it all, he sighed and let his thoughts fall back into the jumbled mess that they became without strict concentration. It was as if he were trying to assemble a puzzle in midair, and just when a picture began to take shape, the pieces would crumble apart and he would have to start over.

"I suppose we could try getting into New Haven without being seen. See if their communications are still down," Sullivan offered.

Everett breathed out a long hiss of air. "Yeah, that's probably our best bet. Hand me another bottle of water before we go, the vending machine inside was out when I checked and I didn't get a chance to come out here today."

Sullivan began to reach for the container of bottles when he stopped, his vision locking on the place where Everett's words came from. "You only drink bottled water?"

"Yeah, every time I've tried to drink the well water from Singleton I get an allergic reaction. It happened the first day I was here. I took a sip of water from one of the fountains and my throat almost closed up. I got dizzy and lightheaded and had trouble sleeping. I couldn't figure it out, until I took a drink again the next day. I asked the warden about it, and he thought it might be the higher iron content in the soil."

Sullivan swallowed a lump in his throat and felt his heartbeat speed up. "Did you have any dreams that night after you drank the water?"

Silence met his question, and before Everett spoke Sullivan knew the answer. "How did you know?"

"Because the night Barry disappeared I had one. It was so vivid it felt real."

"The barren land full of smoke and dust?"

It was Sullivan's turn to be dumbstruck. "We had the same dream."

"Did you see it? Did you see what was over the edge of the cliff?" Everett asked. His voice was thin and full of holes where his words became whispers.

Sullivan shivered despite the warm air around them. "Not really, but I was afraid."

"What the fuck is happening?" Everett asked again.

Sullivan was about to reply when a memory from the day before surfaced like a body in a swamp. The straitjacketed mental patient in the hallway of New Haven, the man's breath hot against his throat. Words, quiet and only for him to hear: *Don't drink the water.*

Sullivan shot to his feet, and he heard Everett recoil in surprise. "Let's go," Sullivan said.

Everett stood but didn't move toward the makeshift doorway. "Where are we going? New Haven?"

"Yes," Sullivan said. "There's someone there that has answers for us."

==

The water was much higher than when Sullivan walked the road that morning. Its surface rippled in the night air with the dropping rain from the canopy of trees. It licked and talked only a foot from the edge of the road, and Sullivan estimated it would cover the ground he and Everett walked on well before daybreak.

They slunk in the deepest shadows, as near to the forest as they could without getting their feet completely soaked. Every so often they would stop and listen for the sounds of pursuit, footsteps behind or in front of them. At these times Sullivan would stare off into the woods, knowing that the fence was there, wondering if something beyond it was looking back.

The gate grew out of the road before them, and Everett stopped a few feet from the card reader, glancing over his shoulder at Sullivan. "We should run the rest of the way. If someone's watching the access notices in the surveillance room, they'll see that this gate is opening. It would be good to get inside and back out of New Haven before they get here."

Sullivan nodded and readied himself. His body still ached from the various bruises and cuts, but the pain sharpened his senses. Any impression of wariness was gone; his body was a battered shell of soreness but on full alert.

Everett scanned the key across the reader. The gate lumbered to the side. "Go!" he barked.

Sullivan ran silently behind the guard, up the narrow road, until the air in his lungs took on an acidic feel. Everett halted a few yards before the clearing opened up into New Haven's grounds. The men panted side by side, and it was then that Sullivan smelled something in the air. He stood and drew a breath in through his nose. Cigarette smoke.

"I have an idea," Sullivan said, and took off at an angle to the right, pushing his way between the lower undergrowth, into the bulk of the forest. Everett followed a few steps behind, the only sign of their progress through the trees the occasional snapping of a wet twig beneath their feet. Sullivan studied the surroundings as they moved. This portion of the forest was mature pines that held branches wider than trucks above their heads. Most of the floor was even and covered with a layer of pine needles. The ground was higher here, and only once, as they skirted the perimeter of the clearing, Sullivan felt his shoe sink into a muddy depression.

A white light began to filter in through the trees separating them from the building beyond and muffled laughter echoed across the yard. Sullivan crouched lower and moved at a slower pace, in a sweeping arc around the voices. Finally, he stopped and waited for Everett to kneel next to him. The guard's face was pale, but the slackness was gone from the muscles in his jaw, and his eyes were squinted and sharp once again.

"What's the plan?" Everett whispered.

"We have to incapacitate the two orderlies that are on break. Can you do it?" Sullivan said, looking directly at the guard next to him. Everett met his gaze and nodded once. "Good. We come from behind, choke them out, and bind them somehow."

Sullivan waited for Everett to argue about assaulting two men he probably knew, if not by name, then by sight, but the guard merely nodded again and stared ahead, his hands clenching and unclenching. Sullivan moved forward, easing around a deadfall and an extremely thick-looking patch of bushes, until he could see the open yard.

The two orderlies from the day before were in their same spots beneath a metal-halide lamp that threw a ring of white light around them on the cement apron. Their shadows were elongated into grotesque forms that stretched almost all the way to the forest edge. Both men had their backs turned to them and were talking animatedly, their arms and hands gesticulating at times.

Sullivan looked at Everett, and pointed to his own chest once and then to the orderly on the right. Everett nodded. Sullivan counted down in silence, with one hand held up so Everett could see the fingers folding in to a fist. *Three, two, one.*

Both men stood and slid out of the trees without a sound. Sullivan's gaze snapped back and forth, from the ground to the orderly's back, assuring he wouldn't tread on a stick that would announce their presence in the quiet yard. Sullivan slowed his pace further when he and Everett were within a few strides of the men, and glanced at the guard. Everett shot Sullivan a look that assured him he was ready. A picnic table sat just behind the orderlies and Sullivan prepared to move around it. As he sidestepped to the right, Sullivan watched his orderly crush a cigarette beneath a white shoe and then begin to turn.

Before the orderly could rotate toward him, Sullivan launched himself up and off the picnic table's seat. He flew across the distance between the table and the other man and crashed into him. The man uttered a surprised grunt, and then a cry of pain as Sullivan followed him to the ground. The orderly lashed out with a quick jab and caught Sullivan on the jaw, but instead of reeling back, Sullivan pulled him closer. Without thinking, he swung an arm behind the orderly's head and neck, clasped his other hand in a solid grip, and pushed his own head into the back of the orderly's outstretched arm. Sullivan turned his body and tightened his grip around the man's neck, effectively cutting off the orderly's air with his own arm. The man flailed and bucked his hips, but after a moment his movements became weaker, and finally stopped altogether. Sullivan unclasped his hands and let the orderly's arm fall away from his own neck.

"What the fuck was that?" Everett whispered as he stepped up beside Sullivan.

"Head-and-arm choke. Don't you watch UFC?" Sullivan couldn't help but smile at the gaping look on the guard's face. "How'd you do?"

"Got lucky, he hit his head on the ground when I tackled him. He's out cold," Everett said, motioning to the other downed orderly.

"Good, let's pull them around back. I saw a gas main coming out of the ground," Sullivan said, stooping to grasp the nearest man under the armpits.

A few minutes later, the two orderlies were handcuffed to each other, their arms laced behind a gas pipe over three inches thick. The rain fell from the slight overhang of the roof and barely missed their unconscious forms as they lay pressed against the building.

"There, they won't even get wet," Sullivan said, snapping a keycard off the closest man's belt.

The steel door unlocked the moment Sullivan passed the key over the reader. He pulled it open a few inches and peered through the crack. A janitor strolled down an otherwise empty hallway, his back hunched as he leaned over a cart loaded with cleaning supplies. As Sullivan watched, he turned a corner at the far end of the hall and disappeared.

Sullivan pulled the door all the way open and stepped inside the building. The coolness of air conditioning hit him full force and sent a shiver through his frame. He rubbed his arms for a moment, trying to dry them and force the chill away, as Everett stepped in beside him and pulled the door closed.

"Let's just act natural. Maybe Andrews hasn't put out an alert for us yet and we'll get lucky. Act like you're supposed to be here," Sullivan said.

"The shit that's been going on, I think I am supposed to be here," Everett said as they began to move down the corridor.

A side door marked "Stairs" stopped Sullivan in his tracks, and he yanked on the locked handle before swiping the keycard over the reader beside the door. It unlocked and he and Everett slipped inside. They took the stairs two at a time, until they reached a landing marked with a large *3* beside a door. Sullivan pushed it open an inch and listened before shoving it wide enough to sidle through.

The third floor hallway was empty, but Sullivan spied the black rectangular box of a camera at the far end, its unblinking eye staring straight at them. As they made their way down the corridor, hugging the right wall, Sullivan hoped that whoever was supposed to be watching the cameras was taking a siesta or a nice long piss. They would know soon enough one way or another.

Sullivan paused at a door on the right side, scanning the room beyond through the glass and wire mesh. The living space was simple and windowless. A caged bulb in the ceiling dropped faint light over everything in the room, which wasn't much. A bed frame was bolted to the floor in one corner and an overstuffed chair sat in the other. Sullivan could see no TV, but could make out a darkened bathroom to the right.

"What do you see?" Everett asked.

"Nothing. I think this is the right room, but maybe the guy's in the infirmary or—" Sullivan's words were choked off as a face pressed against the glass on the other side.

"Fuck!" Sullivan cursed, jumping back from the door, his heart leaping toward the top of his throat. The mental patient who'd pinned Sullivan to the wall the day before grinned at both of them and pushed his nose against the glass again, flattening it like a burst tomato.

"This is who you came to see?" Everett asked. His voice held a hint of accusation, but Sullivan only nodded as he looked at the doorjamb for a card reader. There was none. Sullivan's heart sank as he spied two keyed locks that sat flush with the door's surface.

"Shit, we don't have the—" Sullivan stopped as Everett pulled out a ring with several keys hanging from it.

"Grabbed them as an afterthought from the orderly before we came in," Everett said, stepping up to the door. Sullivan almost hugged the man, and watched as Everett tried each key on the ring in succession. None of them fit.

"Each orderly must have keys for a different floor. Shit!" Sullivan said, glancing up and down the hallway, searching for another answer.

The elevator at the end of the hall rumbled and dinged its arrival.

Sullivan stood on the edge of indecision, and then tipped to one side as he began walking at a steady pace toward the double doors beginning to open. He wasn't surprised in the least to see the orderly that had pulled the mental patient off him step from the car. The man's eyes were glued to his cell phone and he didn't look up until Sullivan was a few steps away.

"What the fuck? What are you doing up here?" the orderly said, tucking his phone away.

"Conducting an investigation," Sullivan said, stepping into the other man's space. "I need to speak with the patient in that room immediately."

The orderly frowned. "Jason? Why, what's going on?"

"I believe he has information concerning my partner's whereabouts," Sullivan said in a steady voice. He tightened his hand into a fist, waiting for the man's mouth to spring wide and erupt with a fray of whipping tentacles.

The orderly merely shifted from foot to foot. "When did you guys come in?"

"About ten minutes ago. We were told someone would be up here waiting to let us in, but we've been standing around ever since." Sullivan hoped the false bravado in his voice was working. He didn't know what he'd do next if the man called his bluff.

The orderly eyed Sullivan and Everett one more time, and then nodded. "Sorry, guys, I was in the shitter. Damn cell phone's still out too." The orderly walked past them as he dug out a set of keys similar to the ones Everett carried. Sullivan hovered just on the edge of the doorway and watched while Everett flanked the man.

The locks slid back and the orderly pointed through the porthole. "Jason, go sit on your bed. You have some visitors." Sullivan saw the bald man inside the room move toward the bed and perch upon its edge like an oversized bird, his arms wrapped around his knees.

The orderly stepped into the room and began to turn toward Sullivan. "I'll have to stay inside while you gu—"

Sullivan cut his words off with a left hook that rocked the bigger man's head ninety degrees. His knees unhinged and Sullivan caught him before his face impacted with the tile floor.

"What are you doing?" Everett said as he shut the door behind them. The guard's eyes were wide and his hands trembled as he nervously ran them up and down the front of his uniform.

"He was going to stand here the whole time. He could've locked us in in a second if a call came through on his radio," Sullivan said after laying the orderly on his side.

"That was a sucker punch. Not really fair but necessary. He deserves it, though. That bastard eats my mashed potatoes every time I get them. It's like clockwork."

Sullivan and Everett turned their attention to the man on the bed. His eyes were running up and down the prone orderly's form, and something along the lines of a smile played at the corners of his wet mouth.

Sullivan walked to the edge of the bed and squatted in front of the man, blocking his view of the orderly on the floor. "Your name is Jason, isn't it?"

The man licked his lips a few times, and then leaned in so close, Sullivan almost retreated, but he managed to hold his ground. "Yes, Jason Godring at your service, and I knew you'd be back to see me, or you wouldn't, which would mean you'd died."

Sullivan could smell Jason's stale breath, but it was an afterthought. Something else struck a chord deep within his mind. "Your last name is Godring? Are you related to Oliver Godring?"

A wide smile spread across Jason's face. "He was my father."

Sullivan blinked. "Your father? The man who helped build Singleton and New Haven?"

Jason nodded. "Oh, he built more than that. So much more than that."

"What do you mean?" Sullivan asked. Everett moved closer, and stood just behind Sullivan, his head turning every so often to glance at the orderly on the floor.

"His work was secrets. Full of them. But he told me sometimes when I was little. He told me if I was naughty. He wasn't supposed to, but he did. He put me here when he died, put it in his will so I wouldn't tell." Jason's eyes gained a glassy sheen as he spoke and lost their hold on the room around him.

"What secrets? Secrets from whom?" Sullivan asked.

"From everyone. He worked for the government. He did experiments for them. After the Manhattan Project, after the bombs, he worked on the beam. It was his favorite. More favorite than me."

Sullivan looked over his shoulder at Everett, who returned his gaze with an upraised eyebrow. Sullivan turned his attention back to Jason, who now rocked back and forth, his arms still bear-hugging his knees.

"Jason, why did you tell me not to drink the water yesterday?" Sullivan asked.

Jason stopped rocking and looked directly at Sullivan. "It contaminated the water. It makes you dream the dream."

"What did? What contaminated the water?" Sullivan asked, and saw Everett move closer in his peripheral vision.

"She did. My father said she was beautiful. He said she was going to make a different world for us, change everything. He told me if I wasn't good that he'd feed me to her."

The radio on the orderly's hip squawked, and all three men jerked at the sound. There was a rip of static, and then a woman's voice leaked from the small walkie-talkie.

"John, are you on three? Charlie and Jake aren't responding."

The orderly on the floor moaned, and the arm he wasn't lying on flailed weakly before dropping back to the linoleum.

"We have to get out of here," Everett said, pulling at Sullivan's shoulder. Sullivan shrugged him off and turned back to Jason.

"Jason, what's happening at Singleton? Do you know? There's something inside the people there."

Jason shook his head and scooted away so that his shoulders pressed up against the wall. "Don't know, but she does. She knows everything."

The woman's voice came from the radio again, more urgent this time, demanding that the orderly respond.

"Sullivan, we have to go now!" Everett said.

"Jason, where do we find her?" Sullivan asked, sliding close to the older man on the bed.

Jason looked down at the bedspread, his mouth working silently. Finally he brought his gaze back up to Sullivan's face. "She's underneath, in the dark."

The orderly on the floor groaned and planted a hand beside his body. Sullivan stood and followed Everett to the door, but before leaving the room, he turned back to Jason, studying the shell of a man, seeing only the young boy who remained inside.

"Thank you, Jason," Sullivan said. He didn't wait for him to respond.

The corridor was still empty as Sullivan and Everett ran to the door that accessed the stairs. As Everett swiped his key across the reader, the elevator hummed, nearing their floor. Both men slid through the door, onto the dimly lit landing, and held their breath. Several sets of feet approached and then receded as they passed the door by. Sullivan let out the breath he was holding as they began to descend the stairs, their shoes barely touching the treads.

The hallway they'd entered by was vacant, and after a few seconds, the fresh air of the night hit them both square in the face as they stepped outside. The rain still fell in mist form, and no moon was visible through the blanket of clouds above. Neither man spoke as they fled from the building's back entry, and just to be safe, Sullivan led Everett back into the woods and began to curve toward the access road to the right. When they were sure no one pursued them through the trees, they both slowed their pace and fell in alongside each other. The leaves and branches around them dripped and nodded as they passed.

Everett looked over at Sullivan and finally broke the relative silence. "What the fuck was the purpose of that? That guy's a raving lunatic."

"He's the son of the man who built both these facilities. Oliver Godring is the source of all this, I know it."

"He could have been lying, for all we know. He might've said he's Elvis's illegitimate child if we'd asked," Everett said, pawing at a low-hanging branch.

"He's not lying. You heard him, his father had him locked up there after he died because of something he knew. I doubt if he was even crazy when he was committed, although he's definitely affected now."

"That's an understatement," Everett said.

"Look," Sullivan said, stopping and grasping the guard's arm. "If you want to find your brother, this is all we have to go on. That's how you solve things like this, you take what you have and go with it."

"What do we have? The say-so of a paranoid schizophrenic about some 'she' that's polluting the water? And what do you want to do with this information?"

"I think we should go back into the prison, find Andrews if he's still alive, and then search the solitary level."

"Search it? For what?" Everett asked, his voice bordering on incredulity.

"For something underneath it."

Everett's face was hidden mostly in shadow, but Sullivan could imagine the anger that graced it. After a moment, the guard shook his head. "You're crazy."

"Am I? Do you want to find your brother or not?"

"Of course I do!" Everett roared, taking a step forward.

"Then listen to me," Sullivan said. "You saw your co-workers leading the physicist into solitary."

"*Thought* I saw," Everett corrected Sullivan in a lower voice.

"If there is one place in the prison that might have a hidden entry, it would be the lowest level." Sullivan heard Everett sigh and saw his shoulders slump a little. "And if there's a place underneath the prison, that's where your brother would be. It's where Barry would be too."

The wind came up and tossed the tops of the trees violently. Sullivan waited, and when the wind died, Everett spoke.

"Okay, so what's your plan?"

"We need more weapons," Sullivan said, walking again.

"There's a little armory closet on the first floor. I have a key for it."

"Good. Maybe you can get the guns while I get Andrews," Sullivan said, as they stepped out of the woods onto the road.

They walked side by side on the muddied gravel. It was over a minute before Everett spoke again; this time his voice was softer. "Sullivan, I'm sorry I was such an asshole to you and your partner when you got here. I guess I just didn't want any interference from the outside messing up my search for Alex. I lost faith in investigators after they told me that he'd turn up and just to wait it out." He paused, turning his head toward Sullivan. "Your partner seemed like a decent man."

Sullivan nodded. "He was—is." *Don't you give up on him now. Not now. You bring him home to his wife and kids.*

Sullivan realized a moment later that Everett wasn't beside him, and turned to look at the guard. Everett's eyes were locked on something ahead of them, and Sullivan spun to look in that direction.

The gate had just come into view. It was still open.

"Fuck," Everett said, drawing even with Sullivan. "That's not good at all."

"Why, does that mean someone just came through?"

"No, it closes on its own after ten seconds. It only stays open if you lock it at the keypad or from the surveillance room."

"So unless someone's here right now, I'm guessing they locked it from inside the prison," Sullivan said eyeing the surrounding woods.

"Looks that way."

Sullivan reached up and rubbed the scar over his eye, massaging the skin and muscle near the temple. "Then I guess they're expecting us," he said at last. "Let's not disappoint them."

Chapter 11

The cafeteria was still and dark when they stepped inside the emergency exit they'd fled through hours before. Both men shook water from their hair, as the rain had begun to fall in earnest again. When they'd rounded the far side of the prison, Sullivan glimpsed the sandbags succumbing to the flood, water rolling over the barricaded edge in wide swaths. He guessed they had very little time before the water would be knocking on the prison's front doors.

Sullivan reached instinctively to his side where his weapon normally rode, and found only empty air. Remembering the guard's handgun at his back, he grasped the handle and drew it. Everett stood beside him, his pistol pointed at the floor.

"Ready?" Sullivan whispered.

"Ready," Everett replied.

The two men hurried across the expanse of the room, the light tapping of their footsteps the only sound. The hallway to the main holding area was empty and quiet also, and as they passed the infirmary door, Sullivan couldn't help looking at it. He almost expected it to fly open and Amanda to be standing there, her head wreathed in twisting shapes. The door to the holding area stood ajar, and both men slowed, sidling up to the entry. Sullivan risked a glance into the enormous space and drew back. Everett stared at him from across the hall.

"It's empty," Sullivan said in a low voice.

Everett frowned. "Empty?"

"As far as I could tell," Sullivan said. He listened to the humming silence, nudged the door, and stepped out into the open.

He was right. The entire holding area was devoid of life. Only the emergency lights burned in the darkness, but they were bright enough to see that no one was there. No guards stood at the desk or beside any of the security doors and none walked the grids overlooking the floor. Most disturbingly, the cells were also empty. Each and every inmate had vanished, leaving only open doors that stared like dead eyes into the walkway.

Everett cursed quietly and held his gun at arm's length, swinging it into the darkest corners. "Where'd they all go?" Everett asked, still incrementally turning to study the surroundings.

"I don't know," Sullivan said.

"Did they start the evacuation?"

"We would have seen them outside. Let's go, this isn't right," Sullivan said, moving toward the security door. His keycard scanned successfully and the lock released with a click. Sullivan peered into the lobby. The main desk was empty, the computer screen upon its surface dark. He stepped into the lobby and Everett followed, letting the door ease shut behind them. The warden's door was closed, but a little light leaked out from beneath it.

Sullivan turned to Everett. "You get the guns and come to Andrews's office. We'll try to make a plan from there."

Everett nodded and spun away, disappearing around the corner toward the interrogation rooms. Sullivan hefted his weapon and realized how much he missed his own gun. The pistol didn't feel comfortable in his hand, but it was all he had.

He took two steps toward the warden's office, when the door leading to the overnight quarters flew open on the other side of the room. Two guards rushed out, handguns drawn, flashlights shining in his eyes.

"Put it down!" one guard yelled as Sullivan's muscles tensed. He considered diving and throwing a shot at the two men, but then realized he recognized the guard's voice.

"Officer Hunt?" Sullivan asked, shielding his eyes.

The guard nearest him lowered his flashlight as well as his weapon. "Agent Shale. Glad we found you, but I need you to drop your gun."

Sullivan glanced at the other guard and saw that he carried a riot shotgun, its twelve-gauge eye still focused on his chest.

"Okay, here you go," Sullivan said, kneeling slowly to the ground. He set the gun on the floor and slid it toward the two guards. Hunt bent and retrieved the weapon.

"Warden Andrews needs to speak with you," the guard with the shotgun said as he lowered its menacing barrel toward the floor. "You have any other weapons?"

"No," Sullivan said, relief blooming in his chest like a spring flower. Hunt and the other guard looked anxious, and the fact that they wanted him to see Andrews was encouraging. He wished he could've caught Everett before he'd gone in search of more artillery.

The two guards walked to Andrews's door and opened it, letting the yellow light spill out onto the floor. Sullivan stepped past them into the office, his relief growing at the sight of the warden behind his desk.

"Sullivan, come in," Andrews said, rising tiredly from his seat. "I'm glad you're all right."

Sullivan walked up to the desk, as Hunt and the other man entered the room and shut the door. "Sir, there's something very wrong here. I found out a few more things, but right now we need to gather as many men as we can and search the solitary level."

Andrews's eyes were half closed, as if standing were a job in itself. He gradually folded his lanky frame into the chair and stared across the desk at Sullivan. "Are you and your wife divorced, Sullivan?" Andrews finally asked.

The question was like a shot of cold water during a hot shower. It caught him off-guard and made his mind stutter step. "What?" Sullivan asked.

"Your wife," the warden continued, and now it seemed that the older man was getting comfortable in his chair. "You said you were no longer married. Are you divorced?"

Sullivan licked his lips and felt the scar above his eye tingle. "Sir, what does that have to do—"

"Just answer the question," Andrews said, as a cold smile that Sullivan would have called benevolent hours ago appeared on the older man's face. Behind him he heard the safety on one of the guard's weapons click off. Sullivan felt his guts compress and his scalp tighten.

"No, she's dead," Sullivan said.

The warden nodded, the smile lingering on his lips. "Good, I'd hoped so."

"What did you just say?" Sullivan asked incredulously. He was sure he'd heard the warden wrong.

"Have a seat, son," Andrews said, gesturing toward one of the chairs across from the desk.

"Sir, I don't know what you're playing at, but—"

"Have a seat or one of the men behind you will put a bullet in the back of your head," Andrews interrupted.

Sullivan stared at the older man. He felt his jaw wanting to hang open, but kept it shut. He wanted to scream, to curse himself for being so stupid. He wanted to jump the desk and throttle the warden where he rested. Instead, he sat in the chair behind him.

"You don't seem like a man that fears death, Sullivan. I admire people like that. I'm not one of them. Death has terrified me since the moment I saw my grandfather fall down dead of a heart attack. I was seven at the time. I remember thinking I never wanted to have the look on my face that he did when he was lying there clutching his chest. That fear, the fear of what's beyond. It scares the hell out of me." Andrews sat forward and rested his hands on the desktop. His eyes were soft in the low light, pleading almost. "How did your wife die?"

"Fuck you," Sullivan said through clenched teeth. Somewhere behind him he heard a hammer cock.

"Now, now. We don't need rudeness invading a polite conversation. I told you how I lost my wife, it's only courteous that you do the same."

Sullivan felt his breath beginning to deepen. His heart felt like war drum in his chest, not fast but hard. "She killed herself."

"Hmm. I'm very sorry to hear that." Andrews turned his head to study the pictures hanging on the wall. "What would you say if I told you, you could have her back?"

Sullivan stared across the desk at the warden. "I'd say you're off your fucking rocker, old man."

Andrews laughed and turned his attention back to Sullivan. "I'd have said the same thing six years ago before I came here, son. You see, a man's view of the world and reality is so narrow that he sometimes misses things that are just outside his peripheral line of sight. Things that are broader and so beautiful, they're beyond reckoning."

Beautiful. Hearing the word chilled Sullivan after the past few days. It no longer held any good connotations.

"Oliver Godring had wide vision. He was a brilliant man in his time, and would have rivaled any mind today. I admire him more than any other human being on the planet."

"He locked his own son away in a mental ward," Sullivan spat.

Andrews nodded and licked his lips. "Regrettable, but necessary for his work to continue."

"His work for the government? No secret is worth forsaking your own son for," Sullivan said.

Andrews studied him for a moment, then said, "Not the work he did for the government, the work that came after. The work for her."

"What are you talking about?" Sullivan asked.

Andrews smiled again. "Oliver Godring was a brilliant nuclear physicist commissioned for a project after World War II. It was top-secret, and only his staff and handful of people in Washington knew about it. They wanted him to build a weapon based on the atomic bombs dropped on Hiroshima and Nagasaki, but those who had hired him were dissatisfied with the aftermath of the atomic holocaust. It was too messy, with too many casualties. Oliver birthed an idea that pleased them to no end: the beam."

Sullivan blinked. Jason had mentioned the same name. "What was it?"

"More or less, it was a focused beam of atomic energy, able to pinpoint a certain target and evaporate it to an atomic level. Oliver's initial tests had the panel in Washington salivating. They poured millions of dollars into his research. They wanted something they could attach to a satellite and, say, have it orbit over mother Russia, since at the time the Cold War was in full swing. Being able to obliterate a building in the capital or a single home was too attractive an idea to ignore. In late August 1958, Oliver ran his first full-strength test. His testing station was buried five hundred feet underground in a natural cave system. When he triggered the device, it killed every member of his team except him, and instead of destroying the target he'd focused the beam on, it did something entirely unexpected. It opened a doorway."

"A doorway? A doorway to where?" Sullivan asked.

"Oh, you've seen it yourself, in your dreams, no doubt," Andrews said, tilting his head to one side.

Sullivan's mouth instantly dried out.

"I fed you water from our well here, in the coffee you and Agent Stevens drank the first time you sat in this room. That water comes from beneath the prison, over five hundred feet down, where she lives. Her waste mingles with the water table, and when we drink it, we can see, we can feel, and we become more."

Images of the burnt landscape shrouded in smoke ran through Sullivan's mind. The dream had seemed so real, and now he knew why.

"You've even met her, Sullivan. Out in the woods yesterday. She was kind enough to herd you back to us at my request."

Sullivan's hand moved to the wound on his shoulder. "Am I infected now? Are those snake things inside of me too?"

Andrews laughed congenially and shook his head. "No, son. It takes weeks before the water has the full effect on people, before you begin to receive her gift. After you've drank enough, then you start to … alter."

Sullivan felt his stomach flip at the thought of what he would do if he felt a crawling sensation at the back of his throat. "What gift? What do you mean 'alter'?"

"Ah, so many questions. You remind me of me six years ago, when I first came here. I'll answer you this way. You saw her home. It's dying. Her kind is gradually becoming extinct. When Oliver opened the doorway, she slipped through and showed him. She showed him that she needed help in continuing her species. After the failure of the beam project, he built this prison directly on top of the test site, along with New Haven. People were necessary for the plan that he devised, and prisoners were the best candidates. What you saw inside of the people here is a blessed conversion. Anyone who drinks enough of the water gradually becomes a version of her kind, her children."

Sullivan felt like vomiting, and the anger that felt so strong when he'd first sat down evaporated, replaced with overwhelming revulsion. Now, he knew why the prison was so quiet, the inmates restrained. They were connected in a way so gruesome, it defied rational thought. "It's trying to further its species through some kind of fucking human aberration?" he finally managed.

Andrew's smile vanished at Sullivan's words. "The side effects of drinking her waste was a most unexpected turn of events. The people here will be her first spawn, but the doorway must be opened for more of her kind to come through. A male must be brought here to fertilize the eggs she's been carrying for over fifty years. It's imperative for the continuation of her species."

Sullivan sat back in the chair, swallowing his gorge. "Jesus Christ, you're insane."

"On the contrary, son. I'm the first of the many that will welcome her and her kind into the world. I'm the emissary of goodwill. She's allowed me sanctity for my service. I've continued Oliver's work and allocated the necessary ingredients for the greatest revolution the world has ever known. You don't know what she's capable of, Sullivan. The world we live in is war torn, grief stricken, and cruel. When her race is reborn here, they will spread control and peace, since they do not know the meaning of murdering and killing their own kind. They have power beyond human knowledge, the power to heal, to rebirth, even to bring back life."

Sullivan gaped at him. "That's what this is about, then? You think that this thing is going to heal you and bring back your dead wife?"

Andrews bolted up from the chair, surprising Sullivan with an agility he didn't think the older man possessed. "Yes!" Andrews bellowed. "Life is a fucking joke, boy! A sick joke played on everyone who walks the earth. There's no salvation except the kind you make for yourself! I'm a good man. I treated others with kindness. I loved my wife. And look where it got me. She's been gone for years, stripped from me like a leaf in a hurricane, and now I'm dying! This is the thanks I get for being righteous, a good man!" Andrews shook with a rage barely contained. The warden's throat bobbed with emotion, and then he sank back into his chair behind the desk. He bit his lower lip, and Sullivan saw that whoever the warden had been years ago was gone, replaced by something broken and desperate within a battered shell. "She's shown me her capabilities and promised me," Andrews continued in a lower voice. "After the doorway is opened, she will cure my cancer and resurrect my Maddy."

The newspaper in Everett's hiding space suddenly appeared in Sullivan's mind, and he felt as if he'd been struck. "That's why you kidnapped the nuclear physicist, to try to repeat what Godring did all those years ago."

Andrews nodded. "Oliver was a scientist, I'm not. He died unexpectedly, in a plane crash. He was in the process of gathering supplies for rebuilding the beam. I have no doubt she would have brought him back, but Oliver was obliterated in the crash. She went into a deep hibernation following his death, and only awoke when one of my men—Officer Bundy, in fact—discovered the passageway leading down to her lair from the solitary level. When I first saw her, I was terrified, but after she showed me what was possible, I knew what I had to do. It took the better part of five years to acquire everything that was needed—plutonium is especially hard to come by these days. The nuclear council being held in the southern part of the state was just plain fate. Dr. Bolt has corrected the malfunction that killed Godring's team. The storm and flooding is giving us our opportunity for the rebirth to begin, another fateful turn in our favor, as was your arrival here, Sullivan."

Sullivan's mind reeled against everything the other man said. It revolted at what Andrews's words implicated, yet he had no other explanation for the events and things he'd seen. But the last statement the warden made was what finally turned Sullivan's blood cold. He squinted at Andrews, as fat drops of rain fell outside the windows and thunder cleared its throat somewhere off to the west.

"What does this have to do with me?" Sullivan asked, his voice sounding surprisingly steady in his own ears.

"The night Mr. Alvarez was killed, most of our staff was busy sandbagging the perimeter, as I told you. We normally have an offering for her once a month. It was my fault that her meal was neglected, and she was forced to search for food. With the rain and flooding, game has become scarce outside our borders, so she found the only food available through the drain in Alvarez's cell. You would never have been called had we known that our young Hunt over there would notify Sheriff Jaan. You see, Nathan was in the process of becoming. Unfortunately, the sheriff had to be disposed of, along with your crime-scene team, I regret to say."

Sullivan had to dig his fingers into the chair's arms to keep himself from bolting over the desk and beating the warden's face into the back of his skull. Don was dead, along with his assistants. Now, he knew why Barry hadn't been able to raise the sheriff on the phone after he'd left. No doubt, the elderly law man was either at the bottom of the flood outside or somewhere much, much worse.

"Very unfortunate," Andrews continued. "But what I'm offering you is something no other person could ever offer before." The older man leaned forward with fiery intensity burning in his eyes, which Sullivan recognized now as madness. "I can give you your wife back, Sullivan. I can give you immortality. She's granted me a lieutenant in the new world, and I want it to be you."

"Why?"

"Because you're cunning, you have drive, and you're definitely a scrapper. You handled three of my best employees with ease, not to mention our friend Mr. Fairbend. I wanted to thank you for that too, Henry was becoming a problem. First he antagonized Alvarez in the cell, which began all of this, and then when your partner was acquired, he couldn't even get away quietly. Luckily, Officer Bundy was nearby yesterday morning and heard the shots. He managed to dispose of Fairbend's body before you were able to inspect it further. In all actuality, my preference before you was Everett. Since he had such an extreme allergic reaction to the water, he was a natural choice for a human lieutenant. He's a lot like you in many ways—smart, strong, good moral fiber. Although, I'm disappointed that he thought I didn't know who his brother was—I knew the moment he applied for the transfer here."

Sullivan shook his head. "What did you do with Barry?"

"He's in her service now. He's doing his part in assuring the doorway opens as planned."

"You're lying. He'd never agree to this," Sullivan said, his voice rising a notch.

Andrews only smiled. "You'd be surprised, Sullivan. Like I said, you don't understand her power. Just think of it, Sullivan, you would be one of the first to embrace the revolution, you'd have your heart's desire in the new world. People would worship you as a god, you'd never have to fear death, and you'd have your wife back."

Sullivan lowered his head so that his chin nearly touched his chest. He stayed that way for a moment, but when he raised his eyes level with the older man across the desk, there was no fear in them. His breathing was deep and even, and his heart beat slowly, in time with his words when he spoke.

"My wife was mentally ill. When I met her, she was medicated for manic-depressive tendencies. I fell in love with her knowing that it might be a hard life, a life full of pain, and I never looked back. I didn't look back when she drank so much that she did this to me with a broken wineglass," he said, motioning to the old scar above his eye. "I didn't look back when she tried to slit her wrists and, when I intervened, she spilled part of my intestine into open air. I didn't look back when she finally jumped from our twentieth-floor-apartment balcony and landed headfirst on the street below." Sullivan gritted his teeth as tears shimmered at the corners of his vision. "My wife is finally at peace in a place where her mind cannot hurt her anymore. So forgive me for not being tempted by your offers. You have nothing that I want, and I'm not afraid of you or whatever you have hiding down in the dark."

The warden's eyebrows creased together and he grimaced as if in pain. Sullivan readied himself. This was the end, he could feel it. He'd been given his shot at riding along, and he'd missed the train, on purpose. He listened for the sound of movement behind him, in case the killing shot would come from one of the guards, and watched Andrews intently, to see what the man's next move would be.

"Well, I'm sorry to hear that, Sullivan," Andrews said. "Truly, I am. I had high hopes for you, but as they say, the show must go on." Andrews pulled open a drawer and drew out Barry's handgun, cocked it. Lightning arced from west to east in the sky and strobed in the office with vibrant pulsations. Everything slowed, jumping a few seconds in time with each beat of Sullivan's heart. The eye of the barrel stared at him as it rose to meet his gaze. Andrews squinted down the sights at Sullivan and applied pressure to the trigger. Sullivan's muscles tensed as he breathed in, held it.

Sullivan dropped sideways to the floor and heard the gun go off. The roar of the gunshot faded and Andrews howled in anger. At the same time, the door to the office exploded inward, and Sullivan twisted on the floor to see who had entered.

Everett stood in the doorway, his hands clutching a riot shotgun. The guard next to the door spun as Everett leveled the shotgun and fired a load of buckshot into the man's chest. Blood and matter flew across the room, as if sprayed from a hose. The sound was muffled, the blast deadened by the body before it. Sullivan heard Andrews fire again, and watched Everett twitch as if energized by electric current. Sullivan crawled backward toward the wall, and caught sight of Hunt retreating as he drew his pistol even with Everett's head. Sullivan kicked the chair beside him in Hunt's direction, and the young guard flinched. His shot strayed and tore a runner of cloth from Everett's shoulder, along with a spray of blood. Everett staggered in the doorway but managed to bring the shotgun up and blast one of Hunt's legs. Sullivan saw muscle and bone rip free of the guard's pants leg as the joint in his knee folded the wrong way, sending him to the floor with a cry.

Movement caught Sullivan's eye as Andrews rounded the desk, pointing the handgun down at the floor like an exterminator hunting for a pest. Sullivan rolled behind the small table that sat between the chairs, as the warden fired. A line of acid traced a path across his forearm, and he looked down to see blood seeping from a shallow trench in his flesh. He heard a grunt of pain from the doorway, and listened as Everett collapsed while racking a fresh shell into the chamber.

Andrews loped for the door, and Hunt sat up, numbly staring at his ruined leg and the spreading lake of blood on the floor around him. Everett fired again, and Sullivan saw Hunt's face obliterate and his body go languid, the last twitches of life escaping in shivers through his frame. Another gunshot resounded in the room, and Sullivan propped himself up just in time to see Andrews disappear through the doorway, his tall frame hunched as he ran.

Sullivan bolted to his feet and nearly slipped in Hunt's blood. He sidled into view of the lobby and snatched Everett's shotgun from the floor. He scanned what he could see of the lobby and his stomach lurched as a clicking sound met his ears. *Andrews is going into the holding area,* he thought, but kept the gun trained on the door, just in case, as he knelt beside Everett.

The guard's face was ashen. His lips were becoming blue where they weren't covered in blood from the inside of his mouth. His eyes were open and focused on Sullivan as he came near. Sullivan searched the guard's body for a wound, and finally spotted an entry hole a few inches right of his breastbone. Blood bubbled from the spot with each of Everett's forced breaths. He was also holding the right side of his abdomen, which shone with wet intestine when Sullivan pulled his hand aside to examine it.

Sullivan grimaced and looked into Everett's eyes.

"It's okay," Everett said, all power behind the words lost in the wheezing of his filling lungs. "It's okay. Just get him."

"We're gonna get you help," Sullivan said, cradling the guard's head with his hand. He knew the words were in vain. There was no help here, or on the way, for all he knew. The words were automatic, a thin comfort to an already dying man.

"Alex," Everett said, his eyes beginning to look beyond Sullivan. "Alex."

"He's all right," Sullivan said, not knowing if Everett was seeing something that lay outside of the walls of the prison or merely asking for his brother. "He's just fine, Everett. You did good. Thank you."

Everett nodded and a thick gurgle came from his mouth as he tried to draw in another breath. His spine arched as the oxygen refused to come, and then his muscles were like water. His body relaxed and blood ran over the rim of his lips. His eyes closed halfway and stopped.

Sullivan swallowed and glanced up at the silent lobby as he wiped blood off Everett's chin. He stood and pulled a cushion from the nearby overturned chair, and propped Everett's head off the floor. He looked at the dead man, a gambit of emotions careening through him, most of all guilt. He had convinced Everett to come back inside. Sullivan squeezed his eyes shut and opened them again. There was no time for this; he'd suffer for it later, but now he had to move.

He found a dozen shotgun shells in Everett's pants pocket and transferred them to his own. Without another look back at the ruined office, with its quiet occupants, he stepped out of the door and into the lobby.

Water splashed around his feet as he moved. Looking to his left, he saw its source. The flood was at the door and flowed beneath it with ease. Nearly an inch of water coated the floor of the lobby, and it spread like mercury in all directions. Sullivan sloshed through it, his feet going from damp to completely soaked in an instant.

The security door opened smoothly, and Sullivan stayed behind the safety of the doorjamb, waiting for a shot to rip through the open space. None came. Tentatively he poked the barrel of the shotgun into the next room, and then followed it in a low crouch. He swung the weapon toward the open hallway on his right, then scooted around the guard desk, ensuring that no one hid behind its bulk. He listened to the silence of the holding area; the only other sounds were his quiet breathing and the renewed vigor of the storm outside.

In short bursts of movement, he crossed the holding area, pausing within the entry of a vacant cell every few yards. He expected gunfire at any moment, and when none came each time he moved, it only heightened his sense of unease. A dark shape in the middle of the floor stopped his progress. Barry's gun lay abandoned, its barrel pointing back the way he'd come. Without hesitation, he scooped the 1911 off the floor and tucked it in the waistband at his back. At last he came to the end of the cellblock, where the building expanded into a T-shape. He risked a glance around the corner, and saw the guard at the bottom of the stairway below him taking aim.

Sullivan pulled his face back as the bullet sawed through the corner of the cinderblock he hid behind. Chips of paint, concrete, and mortar stung his cheek. He blinked the dust from his eyes and listened. After a moment of indecision, he let out a choked cough and dropped the shotgun. The weapon clattered to the floor, falling into view of the stairway. Sullivan reached behind his back and drew the handgun from his waistband without a sound. A few seconds later, he heard boots coming up the steel stairway, their echoes drawing closer with each step.

Sullivan swung around the corner and sighted down the handgun's barrel at the guard who was just stepping onto the landing. He had a heartbeat to register the wide eyes of the guard, and then the gun recoiled twice in his hands. The other man issued a strangled yell as the bullets tore through his chest, and he plummeted backward down the stairway. The sickening crunch of bones breaking on steel met Sullivan's ears as he watched the body's descent. The guard came to rest face-down on the second landing, his arms groping for purchase on anything within reach, as blood spread out from beneath his chest. Gradually his flailing weakened, and then ceased altogether.

Sullivan tucked the now-heated handgun behind his back once more, picked up the shotgun, and made his way down the stairs. At the corner of the landing, he stepped into view of the lower level, the twelve-gauge held before him. Nothing moved below. The lower level was still and dimly lit. All of the doors to the solitary cells were closed, and only smooth concrete lined the opposite side of the corridor.

Sullivan paused only to nudge the dead guard with his foot before pelting down the stairs. With a glance through the glass porthole of each solitary cell, he proceeded down the line until Alvarez's death scene came into view. Blood and gore still coated the walls, but the colors had dried to a monochrome of blacks and grays. Bright speckles of bone shards stood out like stars in a night sky. Sullivan walked to the end of the hallway and stopped at the back wall. He turned in a circle, listening to the low hum of the emergency lights, and studied the walls. He made his way back up the row of cells, until he stood at the foot of the stairs. Turning, he scanned the seamless enclosure again. Nothing.

Looking down, he noticed a discolored path on the floor. He knelt and realized what he was looking at. The darkened area down the center of the hall was marks, dirt, and prints from hundreds of shoes treading the same spot. A single-file line. Sullivan stood and followed the path all the way to the far wall, where the footprints terminated in its corner. He looked up and stared at the wall. Licking the palm of his hand, he began to pass it across the concrete, an inch from its surface. He moved to his left, to where the wall met the adjoining surface of Alvarez's cell.

The moisture on his palm cooled.

He pushed his face closer to the corner and breathed deeply. An odor that reminded him of a bag of mushrooms that had sat too long in the fridge met his nose, a musty, half-rotten smell, and something else. Something tangy and pungent. He'd never smelled anything like it in his life, but couldn't deny the sinking feeling it gave him in the base of his stomach. The odor inspired fear.

Sullivan stepped back from the corner as an idea struck him like a mallet. With a glance into the last cell, he moved back and gauged the distance between the back wall of the hall and the inside wall of the cell. They didn't match up.

"You're brilliant, Everett," Sullivan whispered, as he put his hand against the corner of the wall and pushed. Nothing happened. He shoved again, expecting the concrete to shift or give in some fashion. Instead, it remained immobile and his feet slid in the dust on the floor. Breathing heavier, he took a step back and scanned the rest of the surroundings. The shoe and boot marks trailed into the wall below his feet. The walls intersecting before him were smooth. Over his head, plumbing and electrical conduits snaked off in multiple directions.

Sullivan squinted into the space above him, at a branch of water pipes. There were three brightly colored shutoffs mounted in the juncture of the pipe system; two were circular and yellow, while the other was a lever painted a vibrant red. He traced the pipes heading off in the direction of the stairway, and then looked more closely at where they originated. Behind the main branch, another, much smaller, pipe led into the wall above the corner he stood before. On its top, hidden by the pipe itself, was a black handle no bigger than one of his fingers. The area around it was devoid of the dust and spider webs, which adorned every other surface in the ceiling.

Sullivan reached up and turned the handle to the right. It moved with the ease of worn use, and there was a clack from directly in front of him. The thin stream of air he'd felt earlier on his palm now brushed his face, the smell from within stronger, urging his heart into a gallop. He gripped the shotgun again in both hands. With a push from the barrel, the false wall swung open, revealing a yawning black rectangle barely two feet across.

A sound like cloth tearing came from his left, and he spun, expecting a horde of infected guards and prisoners to be rushing him. Instead, he saw nothing, and after a moment of listening and watching, he realized what the sound was.

Water poured down the stairway and washed toward him, its edge like that of a sharpened knife. There would be no stopping the flood from moving where it wanted to go; and where it wanted to go, needed to go, was down. Down.

Consciously breathing in one last lungful of semi-pure air, Sullivan ducked his head and stepped into the darkness.

Chapter 12

A metal staircase fell away into the mouth of the earth, and Sullivan descended. The wan light from behind him outlined his shadow and threw a monstrous version of his shape ahead of him. He stopped every few steps to listen, his hearing his most valuable sense in the darkness. The faint rush of water running ever closer from behind him hid all other sounds. Sullivan peered ahead, faint shapes dancing in and out of the penumbra of darkness. He gripped the shotgun so tight, he felt one of his knuckles crack and the sound was loud in the quiet.

He took another step, expecting the stairway to continue, and stumbled, his foot scuffing against solid ground. An extremely damp earthen wall met his searching hand after another stride and he stopped, letting his eyes adjust further. After a moment, he was able to make out rough impressions of the space in which he stood, and he turned, absorbing it.

He was in a tunnel, perhaps twelve feet across. The walls were uneven and lined with chunks of rock, an irregular mosaic composed of quartz and granite. There were places a few yards to either side that had caved in, the ground spilling its organs onto the tunnel's floor in heaps of sand, stone, and clay. A vertical shape a few feet away made Sullivan's finger tighten on the trigger, but he quickly realized it was only a steel support pillar, its wide plated ends pressing against the unbearable weight overhead.

He stepped to the side, realizing that the light from the top of the stairs wasn't sufficient to illuminate the area his eyes were taking in. A faint glow emanated from farther down the tunnel. It lit up a small halo at what he guessed was the end of the passage but he couldn't be sure from this distance. He also saw that the tunnel dropped off sharply, almost at a forty-five-degree angle. He stepped around the support beam and began to move downward.

The floor was soft beneath his feet as he walked, and every so often he could feel one shoe sink into a footprint of someone who'd trodden in the same spot. He could see more alcoves on both sides, some where the tunnel was partially collapsed and a few that looked like natural pockets in the soil. The sight of the piled earth made Sullivan's heart quicken. He could imagine the sickening feeling of dirt falling onto his head moments before the entire ceiling crashed down, burying him under its crushing weight, smashing his breath from him, his own personal grave where no one would ever find him.

The light became brighter now. He felt he was nearly halfway down to wherever down was. His heartbeat was still the loudest thing in his ears as he moved around an especially large cave-in on his right side.

A shape came out of the alcove and hit him so hard that he heard his teeth crack together. The shotgun flew from his hands and spun away, as he fell onto his side, his head rebounding off the opposite wall. Sullivan twisted underneath the weight above him and felt cold hands trying to grip the tender skin of his throat. He bucked his hips and shifted, grabbing the assailant's leg. With a shove, Sullivan levered himself into a sitting position and tossed the flailing body off him. He groped at the small of his back, his heart dropping when his hand found only air where Barry's handgun was moments before. He climbed to his feet, bracing his hand against the wall of the tunnel, as the shape across from him rose at the same time. Sullivan's hands balled into fists as the shadow moved closer and a face gradually became visible.

Officer Bundy's grinning visage leered at him through the dead air.

"Fancy meeting you here, Agent," Bundy sneered, his lips a twisted line above the V of his goatee. Sullivan said nothing, merely circling to his left, his fists at waist height. "I was hoping I'd catch you. The warden said you might be comin'. I thought you wouldn't be smart enough to figure out the door up there. Proved me wrong though."

"Where's Barry?" Sullivan asked, his jaws latched together by anger and adrenaline. Every inch of his body ached from the abuse of the last two days, but he moved steadily in a slow circle around the other man.

"Oh, him? He's about cashed in. Did us proud, though, served her well. He won't be remembered for his little part in all this, but I can relay a message." Bundy leaned forward as dark shapes began to dance out of his open mouth. "She says 'thank you.'"

Bundy lunged across the space between them, but Sullivan was ready. He lowered his good shoulder and caught the guard low in the stomach, just above the hips. He heard Bundy's air whoosh out past the tendrils spinning and snapping from his mouth, and the sound gave Sullivan power as he kept pushing, his legs pistoning as he drove the guard into the opposite wall.

Sullivan felt hands scrabbling at his sides for purchase and stinging bites on his upper back, as Bundy's sharpened appendages lashed out and cut furrows in his flesh. Sullivan turned from the wall and slammed the guard to the ground in a vicious forward toss, relishing the sound of the other man's head connecting with the earth. A rage Sullivan was unacquainted with before that instant welled up and over him, washing everything away except the will to crush, destroy, and kill. One moment he was holding Bundy down, and then next the heel of his shoe was striking the guard in the face over and over. The tendrils attempted to latch on to Sullivan's leg, but he pulled back, feeling a few separate from their moorings, and continued to stomp the man's face. The hard cracks of bone became softer, wetter. Sullivan's breathing came in ragged gasps, the oxygen fueling the burning anger.

When he felt too tired to raise his foot again, he stepped back and fell to the floor. In the soft glow of the light from below, he could see Bundy's body and a dark stain on the floor of the tunnel where his head should have been. A few languid tendrils rolled over like dying snakes, and then were still also. A hard object was under Sullivan's hand, and when he pulled it from the dirt and moved it closer to his face, relief swam warmly through him. There was no mistaking the distinct shape of Barry's pistol. Sullivan shook the layer of dirt off the gun and wiped it as clean as possible.

A brief search yielded the twelve-gauge near the left wall. He glanced around, expecting another shape to step out from one of the nearby recesses; but when none did, he began to move again, slowly at first, and then with more speed, more urgency. Barry was close, he was sure of it.

Dirt flew up from his heels as he pelted down the tunnel, heedless of the sound his approach might make. The light ahead grew in intensity and he recognized it as halogen, its cold luminosity brightening with each step he took. Soon, the end of the passage was in sight and he slowed his pace, rocks and sand cascading past him. He blinked and swallowed bile that rose with the renewed smell he'd first detected at the top of the stairs. It was ten times stronger here, rancid and thick. It smelled like unwashed flesh and ammonia. Fear invaded him and urged him to run, the animalistic aggression he'd battered Bundy to death with now telling him to flee. Sullivan bit the inside of his cheek and tasted blood. The pain brought him back and pushed the desire to escape to the wings of his mind. He was close now.

Tentatively, he moved into the mouth of the passage and stopped, stunned beyond movement or thought.

A natural domed chamber opened up beyond the end of the tunnel, soaring seventy feet overhead and spanning two football fields in either direction. Massive stalactites hung like black icicles from the ceiling, in some places brushing the floor with their tips. The floor of the cave was relatively smooth, with a few rough platforms composed of a grayish rock. Two unevenly hewn steps dropped away several yards inside the room, and boulders of all sizes lay strewn about like a giant's toys amidst the shadows cast by three enormous work lights. Inside the ring of lights, some fifty yards away, sat a long and low contraption, the likes of which Sullivan had never seen before. It was rectangular and made from what looked to be yellowing sheet metal. A fluted cylinder helixed by stainless-steel support struts extended from the far end, which pointed into the center of the cave. A thick shield made from some transparent material rested at its rear and a complex array of controls sat below it. Sullivan could make out a crosshatch design on the shield, which lined up with the barrel in front of it.

Beyond the machine lay a sea of humanity.

Hundreds of people, nearly all men, milled around in huge groups. Sullivan could hear murmurs of conversation and laughter at times. It looked to him like a congregation before a sermon. He saw a few men shaking hands and smiling as they nodded and hugged one another. Until then, there had been a part of Sullivan that hadn't wanted to believe, couldn't believe it was true. As irrational as it seemed after all that he'd witnessed, he'd hoped that he'd find nothing for his troubles. But the sight below him confirmed everything Andrews told him. Guards mingled with inmates, nodding at them and congratulating them. Sullivan's mind rebelled against the last, most horrifying thought: if everything else was truly real, then where was *she*?

He scanned the room from top to bottom, but could see nothing that resembled the indistinct form he'd glimpsed the day before. His eyes crawled across an area several yards away from the mouth of the passage and he stopped dead, the saliva in his mouth evaporating.

Barry lay naked on the ground, his face upturned toward Sullivan, his eyes closed. Sullivan tried to swallow, and then glanced around the chamber. None of the people below seemed to be looking in the direction of the tunnel. Sullivan laid the shotgun on the floor and crouched, his eyes scanning the crowd just to be sure. Blocking out all other thoughts, he scurried out of the passage and into the light of the cave. His legs burned from exhaustion, along with his wounds, but he kept moving until he was at Barry's side. In the moment it took him to grasp his friend beneath the armpits and drag him the few yards back into darkness, Sullivan tried not to think about how light Barry was. When they'd arrived at Singleton, Barry weighed at least 250 pounds. The man he carried now felt a hundred pounds lighter.

The opening to the tunnel closed over them, shrouding them in comforting darkness, but Sullivan kept pulling, glancing over his shoulder and locating a deep recess in the wall. He pulled Barry inside and gently rested his shrunken body on the ground. Sullivan gazed at his friend, too stunned to even move for a time.

Barry's skin was alabaster, and Sullivan couldn't help but think of the corpses in the vampire flicks he'd seen as a kid, all of them whiter than snow, drained completely of blood. There was no trace of the sunburn the other man had suffered. His face was a skull, and the skin, once plump and healthy, was now drawn tight across angular bones, the eyes sunken in their sockets beneath limp eyelids. Barry's belly was a loose bag and his legs were stick thin, the kneecaps popping out obscenely like two stones beneath a sheet. He'd lost all of his hair, and the only color in his entire body was where blood welled from beneath his fingernails. His chest did not move.

Sullivan drew in a shaking breath and sat beside his friend, the muscles in his legs finally giving out. Tears sprang to his eyes and he wiped at them absently, trying to deny the reality before him. What had happened to him? What could do this to a man in less than twenty-four hours? A vision of a massive spider sucking the insides out of its prey came to Sullivan's mind and he flung it away, nearly gagging.

"What the fuck? My God. What happened to you?" Sullivan asked, reaching out to touch Barry's shoulder. The flesh was spongy and as cold as stone. Sullivan drew his hand back and shook his head, already imagining what he would have to tell Barry's wife, what she would have to tell their children. And it was his fault, again.

Sullivan felt the hope he'd held out for finding Barry alive crumble, and he began to cry. Between tears he tried to speak. "I'm so sorry, man. So sorry. ... I wanted to help so bad, to find you, but I couldn't. ... Jesus, I'm so sorry. I'm always too late." Sullivan dragged an arm across his eyes, his voice choked. A thought floated up from the darkest part of his mind, the part he normally kept locked tight, and he spoke without contemplating why it came to him now. "I think you knew Rachel killed herself. I never told you, but I think you knew. She was so troubled and we fought for so long, but it finally won. The problems in her head were too much for her, and I understood, I did. I couldn't imagine what she went through every day, and drinking sometimes helped, but most times it didn't."

Sullivan felt his tears begin to lessen, something rising from within him inexplicably after all this time, dredged from the depths of his soul by the raking hand of death. "The day she died, I walked in the door and she was standing at the balcony. She had a dress on that I liked. I set the groceries down on the table and just stood there. She stared at me over her shoulder, the look in her eyes when she'd seen something terrible, and I just looked back. I didn't rush to help her like every other time. I waited. I told myself later that it was my way of lashing out at her after she'd hurt me so many times, that I paused to show her I was strong, and she couldn't scare me anymore. But a voice that's still inside my head says I did it because I knew. I knew she'd do it."

Sullivan let out a long breath that seemed to drain him of everything. He felt like a dried husk without anything left inside to hurt. "She jumped. I stood there for a split second, and then I ran, trying to catch her, but she was already gone."

Sullivan reached over and touched Barry on the shoulder again. "I'm so sorry I couldn't save you either."

Barry's eyes flew open and he gasped, grabbing at Sullivan's arm.

"Fuck!" Sullivan cried and fell back, but immediately recovered from his shock and slid forward on his knees to Barry's side. His friend's eyes were so shot with blood that they looked black in the dim light. They rolled back and forth, searching with fear for something, and Sullivan glanced over his shoulder to assure himself that they were still alone.

"She's here," Barry whispered, his words strangled as something gurgled in his throat. "It's time."

Sullivan put a hand beneath Barry's head and lifted it so he could look into the other man's face. "I'm going to get you out of here, buddy. You're going to be just fine."

Barry's eyes found Sullivan's and held them, his cracked lips parted as small bursts of air escaped them. "No, you have to stop her, you have to stop the doorway! There's no time for me!" Barry's voice rose in pitch, although he lacked the strength to muster any real volume for his words.

"I won't leave you," Sullivan said, shaking his head.

"You have to, now. You don't know what will happen if her kind comes through. They're locusts. That's why their world is dying, they've stripped it of everything. They'll do the same here. They'll eat and eat and eat until there's nothing left. They multiply so fast. They destroy worlds." Barry's Adam's apple bobbed and he coughed up milky white phlegm, which coated his chin. Sullivan wiped it away and put his other hand on Barry's cold cheek.

"How do you know all this?" Sullivan asked.

Barry's eyelids fluttered open and he moved his arm to his side and jabbed at his back. "She showed me while I worked with the other man to get the machine running. She connected to me."

Barry pointed again to his back, and with growing horror Sullivan rolled him onto his side. He searched the pale skin there, and was about to turn Barry back over when he noticed a blackened bruise near his tailbone. When he leaned closer to inspect it, he had to clench his jaw to keep from crying out in shock.

The skin around the base of Barry's spine was flayed away. Vertebrae even whiter than the rest of the agent's skin poked free, like an island jutting from a bloodied sea. The wound was circular, and Sullivan could see strands of dark veins radiating outward into Barry's lower back.

Sullivan laid Barry gently onto his back once again, and noticed his friend's breathing was faster. A dry whistle emanated from him, as if there was a bone protruding somewhere inside where it shouldn't be.

"Tell them I'm okay, tell them I love them and not to worry. You stop it, Sully. Stop it for me and for my family, for everyone." Barry's red eyes slowly rolled up until his eyelids mercifully closed over them. His emaciated body hitched once, and then sagged like a sail in a dying wind.

Sullivan's breath withered out of his lungs as he pressed two fingers to the side of Barry's neck. He waited there, hoping that he would feel a dull beat through the artery, but there was nothing. Sullivan's face crumpled and he stifled a sob as he sat back. The weight of Everett's and, now, Barry's deaths was almost unbearable. He felt like a bridge having its support struts pulled away one by one. He imagined his mind would finally snap at any instant, and he would welcome the oblivion madness would bring. It would be a blessing to swim in its embrace and forget everything he'd seen.

A yell from the cavern snapped him out of his trance. He looked toward the glow of the light, and then back at the body before him. Flashes of the man Barry had been ran through Sullivan's mind as he squeezed his friend's shoulder one last time. The urge to take his body with him was overridden by what he knew Barry would say if he were still alive. Sullivan stood and stepped back into the tunnel, and felt liquid begin to run over his shoes.

Water poured down the grade above him, soaking the dirt floor as it flowed past, searching for the lowest point it could reach. He sloshed across the tunnel to the spot where he'd placed the shotgun and retrieved it before the ever-growing river behind him clutched the gun in its cold grasp. He once again made his way to the mouth of the passage and looked down.

The people were amassing in front of the oblong machine, their faces turned away from him, toward the far end of the giant cavern. Andrews stood there on a semi-flat rock that raised him above the rest of the waiting eyes. To Sullivan, he looked taller and stronger than he had in his office; his shoulders were no longer slumped and his back was straight. His hands were outstretched toward the crowd before him, and even from this distance, Sullivan could see the maniacal shine that glossed the warden's eyes.

"Friends!" Andrews's voice boomed and echoed in the rocky cave, giving a powerful resonance to his words. "This is the beginning! A revolution of the sort the world has never seen before! You are the beginning, and you'll be hailed as visionaries in the new world!" Andrews lowered his hands and smiled at the faces upturned toward him, like a preacher doling out eternal salvation. "Death will be thwarted for your loyalty and disease will be wiped from our history, starting today! We will go forth bearing her gifts and renew the life of our new brothers and sisters!"

The congregation shouted in one voice, making a dissonance of repercussion that caused Sullivan to wince with its noise. Soon, the voices changed from exuberant shouts to a low buzzing that was laced with an underlying hiss. As Sullivan watched, he saw every person below him tip his or her head back and yawn widely. Tendrils erupted en masse from hundreds of mouths. They sawed the air as they whipped and caressed the faces of their hosts. Sullivan's stomach turned at the sight and he felt his legs wanting to propel him up the way he'd come. He waited, as their humming chant rose in volume and the snapping appendages tore the air more violently.

A noise suddenly rose above the crowd's song. It was a deep thrumming that Sullivan felt in his chest, the sound of a wounded whale crying out across miles of an empty ocean. Its bass vibration stuttered and ascended in pitch, until he thought his eardrums would rupture, and then it was gone. He waited a beat as the cavern fell silent but for the thousands of tendrils whipping in ecstasy, and then he saw it: movement in the ceiling high above them all.

At first he thought it was an illusion, a dancing of shadows amassing and then recoiling in the light, but then it moved downward along one of the huge stalactites. The shadow crawled languidly, not without purpose but with easy assurance of power. It crept into the glow of the work lights, and as its full form was revealed, Sullivan stopped breathing. It was like having a fractured picture become whole again and finally seeing it for what it truly was. In this case, it was his memories that were broken and rearranged within the dream of the other, dying world and the glimpse he'd caught of the thing near the fence.

It was long, at least twenty-five feet from tail to nose. Its general anatomy resembled a centipede, but instead of its torso being a continuous line, it was segmented into two parts. Its back half bulged with angular protrusions that were covered with black plates, much like a crab's shell. Its tail then narrowed to a wicked-looking point that drew back on itself into a hook. The front half of its body was flared and shaped like an arrowhead. Multiple black spines shot out of its back, pointing forward, and Sullivan shuddered, remembering how they had looked poking from the water he'd almost treaded into the day before. Multi-jointed legs extended from its body every few feet; the two foremost limbs were thick and by far the longest. Both appendages ended in sharp tips that chipped and bit into the solid rock the creature climbed upon. Several smaller sets of legs curled tightly beneath its undulating body, seemingly protecting its plated belly. But it was its head that kept drawing Sullivan's attention. Two soulless eyes the size of softballs perched at the far ends of a triangular skull. They were black mirrors without defined pupils, but he could see them shifting every so often to take in its surroundings. The skin of its head shone as if it were polished marble, and an open maw gaped below two hooked antenna. Its mouth was toothless and appeared soft. A shockingly human-looking tongue licked at its edges and flicked out into the air, as if tasting it.

Another blast of its stench rocked Sullivan back from the edge of the cavern and left him in the dark, gagging and near hysteria, as he watched the creature finally articulate onto the cave floor. Its head turned in an insectile manner toward Andrews, who smiled and bowed to the abomination. Again the deep vibration hammered the air in the cavern, and Sullivan wondered if the warden could understand it, for the man nodded and gestured toward the mouth of the tunnel.

Panic lanced through Sullivan as the thing turned in his direction and scuttled toward him at an alarming speed. It spider-like legs tore into the floor and propelled it forward like a black wave.

It was coming for him.

Andrews had somehow known he was here and communicated it to the horror. She would pull him from the tunnel like a man stabbing a pickle from a jar, and then devour him, to the tumultuous cries of her horde.

Sullivan stumbled back farther and slipped in the water that now rushed around him. He fell and aimed the shotgun toward the mouth of the passage, waiting for the monstrous head to fill the space. Seconds ticked by. Nothing appeared. He pulled himself to his feet, all the while keeping his sights trained on the opening before him.

The floor of the cavern came into view and he stopped, crouching as he realized how close she was. The creature had her back to him, and at this distance he could now make out intricate designs in the black plates of her armored hide. What he'd thought were large interlocking shells he now saw were made up of many smaller diamond-shaped scales that moved and flexed with every shift of her weight. The spines that appeared hard and immobile were, in fact, twitching forward and back with jerking movements. He watched in awe as she sat back, balancing on her tail to unfold the short legs beneath her stomach. What at first he'd thought was a protective measure he now saw for what it was: she was holding something.

Her legs uncurled and released the naked man she clutched to her belly. He stood on wobbly legs, which threatened to release him to the floor. In many ways he resembled how Barry looked: he had no hair and his skin was whiter than new snow. Skin sagged at his buttocks and stomach, which suggested extreme weight loss. Although his head fell to his chest as soon as he was free of the thing's embrace, Sullivan was still able to recognize him.

It was Dr. Arnold Bolt, the missing nuclear physicist.

Bolt wavered again and began to tip, but then something shot free of the thing's mouth and slid behind him. It was like the man had been electrified. Every muscle in his body tensed and flexed through his thin layer of skin. His head snapped back and his mouth flew open in pain. And just as suddenly, he relaxed. The scientist turned in a short circle and walked to the control panel mounted to the rear of the machine.

A pale rope extended from the thing's mouth, attached to the base of Bolt's spine. Sullivan could see some sort of coupling between the man's tailbone and whatever extended from the thing. Barry's wound suddenly became all too clear and Sullivan shook his head, anger rising up within him. They were marionettes. It was using people like puppets to do its bidding. Sullivan watched as the machine began to hum and a few loud clicks resounded from its shrouded interior.

It was starting; he had to move now. Sullivan ran through his options as fast as humanly possible and came to the same conclusion each time. There would most likely be no way he would live through this. His only hope was to destroy the machine and then fight until he was overwhelmed by the monstrosity below or its acolytes. Sullivan steeled himself, loaded four more shells into the shotgun, checked that the safety was off, and stood. He said Rachel's name one time in his head and stepped out into the light.

A snapping sound came from the machine and there was a flash of light that lit up every surface in the cave. A wave of heat hit Sullivan in the chest and he heard his hair and eyebrows crackle as they singed at their ends. He fell back and landed in the mouth of the tunnel, and stared down at the scene before him. The crowd was parted to either side of the machine's barrel, and they all watched something at the far end of the chamber in awed silence. Sullivan drew his eyes to where they looked.

A hole as black as a patch of night sky had appeared where only a large pile of rocks and boulders were before. Its surface was flat and about ten feet across. Its edges waved like water, and at its oily center the darkness within moved and swirled hypnotically.

Sullivan leapt to his feet and shouldered the shotgun, meaning to shoot the machine's controls, although it seemed pointless. The doorway was open and he deduced that the machine had nothing to do with what happened now. Bolt still stood transfixed behind the sighting shield, but he suddenly slumped forward, steadying himself with two weakened arms as the thing behind him detached its probe. All at once the air was alive with swinging tendrils that erupted from the thing's mouth. Each ropy arm was almost as long as the creature itself, and tipped with different shapes of razor-sharp bone. As he saw one tendril that ended in a blunt stump, Sullivan remembered the object from Alvarez's mouth. He lowered the shotgun, in shock, watching the snake-like appendages lash out and begin to slash at the scientist's soft flesh.

Blood and tissue flew in all directions. It looked for a moment like the physicist was caught in a man-sized blender. Bolt tried to scream as his legs attempted to give out, but the creature stabbed a twisted barb through the man's chest and held him in place as it worked, cutting off his cry before it ever left his mouth. Soon, the whiteness of bone became visible in the glow of the lights. One of Bolt's arms fell from its socket and was carried away, only to be shoved into the waiting mouth of the creature. A second later both of his legs were ripped in different directions by the prying arms, and were consumed. Red and blue intestines spilled free of the scientist's stomach and were wound into a ball before disappearing into the thing's gullet. Sullivan watched, mortified, as Bolt's head, surprisingly free of gore and cuts, came loose from his shoulders and fell. It was snatched in midair at the last instant by a lancing tendril that drove through one of the man's eye sockets.

The last of the scientist's body vanished, as though he'd never been there, and the creature's dancing feelers retreated out of sight into its mouth. Sullivan raised the shotgun again to fire, the smell of blood heavy in his nostrils, but then noticed a flowing movement beyond the machine.

The crowd was kneeling on the rough floor, their heads all turned in the direction of the doorway, where something moved deep within its folds. A hinged black leg poked out of the hole and rested its pointed tip on the ground. After a few seconds, the rest of the creature became visible and slid free of the oily doorway, as if being born into the world. It was half the size of the original creature, but otherwise identical. Its black carapace shone in the light, and it made a mewling sound that sprung goose bumps across Sullivan's flesh.

The thing beside the machine scuttled toward the doorway, knocking several men over as it hurried through the crowd. The two creatures met in the center of the floor and locked eyes, their movements becoming slower and more graceful. They leaned from side to side on their long legs and both emitted a low humming that was more felt than heard.

Sullivan swore and leapt down the short steps in front of the tunnel's mouth, landing in a puddle of water and gore from Bolt's remains a few feet from the machine's control panel. The water's flow leaked all the way past the base of the stairs and was expanding quickly. He skidded to a stop and huddled for a moment behind the protective shield. His mind spun with thoughts of how to stop what was happening. He'd missed his chance to destroy the machine, and now there was another creature to contend with. He tried to control his rapid breathing as he stood and peered over the top of the panel, through the sighting shield.

The creatures had finished their greeting, and now the smaller of the two extended itself up as tall as its legs would reach, behind its larger mate. A slit in the smaller creature's belly opened and Sullivan realized, without a doubt, that it was male. A jutting protrusion roughly four feet long extended out into the open air, its rigid form pulsing in the low light. The tip of the organ dripped a grayish fluid before it disappeared into a fold of flesh beneath the female's thrashing tail. The male wrapped its crustacean-like legs around the bulging female's body and hugged her close as his entire body shuddered.

Sullivan fell back to his haunches, abhorrence thick in his chest at the sight of the two alien beasts mating. He had to do something now. The puddle that he knelt in finally crept to the bottom edge of the machine and kissed the metal there. A hiss of steam and the smell of ozone met Sullivan's nose. He looked down to see the water bubbling around the first inch of the enormous gun's housing. The steam scalded his flesh beneath his pants leg and he moved back, an idea taking shape in his mind. He risked another glance through the sighting shield and was alarmed to see that the two creatures had uncoupled and were both facing the doorway, which now fluttered more forcefully at its edges. Several more sets of legs appeared in its opening and began to descend to the floor. Without another moment allowed for thought or consequence, Sullivan stood, his eyes finding the red button at the center of the console. He slammed the heel of his hand down on it.

There was a rapid clicking sound and a sequence of flashes that throbbed at rear of his eyes. Blinking, he tried to focus on the doorway. A cloud of smoke billowed from a shimmering oval shape that hung where the black hole had been. It was like seeing a condensed mirage normally reserved for an expanse of desert in the hot sun. Five twitching segmented legs lay on the floor beneath the anomaly in a pool of dark fluid. Fevered vapor rose from the stunted ends where they'd been cut mid-step. Clouds of boiling steam shot up next to Sullivan as more water flowed around the overheated machine, engulfing him in a heavy cloud. Every eye in the cave swung toward him, along with four alien orbs that narrowed with hatred so pure he could feel it.

Warden Andrews struggled to his feet and pointed with a bony arm at Sullivan. "Kill him!"

Sullivan heard the shuffling of hundreds of knees as the crowd rose to its feet with murderous speed. He looked to his right, and then to the left, until he spotted a rock the size and shape of a large textbook. He snatched the rock off the ground and carefully laid it across the red button on the console, successfully pinning it down.

Sullivan dove away from the machine as a series of snaps rang out in its steel belly. The harsh ripping of electricity outside of its insulation met his ears, and a massive cloud of steam flew up nearly two stories in the air as more water washed down to cool the atomic device.

He gained his feet just as a group of guards and inmates rounded the side of the massive weapon and ran toward him, their eyes silvery with loathing. Sullivan leveled the shotgun without bringing it up to his shoulder and fired.

Two prisoners at the front of the group sprouted red leaks that poured through their uniforms. Their legs pumped several more times before they collapsed in heaps, their bodies dead before their minds could comprehend it. A guard drew his sidearm and threw a wild shot at Sullivan, who ducked, feeling the passage of the bullet beside his face. The shotgun boomed in his hands and he watched the guard scrabble at his throat as several tendrils shot out of the holes left by the buckshot. Sullivan fired three more times, leveling the rest of the group that had rushed him. His hands felt wooden as they dove into his pants pockets and fumbled for more shells. A huge shape loomed on the other side of the mist forming in the cave, its legs articulating at a speed that was scary for something so large. Sullivan stuffed the last shell into the bottom of the shotgun and pulled the stock to his shoulder, waiting to see the black of the thing's eyes before he fired. The head of the male creature came into view through the haze, its mouth open, revealing swaying ropes that slashed like daggers through the air.

A loud thumping sound arose from Sullivan's right, and he turned his head just in time to see the machine's steel cowling buckle and mushroom outward with a pop. A heavy access door shot from the side of the weapon, like it was flung from a colossal sling. It sang across the cave in a runner of smoke and sliced through the male creature's torso without stopping. The monster's body fell in two halves, and it uttered a sickening growl deep in its chest. The smell that gagged Sullivan earlier washed over him and he covered his mouth to keep from vomiting, as a thick wash of black fluid flooded from the creature's torn body. Somewhere deeper in the cavern a blaring roar resounded. It was the sound of distilled rage.

The machine's outer assembly continued to melt, and Sullivan watched as the long barrel tilted and finally struck the ground with a hollow boom. Water flowed constantly around the machine and continued to kick up vast amounts of steam that reached all the way to the ceiling and crept outward at a steady rate. A few screams were audible on the opposite side of the cave, which was obscured by the curtain of vaporized water, and Sullivan knew the steam was doing its work.

He ran past the fallen body of the male creature and jumped over a still-twitching leg, firing the shotgun into a cadre of hissing inmates as he went. Through the crawling fog enveloping the cavern, he spotted the female creature—*she*. She was moving away from the encroaching steam, farther into the darkness that cloaked the far end of the cave. A shot rang out somewhere to his right, and a few pieces of rock kicked off the stalactite he was running past and showered the top of his head. He spun and fired blindly in the direction the shot came from, and kept moving. In that instant as he turned, he saw that a large portion of the crowd was trying to circumvent the scalding steam that continued to boil off the melted weapon. He realized that they were heading toward the tunnel's entrance, but there was no getting past the atomic-fueled mist.

Up ahead, the remaining creature scrambled over a pile of rocks two stories high and disappeared into the darkness that hung thick because of the slanting earthen roof toward the floor. Sullivan sped up, not willing to lose the impregnated abomination. *Can't let it get away, can't let it get away,* he repeated in his head, hoping the mantra would somehow allow him to stop her before she made it to the world above.

He rounded the last boulder that stood between him and the rock pile the creature had disappeared over, and slid to a stop. No less than fifty inmates and guards stood in a half circle before the rock pile. All of the guards' handguns were trained on Sullivan, and Warden Andrews stood at the center of the group.

"Shoot him!" Andrews screamed.

Sullivan dove behind the nearby boulder just as bullets cracked and whined off the rock's skin. Sullivan crouched there, his heart thundering in his chest, each breath like a lungful of acid. He checked his pockets for more shotgun shells but found none. *We had a good run,* he told himself, *but this is the end of the line.* Bullets continued to chip away at the protection of the boulder, and he drew Barry's handgun from his waistband. If he was going out, he'd go out killing as many of the infected as he could. Just as he was about to step out and unleash hell, he heard a loud sizzling sound and looked to the far end of the cavern.

A gush of water barreled out of the tunnel's mouth and engulfed the atomic gun. The melting reactor in the center of the weapon, along with the molten steel surrounding it, vaporized the floodwater instantly and sent a near-solid plume of steam in every direction. The infected men and women who stood to either side of the machine were overtaken in a flash, and Sullivan heard their dying screams as the steam blistered every inch of their bodies. A few tried to run in his direction but were swallowed by the billowing mist as it expanded exponentially, covering the cavern from top to bottom in its cleansing haze. The wall of steam rushed steadily onward, until Sullivan could feel its heat begin to curl the hair on his head. Pushing the 1911 back into his belt, he spun away from the rock and ran headlong into the mass of waiting men.

The surprise of rushing his attackers was the only thing that bought him the few seconds he needed. Most of the inmates and guards were staring at the approaching cloud of boiling mist when Sullivan stepped out and began firing. His last few rounds from the shotgun caught four of the armed guards in the chest and head before they'd taken aim. He dropped the empty shotgun on the ground as he ran toward the remaining cluster of men and drew the heavy .45. He saw a glimpse of Andrews's long face folding in anger and frustration, and then it felt as if an oven had been opened behind him. Sullivan saw the group split in half and run in either direction, away from the encroaching steam. Without pausing to fire any more rounds, Sullivan ran up and over the hill of stones before him, his feet finding purchase on the various edges in the deepening dark.

When he reached the top, he paused only to assure himself that the creature wasn't waiting on the other side, then plummeted down without seeing where he stepped. A loose rock gave way beneath his left foot and he uttered a short cry before falling to his back, the entire rear of the pile sliding downward in a rumbling avalanche of stone. Sullivan managed to keep his balance and landed on his feet as soon as he hit the floor. Several rocks hit the back of his legs, but none were large enough to knock him flat. To either side he heard cries of terror and saw scurrying forms in the dark, seeking shelter from the burning tide that came closer with each second. He moved straight ahead, following the course the female creature was traveling on before she'd vanished from sight.

The darkness closed in over him as he navigated as fast as he could around waist-high rocks and over small cave-ins that littered the floor. He could tell that the floor was gradually moving up. The slope rose at a small angle and the craggy ceiling came down to meet the floor. Sullivan prayed as he ran that he would find the exit that Andrews had mentioned without knowing it. If the creature sometimes hunted in the forest around the prison, then there must be an alternate route from beneath the facility.

A series of boulders surrounded his path, and in the dim light he saw that the track he was on narrowed ahead. The screams of the cooking men behind him were a mingling staccato of agony that would not stop. Just as one voice became silent, another would take up its course and rise to a crescendo before falling away. Sullivan took two more steps and stopped, the heat at his back a reminder that death was less than thirty seconds behind if he didn't find a way out. He squinted into the darkness around him and saw a deeper shadow a few yards to his right. Holding out the handgun before him like an unlit torch, he continued, his other hand groping at the nearby wall that closed in around him. He followed the curve of the tunnel, and the true darkness of being underground closed its fist over his vision. He stumbled over something and kept going, the floor becoming more hazardous with small outcroppings of rocks.

After a few more halting steps, he tripped, and when he put his hand against the ground to stop his fall, he knew he'd found the way out.

The leaf beneath his palm crackled with dryness, but its texture was undeniable. After he steadied himself, he pushed the handgun deep into the back of his pants and started climbing again. The incline was steeper than the man-made descent on the far side of the underground cavern and more riddled with rocks and debris. A misty light came from somewhere above and he could see the tunnel he traveled through was large enough to accommodate the bulk of the creature. The only question was how far she'd gotten ahead of him. With a renewed vigor, he leapt toward the next outline of rock, ready to surge forward and close the distance between him and the beast.

A cold hand gripped his ankle and yanked him backward.

Sullivan grunted as he fell to the floor, his body colliding with its jagged embrace. He felt pain radiate outward from his ribs and rebound at the top of his head, only to make the circuit once again.

"You fucking worthless prick!" Sullivan rolled over to find Andrews standing above him, the older man just a shadow with two burning eyes full of hatred. "You ruined everything, you self-righteous shit!"

Sullivan kicked at the warden with half the strength and speed he normally possessed. Andrews caught his ankle in two bony hands strengthened with animosity.

"Now, you're gonna burn with the rest of us for taking Maddy away from me!"

Andrews hauled on Sullivan's leg, and Sullivan felt himself slide several feet, his back scraping over several razor-edged stones as he went. He tried to grab the gun at his back but it was pinned beneath him as he slid. He kicked out again, but the older man merely laughed and pulled, skidding them both down the slope, and now Sullivan could feel heat building from the chamber below. The only escape for the radiation-tainted steam was the natural vent they were in now. Panic began to grip Sullivan with thoughts of how his skin would feel as it blistered and bubbled under the scorching touch of the steam. He could already see the flesh dropping off his bones like an overdone piece of poultry, as the skeleton that used to be Andrews grinned over its shoulder, its vacant eye sockets swallowing his soul.

Sullivan cried out as his hand closed over a baseball-sized rock. In one motion he pulled the stone from its bed in the soil and drew back his leg. Andrews leaned toward him, staggering from Sullivan's movements. Sullivan brought the heavy rock up and over in a viscous arc that connected with a wet, breaking sound as it met Andrews's face.

He had only a glimpse of the warden's wide eyes above the oblong rock, lodged solidly in the wreckage that was once his nasal cavity and cheekbones, before Andrews tipped backward and plummeted away into the gathering steam below. A choked bellow filtered up to Sullivan, and then was gone, along with the warden's lanky outline. The solid wall of steam continued unabated.

Sullivan scrambled to his feet and climbed again. He felt the back of his pants growing moist and hot, which only spurred him onward. There were men on the earth who were afraid of hell and its fury. Sullivan had been there and seen its occupants, and now ran from it with all the strength he contained.

The tunnel sped by as the howling voice of the irradiated mist chased after him. The aboveground opening came closer and closer, until he was finally free of the tunnel. Cool, fresh air that tasted almost sugary hit him full in the face as he struggled free of the earth's clutches. He fell out of the cave's shaft and onto the ground. Light drops of rain and soft green blades of grass welcomed him, asked him to sleep in their embrace, but he stood and stumbled, drawing the pistol as he went.

After a few wobbling strides, Sullivan collapsed and fell back, his chest heaving and his eyes taking in the rim of gray daylight that dawned in the east. A whistling sound vibrated behind him and he turned, squinting at the hole in the earth.

A blast of steam so thick and solid that it appeared to be a vertical river flew from the passageway. It mushroomed out into the cool air of the early morning and descended upon him, a soft blanket of death.

Sullivan struggled to his feet and ran down the rise he'd rested upon. With a look back, he saw a partial view of chainlink fence topped with razor wire standing on the shoulder of the hill, and beyond that, the morose silhouette of Singleton. He faced back in the direction he ran, the grass groping and tangling at his feet. As he moved he noticed the foliage around him was bent and trampled flat, as if a steamroller had driven through the spot over and over again.

A thick rumbling that rattled his heart against his rib cage echoed through the morning air. He scanned the brush and tangled screen of greenery before him until he spotted it. The creature stood, looking back over a massive shoulder at him from the edge of a roaring stream. Sullivan threw the handgun up in front of him and squeezed off two shots. At the reports, the beast scuttled away with an uncanny speed. He followed, his feet slipping on a patch of wet ferns, as he half ran, half slid down the little hill.

The stream was swollen beyond its narrow banks with the accumulation of rain over the last few weeks. The water spit and flew off rocks and trees that bordered its normal path. Sullivan sloshed through a few inches of water and stopped at the stream's edge, making sure the creature hadn't fled into the current or swam to the opposite shore. A sapling snapped in half farther down the stream on his side, and he began to run again, his breathing erratic and punctuated with a heartbeat that never seemed to slow. He knew now where it was going. Andrews had told him and Barry the first day they set foot in his office. This stream fed a larger river, which emptied into Lake Superior. Lake Superior was attached to the ocean. It was heading for the sea.

The thought of the creature escaping into the depths of the ocean to birth its young made his feet quicken their already hurried pace. The sky was lightening more in the east, a shine beginning to spread across the clouds overhead. He ducked beneath a fallen birch and hurdled a rotting stump. The ground became wetter the farther he went, and all at once he realized he could no longer hear the thing's passage over the sound of his own footsteps.

The bone-tipped tendril hit him in his left side. He felt the jagged edge tear through the thin T-shirt and strip meat down to his ribs. He screamed and fell dangerously close to the edge of the stream. As he rolled to his back, the cool water washing around him and stinging the new wound at his side, the creature stood from its hiding place behind a cluster of fir trees. Like a gigantic scorpion, it articulated closer, its hinged body swinging obscenely. Sullivan leveled the handgun at its head just as the rest of its tongues emerged from its mouth, their bone edges shining in the early light. He fired.

The bullet hit the bundle of appendages in its open maw. The hard ends of each tendril exploded like porcelain hand grenades. The beast staggered and the ruined tongues withdrew from sight, as ichor began to flow from its slack mouth. It coughed, a surprisingly human sound, and nearly fell. It legs bit and tore into the sopping earth as it regained its sense of direction and ran between two towering oaks, raking the heavy bark off as it went.

Sullivan stood and addressed his newest wound with what light he had. The rip in his shirt dripped crimson, and when he touched it he realized the flaps of his skin almost perfectly matched the tears in the fabric.

"Fuck!" he swore, his voice coming back to him off the flowing water and surrounding trees. Another tree fell to the ground beneath the thing's weight, fifty yards downstream. Hissing at the continued burning in his ribs, he began to run again. Without stopping, he ejected the magazine from Barry's pistol and checked the round count. The empty clip met his gaze and he slammed it back home, cursing. There was one shot left, seated in the chamber. He'd have to make it count.

A black slick on the surface of the water appeared, first in small patches, and then in glossy thickening pools that covered the area he ran through. He hoped the creature's own organic shrapnel had cut an artery, or what passed for such in the alien organism. Perhaps he'd finally catch a break and come upon its lifeless body after a few more steps. A loud rushing sound that dwarfed the call of the stream grew. The river was very close. Sullivan caught a glimpse of the creature's swaying form as it attempted to crawl over a deadfall, and he skidded to a stop, drawing a bead on where its head would be. The gun shook with his rushed breathing, and then the thing scuttled up and was gone behind the scraggly branches of the downed tree.

He ran again. His legs felt like hunks of lead, threatening to fold him to the watery ground, and several alarming bursts of light began to flash at the corners of his vision. He couldn't fall now, not when she was so close to the river. If she disappeared beneath its surface, he'd have failed. Failed not only Barry and his family but every other human being on earth.

The roar of the water was everywhere now; the air was alive with it. Sullivan ran around the tip of the deadfall and saw the stampeding flow of the river to his left. Its banks, within inches of overflowing, curved in a scythe toward him, and then swung away to the southeast, where it dropped into the foaming jaws of white rapids. The smaller stream joined its brother from the right, forming a peninsula of land. Sullivan sprinted toward the point and slid to a stop directly in the path of the scurrying creature.

She paused in mid-step, her insect-like form shuddering and contorting with what he assumed was pain. Black liquid drooled in a steady flow out of her ruined mouth, and she swayed drunkenly on unsteady legs. She looked down at him as he stood to his full height and pointed the pistol at her face. Both eyes shone like volcanic glass and glared at him, into him, with hatred so palpable, he felt it bore into his chest. The smaller legs near her back end gripped and pulled at the ground, digging wet furrows on both sides.

Suddenly she cried out. A bellow loud enough to make his eardrums flutter like speaker skins ripped through the clearing, as the creature's long front legs dug into the earth. A harsh tearing sound followed, along with several dry cracks, like kindling breaking.

Sullivan watched, his eyes bulging in disbelief, as the back segment of the creature tore free and fell to the ground. The four sets of legs still attached to the pregnant portion danced and pulled as they struggled to lift the considerable weight.

"What the fuck?" Sullivan said, feeling his head tilt to the side despite himself.

More black blood spewed from the separation and coated the squirming egg sac, which dragged itself toward the surging stream. Sullivan snapped from his trance and sighted down the barrel at the rear half of the creature's body and fired.

The bullet hit dead center in the mass of flexing flesh, with a sound like a melon being struck by a baseball bat. Yellowish pus squirted from the wound in a curving fountain, and the legs holding up the weight of the sac stumbled and fell. The creature spun on shaking legs toward her lower half, studied the wound, and then turned back to Sullivan. Its antenna snapped and slashed the air in fury, and it bellowed again as it took a step toward him.

Sullivan glanced down at the gun in his hand, the slide open and locked back, the empty chamber staring at him like an uncaring eye. When he looked back up, the beast had taken another step, its weight awkward with the missing balance of the rest of its body. His hand snaked down to his pockets, searching for something, anything he could use as a weapon, while he backpedaled toward the roaring river. A small cylinder met his groping fingers, and for a moment he could only look down at what his hand had produced from his pocket.

The .45 shell he'd used to check the bullet holes in the boat gleamed dully in the gray light. Trying not to think about how wet the powder could be inside the case or the chances of a misfire, he fed the round into the waiting handgun and let the slide slam home. The creature was closer, only a few yards away, and he could smell her rotting scent. He looked up into one of the unblinking orbs and felt heat begin to sear the top of his skull. No, not the top but inside. It felt as if layers of his brain were being peeled away, inch by inch, until the very bottom of his head had the sensation of unhinging. He blinked and gritted his teeth as he raised the gun, which now felt heavier than a cinderblock at the end of his arm. An unbroken tendril snaked free of the creature's mouth and raced toward his upturned face, as he aimed and pulled the trigger.

The beast's left eye detonated in a shower of clear fluid. The tendril stopped its flight toward Sullivan's face and fell limp, as the creature wobbled backward. A choked cry, much higher in pitch than its earlier calls, leaked out of its mouth. He watched the thing spin in a half circle and then back before tipping onto its rearmost legs. For a moment it looked as if it would simply sit down, but then it reared up, fighting for balance that would not come. It pitched backward and fell with a resounding crunch onto its still-bleeding egg sac. Sullivan saw the pointed black spines on its back disappearing into and through the skin of its detached body. Its long front legs scissored out in a few feeble movements, and then began to curl inward, until they were folded neatly into its body. Sullivan was reminded of a dying spider, its legs tucked close in a final act of protection. The creature gasped one last time and laid still. Life exited its remaining eye, the black color fading to a cloudy gray that mirrored the sky overhead.

All the strength left Sullivan's legs and he fell to the ground, Barry's pistol still clutched in one hand. The rain pattered down around him and the stream ran to meet the river, which heedlessly rushed on out of sight. He let his senses relax, and stared at the clouds above, which were iron colored but higher than he'd seen them in weeks. In a few spots he could actually see patches of sky shifting in and out of focus with the storm's movements. The forest around him was still, with only the dipping of leaves in response to the rain's touch. A thudding grew above the sound of the river, and he raised his eyes to the tree line.

A speck that he thought at first was a distant circling bird took shape, and soon he could make out the fanning rotors of the helicopter. For a few seconds he thought that the sun had come out, since the rain felt warmer on his face, but then he realized that tears were leaking from both of his eyes. He tried to stand and felt as though every inch of his body was covered in rusted wire. After another attempt, he made it to his feet. He stared at the stilled body, which had come from somewhere he never wished to see again, a place he hoped would wither and die beneath the light of an alien star. Some things were meant to fade away.

Without another look back, he turned and pushed his way through the branches that met him and strained his ears for the sweet sound of the helicopter landing somewhere to the west.

Chapter 13

Sullivan woke with a start, his eyes scanning the darkened living room around him. His living room, his house. He listened, his breath hitching in his chest for over thirty seconds before he allowed himself to relax. He licked his lips and grimaced at the sour taste in his mouth. Barry's gun sat on his right thigh, held loosely in his hand. To his left a half-empty bottle of Jack Daniels rested on a nearby table. The wind outside gusted and made the house around him creak and groan in protest of the approaching storm.

He'd watched The Weather Channel and seen the growing nest of greens and reds that clustered and inched across the screen toward his residence. He watched The Weather Channel a lot. He had quite a bit of free time on his hands now that he wasn't working anymore. Debilitating posttraumatic stress disorder. The psychiatrist only saw him three times and then wrote a dismissal letter on his behalf. He'd handed the letter, along with his ID, to a solemn Hacking, who'd taken the items without looking him fully in the face. There had been no gun to turn in since he hadn't retrieved it from the room where he dropped it at Singleton.

After a few days he'd realized there would be no corroboration for his story. He'd seen a few of the faces of the men who'd come back from the fork in the river. He knew that they'd seen what lay on its banks, but they said nothing. It had been swept beneath a rug so thick and piled with lies, there would never be a way to get the truth from anyone who saw anything that day. New Haven had dropped the charges of assault, breaking and entering, and endangering a patient after he'd gotten his diagnosis. Several weeks of tests and procedures to detect radiation followed. Miraculously, he was free of any toxins and was cleared to go home, to sit and think … and remember.

He reached out and grasped the whiskey by the throat before taking a long pull from the bottle. The liquor burned and helped dull the memories that were always there waiting to pull him into the depths of his mind, where they'd smother him for hours.

But he remembered anyway.

He remembered what it had felt like watching Everett and Barry die in his arms, their lives flowing out of them like water through a sieve. He remembered the things that spewed from the mouths of so many, poisoned by something not of this world, or perhaps even this dimension. He remembered staring into the creature's bottomless black eyes that had peered into him that morning near the river. He drank another swallow of the amber liquid before letting his mind return to why he sat in his living room, his easy chair facing the front door, a gun held in sweating fingers.

Unwilling to truly accept why he was doing it, he'd driven to Minneapolis the week before, letting the car take him without purposely steering it to a destination. Regardless of how his mind tried to hide from it, he ended up there anyway.

The sprawling grounds of Lakewood Cemetery were quiet and motionless the day he'd walked across the parking lot and onto the soft grass. The city hadn't suffered the storms the north had endured, and there were no puddles or standing water—a small blessing. He'd wound his way over two hills, and then followed a paved path that led deep into the cemetery, beneath a towering oak that shaded a spot he knew so well. How many times had he stood there under its unwavering watch? How many tears had he cried as he looked at the stone that bore his last name? He'd hesitated before stepping off the path onto the too-green grass, and when he came into full sight of the grave, it was like a giant tumbler falling into place, locking tight all rational explanations and thoughts that pounded on the wall that now separated him from a reality he could never fully return to.

The house snapped and popped again at the storm's insistence, and he flinched, bringing the gun up from his leg, only to let it rest there again after a minute of listening. This was his life now. A trip to the mailbox to collect his check that paid for the mortgage, a few groceries, and the glowing stack of bottles he never let fall below five in his pantry.

And waiting in his chair at night for something to come to his door.

Although he'd tried to put everything that he'd witnessed at Singleton behind him, the moment by the river wouldn't let him rest except in the full light of day. Because he remembered. He remembered the heat of the thing's mind pressing down upon his, how she'd cut through his defenses and penetrated him. How until the last second he hadn't believed Andrews, hadn't believed an old man hollowed by disease and a sadness so deep that he'd held on to hope, no matter how vile the price would have been.

But he believed now.

He'd felt her inside his head, prying and pulling until he'd been able to fire the shot that extinguished her life. He'd felt her intelligence withdraw from his own; an intelligence so vast and brimming with power, it dwarfed every other experience he'd ever known. But not before she spoke one word to him, a word that echoed to the depths of his soul—still echoed. The word that would exact a revenge so cruel that sanity itself would crumble before it. The word that compelled him to drive to the cemetery where his wife was buried. To see the earth disturbed there, as if something had recently crawled out from below.

He heard the word in his mind, as if whispered by the storm outside, and hefted the gun again.

Rachel.

The End

Author's Note

Where the hell did this one come from, you ask? I'll tell you.

I was looking for a new project while *Lineage* was being edited, and couldn't really decide on something solid. I had three or four ideas that were all decent, but none jumped up and grabbed me by the throat, which is how I know I've found my next story. On Tuesday, June 19, 2012, a rain began to fall in the northern part of my home state of Minnesota. The torrential downpour flooded streets, washed away the ground, and saturated people's basements in our area. It was, quite literally, the worst rainstorm I'd ever seen. But the damage caused in our area was nothing compared to Duluth, Minnesota. In Duluth, streets were overrun with water and cars were washed into sinkholes, and afterward, it was declared the worst flood in almost forty years. In the aftermath of the flood, businesses were closed, along with schools, and homeowners were forced to abandon their properties due to the damage.

The idea for *Singularity* spawned from this disaster sometime after I heard that the town of Moose Lake was almost completely surrounded by the runoff of floodwater. Immediately my mind asked, *What if it wasn't a town cut off by water, but instead a prison?*

The rest came easily.

I really hope that you enjoyed the book, and as always, I would appreciate any reviews or feedback you have to offer. Thanks so much for reading!

Other Books by Joe Hart

Made in the USA
Charleston, SC
20 April 2013